# THREADS

## A NEOVERSE ANTHOLOGY

Short Stories
Volume 1

To learn more about NeoVerse Short Story Writing Competition:

www.neoglyphic.com/neoverse

# THREADS
## A NEOVERSE ANTHOLOGY

Short Stories
Volume 1

A Neoglyphic Entertainment Production
Edited by Aaron Safronoff

NEOGLYPHIC ENTERTAINMENT
CALIFORNIA

Threads: A NeoVerse Anthology
Volume 1

Published in the United States by Neoglyphic Entertainment, Inc.
www.neoglyphic.com

Edited by
Aaron Safronoff & Neoglyphic Entertainment

Art Direction by
Eve Skylar

Produced by
Aaron Safronoff, David Ramadge & Kylie Kiel

Cover and Internal Artwork by
Neoglyphic Entertainment & Artwoork Studio

Copy Edited by
Dominion Editorial

For information on bulk purchases, please contact Neoglyphic Entertainment
contact@neoglyphic.com.

ISBN-13-: 978-1-944606-03-9

10 9 8 7 6 5 4 3 2 1
First Edition
Printed in USA

*Dedicated to all the authors who bravely submitted their stories to our contest.*

*Thank you all for your amazing contributions.*

# Contents

# Foreword

Neoglyphic Entertainment proudly presents Volume One in our anthology series: *Threads: A NeoVerse Anthology*. This collection represents the best among emerging talents in the world of fiction: the winners of the NeoVerse Short Story Writing Competition. We pored over thousands of submissions, and chose twenty winners, employing natural language processing, a group of casual readers, and a panel of industry professionals to focus on premise, story, and technique to render our ranking. The results:

"One Time Hero," by Neil Chase, excels in every dimension. The story of a hero succumbing to the fetters of time, his body enfeebled by a preternatural power ill-suited to the confines of the human form. But he has strength enough to sacrifice himself one more time. A Hero's worth.

"Night Insects," by Edith Clark, draws the reader into the jungles and history of the Philippines during World War II. A rich culture and movement of resistance focused through a single character, Raju, as his deep connection with the natural world acts as both weapon and shield against the Axis.

"Dysphoria," by Chuck Regan, bends the audience through a mobius knot of humanity's future defined by virtual experiences of reality packaged, broadcast, and consumed by people that have never walked the earth, never been unplugged. The physical world made unreal, and flooded by nanogel. My advice? Learn to swim.

"Say When," by Pamela Bobowicz: "Momma always said that coming into this world and going out of it are the hardest things a person can do… But now that she's the one knocking on death's door, I wonder what's really harder: the leaving or the being left behind."

"Gold, Vine, and a Name," by Stephen Case, invokes the magic and terrible power contained within a name. The power to give life. The power to take it away. An assassin's greatest asset, and deadliest liability. The job of a Wordsmith seems safe enough, unless an assassin desires to change his name.

"Hotel Marietta," by Sabrina Clare, plays the heart like a maestro. A triumph of understanding and patience, a social worker reaches out to a tragically orphaned, seemingly autistic young girl only to discover the powerful connection that comes with time and caring. No one listens better than one who doesn't speak. She's been watching, reflecting, and waiting to open, Hotel Marietta.

"HX-59B," by Stefan "Mandevu" Dyk; on a space station bordering the known territories of the galaxy, a lone human guard argues with his AI's orders to prevent alien immigration. This satirically warped looking glass reflects an all too plausible future, cautioning readers that action without thought is madness. And madness works sometimes, even if not the way you'd expect.

"Vanni's Choice," by David A. Elsensohn, transports the reader to a gritty and fantastical land of booby-traps, towers, and sorcery through the eyes of a mercenary thief. Vanni's defeated every defense ever raised against her, and always seized the prize for a price. This time though, the prize is her life.

"Stormsong," by Tessa Hatheway, offers a new, inspired and creepy look at a classic legend of the sea. A vivid fantasy with a surreal and unexpected twist that will make readers question the definition of monster.

"Fallen on the Green," by Tanya King, moves the reader through the stages of grief of a soldier whose spirit remains tethered to his grave. A surreal and emotionally driven work about finding forgiveness. Hatred poisons the soul. And the soul, the soil.

"No Protections, Only Powers," by Katie Lattari, reminds the reader to be careful what you wish for. A mother wants so much for her children:

friendship, love, and happiness. Innocent intentions. Tragic consequences. A twisted tale that tingles all the way down the spine.

"The Queen's Dragon," by Hannah Marie; in struggles of sorcery and politics, sometimes retreat leads to victory, and sometimes, the Queen is sacrificed. But she's left clear instructions for the help: Exact my revenge. Release my dragon.

"A Knight, a Wizard, and Bee — Plus Some Pigs," by K.G. McAbee; what's not to love about this playful, sarcastic view of common tropes in fantasy fiction? Armor clad prima donnas, and senile sorcerers do not impress the young lad, Bee, but at least the pigs are useful.

"The Waiting Room," by T. L. Norman, tethers the reader to a hospital room with a young girl and her mother caught between this world and the afterlife. But they are not alone. The lights are coming. But for whom?

"Retirement Plan," by Chris J. Randolph; science-fiction, espionage, and assassination make for a fast-paced favorite in this speculative work about the influence wielded by the corporate executives of the future. Hostile takeover redefined.

"The Magical Worlds of Theodore Erickson: A New Beginning," by S.A. Rohrbaugh, conjures an unforgettable universe of Hippopotami, pinstripes, and bowler hats capable of delighting the child in each of us. Once you've caught a glimpse of Theodore's Magical World, you can never unsee it, and you wouldn't want to.

"Boneyard Prophet," by Charles D. Shell, folds a fable-like detective story into a work of tangible, speculative science-fiction. The hidden Boneyard, a space station dormant for generations, sparks to action as a fanatic arrives with a plea for divine intervention: a prayer for the Boneyard intelligence to fulfill its destiny. Pursuers arrive alleging lies, and the Boneyard must decide: defend or deny?

"The Carving," by M. Lopes da Silva. Halloween; an excuse to send up the creatures of the night, transforming our fears into tiny treats, offering us all an opportunity to hide out in the open. That is, unless an inexplicable knack forces your hand to carve the real you into the face of a pumpkin. No one can hide from the monsters we are, in, The Carving.

"Refugee and Her Book of Secrets," by Marija Stajic; a provocative tome of secrets wields power over the members of her family, but also, preserves their history when war pays loads to eradicate it. The Refugee will hold onto the book of secrets. She'll hold onto her heritage. Because she may never go home again.

"Call Me Home," by Joseph Swink; Eleanor tries to get by with a little help from her friends from the White Album and beyond. In the wake of her loving husband's passing, Eleanor copes with the news that her son may have followed his father too soon. This bittersweet tale will remind you to call home.

On behalf of all of Neoglyphic Entertainment, a huge thank you to all of the contributing authors, and to you, the all important readers, for sharing your time with us. Enjoy!


Sincerely,

Aaron Safronoff

*"A short story is the ultimate close-up magic trick—*
*a couple of thousand words to take you around*
*the universe or break your heart."*

*~ Neil Gaiman*

*First Place Winner*

# ONE TIME HERO

## By Neil Chase

### ABOUT NEIL CHASE:

Neil Chase is a short story author, novelist, and award-winning screenwriter and actor. His screenplays have won at film festivals and screenwriting competitions world-wide, including the Las Vegas Film Festival, Action on Film Festival, FilmQuest, Fantastic Planet, West Field Screenwriting Awards, and Cinequest. He is most proud of winning the FilmMakers International Screenwriting Awards Grand Prize and the Arthur Rosenfeld Award for Excellence in Dramatic Writing.

When not writing, he's drawing inspiration from his beautiful wife and two daughters. The NeoVerse Short Story Writing Competition is the first short story contest Neil has ever entered.

# ONE TIME HERO

## Neil Chase

*"I learned that courage was not the absence of fear, but the triumph over it. The brave man is not he who does not feel afraid, but he who conquers that fear."*

*–Nelson Mandela*

It was the music that woke him. Tinny, static-filled fanfare better suited to days long past.

He didn't know where it came from, or how long it had been playing. But as his eyes fluttered open on a blurry world, it somehow seemed fitting.

His focus returned with more effort and less speed than he would have preferred, and eventually found a familiar sight.

A dazzling smile on chiseled features. A mane of thick dark hair over piercing, iridescent eyes. Rippling muscles on a frame that towered over the strangers next to him. An aura, warm and radiant over his skin-tight costume, making him look even more the champion.

The picture repeated over and over, in a variety of poses and circumstances. But one thing remained constant.

Orion. The greatest hero the world had ever known.

Old newspaper headlines, magazine covers, faded photographs, children's drawings, and get-well cards tacked onto one wall, covering it almost from floor to ceiling. The *get-well wall*, as he liked to think of it. Comforting and welcome, the memories there almost made him forget his pain.

He could almost hear the cheering crowds and laughter as his eyes played over the headlines—*ORION SAVES THE DAY*, and *HE DOES IT AGAIN*, along with the photos showing the young hero rescuing a child or capturing a criminal.

In others, Orion fought monstrous robots and giant creatures from parts unknown. In yet more, he shook hands with presidents and kings, or simply hugged grandmothers and small children.

Melancholy greeted him as his gaze continued over the wall of memories and the headlines changed. *ORION FALLS. ROBBERS ESCAPE.*

A photo of a burning school. Black plumes of smoke rising high into the sky. Orion on his knees in the foreground, head hung low. New words stood out as the static-filled music faded, replaced by a rhythmic beeping sound. *TOO LATE. DOZENS PERISH.*

A lump formed in his throat and his vision blurred from rising tears. He fought them back, quickly moving on to the next set of pictures.

Orion leaning against a police officer for support. Orion losing a fight against a powerful archvillain. Orion on a gurney, being wheeled into a waiting ambulance.

The music outside the room died down, likely turned off by a nurse or patient to whom the radio belonged.

A final headline had caught his eye before he tore his gaze from the wall. *TERMINAL.*

The lump in his throat grew, and he had trouble breathing. Though he willed his heart to stay its weak drumming course, the tears that threatened to overflow finally broke through.

He knew they meant well. The visitors. The children. The doctors. Even the media. The people that came to the hospital day in and out and were turned away at the front desk without exception. The people whose get-well cards and newspaper clippings and photos and mementos always ended up in his room even if they didn't.

And of course, there was the hate mail as well. Not nearly as abundant as the fan mail, but significant enough to keep security tight in the medical complex.

Most people had forgiven him long ago. But there were those who could never do so, either through first-hand knowledge of his victims or simply through their own rigid moral code.

There was no doubt in his mind. Those innocents he failed to save. Those whose lives he took by either his negligence or as collateral in some greater conflict. They were his victims, as much as if he'd purposely killed or maimed each of them.

As if in response to his thoughts, the doctor's words burrowed into his skull.

"—found out too late."

"It was the powers?" asked the nurse standing next to him.

He knew they were standing there, even if they spoke in hushed tones. The haggard doctor and the fresh nurse.

"Mm-hmm," said the doctor, answering the question with the same obvious certainty as if she'd asked if water was wet or the sun hot.

"I mean, I know that's why he's here," she replied. "But nobody talks about how it's actually affecting him."

Merryman, the doctor, had been working around the clock since his high-profile patient was first admitted some months ago, but to no avail. The wear was written all over his otherwise youthful face. The worry lines, the dark circles under his eyes, even a few gray hairs that hadn't been there before.

He hadn't seen the nurse before. A middle-aged, stern woman in scrubs. And yet, for all her professionalism, she couldn't quite hide the awe in her voice. Being this close to the most famous—or perhaps infamous—man on the planet had a way of doing that to even the hardest people.

"To be honest," Dr. Merryman said, "we don't really know. So much about him has always been a mystery. We don't even know how he did what he did before he got sick. But there's something to the toll those abilities take on his body. The more he used them, the worse the side-effects."

"Like a sprinter running too hard?"

"And too long. Exactly. At first, it was nothing. Little things. A dip in strength or a bad headache. But as the demand for his services grew, it cascaded exponentially. In the end, well, he was more harm than good."

"The St. Nicholas Fire."

"Four alarm. They pulled back the moment he arrived, expecting another miracle. Instead…"

"Who knows how many they could have saved."

The conversation continued, but the words faded. He stopped listening, having heard it all before. Worse, having lived it.

Orion lay in the only bed in the private room. An oxygen mask supplied fresh air to his withered lungs. Tubes in his arms pumped vital fluids into his frail form. The color had long since drained from his gaunt face, his mane of dark hair was all but gone. He was a shell of his former self, ravaged by the effects of his mysterious illness.

Instead of focusing a second longer on the people in his room, his ears picked up another, more welcome, sound. A child's laughter.

His ear attuned to the wavelength, following the very sound waves themselves —out the closed window next to his bed, over the hospital grounds, along a busy roadway running up a steep hill, and to the top where sat a small hub of roadside stores.

There, he heard a young woman making baby talk with a laughing toddler, as she fiddled with some kind of device.

*Click.* The distinctive sound of a seatbelt latching.

The toddler babbled as the mother closed the car door.

He heard her footsteps as she went around the car toward the driver's side door.

*Ting!* Something unmistakably important snapped underneath the waiting car. The mother's footsteps paused for the briefest instant, when—

He heard the car begin to roll on its own, the tires creeping forward over the pavement. A rising dread filled him as he understood the brake line had failed, and gravity had taken over almost at once.

He heard the mother's gasp. He heard her rushing footsteps. He heard her rising heartbeat in her chest.

She was running for the driver's door, still in time to stop events from unfolding further.

He heard her foot strike a rock. He heard her breath catch in her throat. He heard her strike the ground as the wheels continued to roll.

"No!" she cried. "My baby!"

Though the doctor and nurse heard none of it in the quiet, sanitized room, the scream hit Orion like a hammer.

His heart monitor spiked, his heart suddenly galloping away on him. The ceiling lights momentarily flickered.

He turned his head to face out the window, which looked onto the roadway and the hill above. His eyes focused and impossibly he saw the car. It was a blue sedan, parked curbside just outside a small coffee shop.

A recent model, undoubtedly loaded with the most modern accessories and safety features. But those were of little use if there was no driver.

It rolled away, quickly gaining speed. There were no cars in front of it. Nothing to impede its way.

He heard the child's laugh and saw her little hand reach out, copying her mother's desperate pose.

She thought it was a game. Poor child.

The mother scrambled to her feet, far too late. She ran after the car, yelling, "Help! My baby! My baby!"

Orion's hand gripped the bed railing, the knuckles on his already ashen hand becoming even paler.

The nurse noticed his elevated heartbeat. She glanced at the doctor for confirmation, but he was already out the door to continue his rounds.

"Doctor," she said with a trace of worry.

Orion knew he couldn't do a thing to stop this tragedy. His own body wouldn't let him even if his spirit were still willing. And in truth, it wasn't. At best, he'd simply die trying. At worst, he'd cause more victims.

Orion closed his eyes, ashamed of his impotent cowardice, when—

"Mama!"

The joy was gone from the child's voice. What remained was the kind of terror that only the innocent possess and the weak lament. In her black-and-white world, all the small girl knew was that her mother was gone, and that was enough fear on its own. The poor child had no idea of the greater danger around her, and that only made it worse.

His eyes flew open, the decision made.

With a trembling hand, Orion pulled the oxygen mask off his face, followed by the tubes from his withered arms.

The heart monitor alarm went off in response to the pounding of his heart. He was in danger of cardiac arrest from just this small movement.

The lights again flickered, and the machines went haywire as if the room underwent a sudden power surge.

The nurse rushed over to restrain him from doing further harm to himself.

"Doctor!" she cried in a loud, urgent voice as he sat up and dragged his legs over one side of the bed.

Ignoring her, Orion glanced out the window. The car careened down the hill, no one able to stop it. The toddler's mother was already too far behind. The car glanced off a rusted pickup truck, and other motorists swerved as it crossed back and forth between the two lanes.

Horrified, the mother looked past the car to the bottom of the hill where a busy intersection sat, full of crossing traffic.

Orion saw it too. It was going to be ugly.

He clenched his jaw and stood up.

Sparks flew from the hospital machinery. The ceiling lights exploded from the overload.

Dr. Merryman rushed back into the room to help the nurse. He reached for a syringe, already waiting on a tray next to the bed. It was a powerful sedative, meant for emergency use just like this, though in all the time Orion had been bed-ridden they'd never had cause to even look its way. He was so sedate and passive; it became an afterthought.

As the doctor brought the needle toward Orion's upper arm, the frail man threw that same arm out in a pathetic swipe. The doctor and nurse went sprawling into the get-well wall.

Orion took a step forward. He was leaving.

"Orderly!" the doctor called. "Code white! Code white!"

Orion stumbled into the hallway, weak as a kitten. And yet, somehow he was brighter in face and color than only a moment before.

A beefy orderly, much bigger than the feeble patient, rushed over. His powerful hands were just about to grasp Orion, when—

The lights went out in the hallway. Orion extended a hand, calling up some dormant reserves even he didn't know still existed.

With a dazzling ripple of air, the orderly flew back into the far wall with a resounding *thud*, the plaster caving and cracking at the point of impact.

Orion listened past the rising tide of alarm in the hallway to the car on the hill outside.

It was completely out of control, speeding away down the mostly empty road, only a few dozen meters at best from a grisly end. There were mere seconds left.

He heard the mother's cries, and her running footsteps, which were nowhere near fast enough to do anything at all.

Orion willed his legs to move. Despite the groans of protest shuddering through his atrophied muscles and brittle joints, he forced his legs to forget their fragility. Somehow, they responded, and he gained speed with each painful step.

Two security guards came at him, but he brushed them aside with his mind with even more ease than the orderly. With each step becoming surer and quicker by the millisecond, with each use of his long-lost powers, the lights went out in a shower of sparks as he glowed brighter and brighter.

The car was almost at the intersection. It bounced over a curb, then back onto the road. All anyone could do was dive out of the way or turn their heads to avoid seeing the inevitable collision.

The toddler, red-faced and hysterical, wailed as the car took another bad bounce over the curb and took flight into the unsuspecting intersection traffic.

Time slowed to a crawl.

Orion charged out of the hospital, a blur of motion against a backdrop of statues. A beacon in the daylight sun, he pushed himself past breaking.

The car flew through the air, a red family minivan at the end of its deadly trajectory. Orion saw the driver freeze up, mouth agape at what was about to hit him and his clan from the side. Even if he could react fast enough, there was nowhere for him to go. Other cars sat in front and behind.

The hapless driver closed his eyes in that last moment.

The toddler wailed in terror.

Orion gave one last push, the strain tearing him apart.

The girl's mother reached out, horrified beyond all reason, her scream adding to that of her child, when—

A blinding flash of light, brighter than any star in the sky, encased them all. Despite their overwhelming fear, every witness shut their eyes at that moment.

Everything stopped—the screams, the terror, time itself.

After what seemed far too long, they each opened their eyes to see—

The runaway car stopped only feet from the minivan. It hovered in midair, Orion on the ground between them, hands outstretched towards the floating vehicle. He radiated a vivid, warm glow, at once blinding and comforting, like the sun itself.

All traffic ceased as if on cue. People got out of their cars, forgetting them behind. Everyone in the intersection looked on in silent awe. Even the toddler sat in mute wonder, staring at the expanse of bright blue sky out the rear window.

With a Herculean effort of will, Orion gently lowered the car to the ground.

The minivan driver exited his vehicle, his family on his heels. They joined the rising throng of onlookers circling the miraculous sight. No one could believe what they were seeing, and excited murmurs quickly rippled through the crowd.

"It's him," one said.

"Oh my God," said another.

"He's back!" added a third, before the overlapping voices were too numerous to count.

The little girl's mother finally reached the car, out of breath and disheveled. She pulled open the rear door, the child in her arms in moments.

The crowd parted as Orion pulled himself up the hood of the car to see if the child was safe. He opened his mouth to ask, when the mother exclaimed, "Oh, thank you. Thank you!"

He crumpled to one knee, thoroughly spent, though inexplicably even brighter than before.

A collective gasp ran through the crowd. There was no mistaking the frailty of their hero or the finality of this singular act.

"Make way! Move!" Dr. Merryman called out. He rushed through the onlookers with his support staff, wheeling a gurney, IV bags, and an oxygen machine.

The mother looked from them to Orion, the fear and worry painted on her face. She leaned down to offer help.

"Please," she begged. "Don't move. They're coming."

Orion shook his head, trying to get to his feet, but unable. He was so brilliant now; it was making everyone squint or shield their eyes. A few had even turned away. And all started to back up. He was a light bulb glowing far too hot, far too bright.

Even the hospital staff stopped, staying on the periphery of the growing circle. Dr. Merryman waved for the young mother to come back to a safe distance.

She stood her ground, though Orion could see the trace of worry cross her face.

They didn't know what would happen. Would he stop, or would he keep going? Would he blind them? Would he burn them? Would he explode? He could see it on their faces and in their eyes. As much as they loved him, they feared him more.

Only the toddler seemed unfazed, more mystified than anything. She reached out with her small hand, her olive eyes full of childlike wonder.

"Shiny man okay?" she asked without a trace of fear.

He took in the child safe in her mother's arms, and couldn't imagine a more welcome sight. This was what it was all about. What it had always been about. Somewhere along the line, he forgot that, and now felt so grateful for the chance to be reminded.

More light now than flesh, he gave a weary smile, the first in a very long time.

"Never better," he said, offering his own hand.

The child's small fingers wrapped themselves around his index finger, and the smile she gave touched his fractured soul.

Orion laughed once, as pure and clear as the joy coursing through him. In that moment, a flash of brilliance enveloped them all. A shudder ran through the crowd, and a soft ripple of wind moved them slightly back.

And just like that, he was gone.

The muted, solemn faces of all those around her could not extinguish the child's beaming smile, so full of joy and amazement at the miracle she witnessed. With a squeal of delight, her small fingers passed through fluttering ashes of white in the radiant midday sun.

# Night Insects

## By Edith Clark

### About Edith Clark:

Born and raised in the American heartland, Edith Clark spent her early years in post-war Michigan when the world was still reeling from WWII. Her uncle died as a P.O.W. in the Philippine Islands, and though his name was seldom mentioned, his memory was a constant presence in the Clark household.

Edith's father, a zoology professor, encouraged her love of reading, writing, and the natural sciences, and Edith (also known as Edie) eventually earned a B.A. in English and an M.S. in Public Health. Perpetually curious, Edith's interest in her late uncle's fate drew her to books about WWII's Pacific Theater, and to the notorious P.O.W. camp, Cabanatuan, located on Luzon Island in the Philippines. Years of reading fostered her deep respect for the heroic—but largely unknown—women and men who risked their lives in the Philippine resistance.

Edith has written a full-length novel about a young Filipino who becomes involved in the resistance when his friend, an American lieutenant, is captured. Her short story, "Night Insects," was adapted from a chapter in that novel, and is dedicated to the extraordinary Philippine resistance.

# Night Insects

## Edith Clark

The Zambales Mountains, Northern Bataan Peninsula
The Philippine Islands
May, 1944

It was 4:00 a.m. when Raju slipped out of his bedroll, pulled his pants on, and listened for the other men. He heard three of them breathing, and he could just make out the telegraph machine that sat on a table in the corner of the tent, right where it belonged. *Good.*

Something had awakened him, but he wasn't sure what it was. He closed his eyes and listened, concentrating. The wind soughed in the jungle canopy and a few trees creaked in the breeze, but something was missing, and Raju held his breath as he focused, trying to determine what was different.

He lifted his head. *That was it.*

The night insects had stopped chirping. The tree frogs and owls were silent, too. Something had interfered with the jungle's rhythm, and Raju felt a dark presence. He and the others in his camp were in trouble.

The war had sharpened Raju's instincts; these days he noticed things, even small things, that he wouldn't have paid attention to in past years. He and the twelve others in this hidden camp would survive only if they stayed at least one step ahead of their foes.

He opened the tent flap and stepped out into the inky night, walking a few strides to the center of the clearing before squatting barefoot on the ground. He closed his eyes and tipped his head back, inhaling deeply and testing the air. He exhaled slowly, then breathed deeply again, turning his head in different directions.

*Oh yes.* Uphill, not so very far away. He wasn't sure what it was, but something was there that didn't belong.

It would be two hours before the first pale green light of dawn would filter through the jungle canopy. The forest floor was damp; if he left now and went barefoot, there would be little snapping and cracking. None, if he was careful.

Raju moved quietly back into the tent and put on a dark shirt and helmet. He slung his rifle up over his back—it was a 1903A3 bolt action Springfield, and though he had cleaned it relentlessly, he had never once fired it, not even in practice. Maybe this would be the day? He headed to the edge of the clearing where the other tents were clustered, searching for the path leading up the mountainside. There was no light. *Good.* The darker, the better.

Even in the pitch black Raju knew where the path started, and he knew how to move in the nighttime. He closed his eyes and put his foot on the trail, then gradually, gingerly, he shifted his weight and placed his other foot in front of it.

He embraced the darkness for the sake of the many gifts it could send his way. The darkness was his friend and his comfort, and he planned on making it his enemy's worst nightmare. A familiar whispering voice passed through his thoughts.

*Yes, you're right. Uphill slowly, feel your way. Crouch down, place the palms of your hands on the mountain. The mountain will speak to you, listen to what it says.*

A leaf brushed against his face, then another, but Raju was in a different zone now and the leaves, the earth, the night air—all of it felt right to him. He was as tight as a spring, but he felt no fear—instead, he felt the expansiveness of a man who held the clear, silent advantage. He moved like a wild thing, respectful of his surroundings, slowly, eyes closed, his hands feeling the texture and slope of the ground ahead of him.

*You're close now. Trick them with your silence. Be invisible. Move around them. Yes, that's it, go above them.*

And then he felt something moving. It barely touched the edge of his right hand where it was placed flat against the sloping mountainside; then it continued up and over his hand. It was a snake. Raju froze.

Magandang Kapatid na ahas. *Good Brother snake.* Raju smiled and waited. The snake continued over the width of his right hand, then up and over the edge of his left hand, then stopped; and in that sweetly suspenseful moment Raju saw a shadow ahead of him—perhaps maybe not so much a shadow as a denser blackness, maybe fifty feet away. The shape moved carelessly, with no regard for silence or caution. *Good.* Whatever it was, it didn't know Raju was there, stalking it from beneath the tall ferns.

There was the sound of a zipper, and then a liquid sound, like someone pissing. Raju sniffed the air. Yes, urine.

He could still feel the slight weight of the snake across the width of his right hand and halfway across his left hand. Mahal kita kapatid na ahas. Na-save mo sa akin muli. *I love you, Brother Snake. You saved me.*

Raju heard the sound of zipping again, then the shape turned, hesitated, seemed to be fumbling for something.

*S-c-r-a-tchhh.* It was the sound of a match, and for a few moments, the area around a Japanese soldier was illuminated. As he touched the match to his cigarette, Raju could see the man's face in a shimmering halo of light. He was wearing a helmet, and there were more helmets to the left, a circle of maybe six on the other side of the path.

The soldier dropped the match and exhaled. Raju could smell the sharpness of sulfur and the rich aroma of cigarette smoke. And then the soldier was just a shape again, a spot of inky black against the forest, followed by the glowing tip of a cigarette. The snake moved again, slipping over Raju's left hand and away into the jungle.

It was still dark when Raju returned to the guerilla camp. Without hesitating he went directly to the tent where Corporal John Boone was sleeping, shaking him hard by the shoulders.

Alarmed, Boone leaped to his feet, ready to fight, calling for his men. But instead of an enemy, the man he grabbed by the shoulders was one of his own guerillas. It was the young one, the mute boy who couldn't speak a word, and he was signing with his hands like a house afire, a look of urgency on his face. Boone released Raju, then walked over to the table to get a pencil and paper.

By six o'clock in the morning Corporal Boone, Raju, and six other Filipinos were hidden beneath the tall ferns in a spread formation 75 feet above the Japanese encampment. They crouched on the ground, as silent as the shadows that disguised them, rifles ready. The black jungle turned to a misty gray, then to shadowy green as dawn sent narrow shafts of light creeping through the canopy. They could hear the soldiers whispering to one another, could hear the sounds of men getting up to urinate. A few smoked cigarettes. There were seven of them, and they were preparing to head downhill to attack the guerillas.

Instead, the hunted had become the hunters, and when the sun emerged over the eastern horizon there was a fusillade of gunfire; within seconds, all of the enemy soldiers were dead. They hadn't even gotten off a round.

The men wanted to cheer, to acknowledge out loud their dark victory, but Corporal Boone held an index finger to his lips, calling for silence. He turned to Raju and put a hand on his shoulder.

"Raju," he whispered, a new look of respect in his eyes. "Can you track these soldiers backward? Can you show me where they came from?"

Raju understood. Other enemy scouts would have been alerted by the sound of gunfire. They would come looking for their men and Boone wanted to ambush them.

Raju smiled and nodded, and although no one could understand him, he signed: "*Yes. Easy job.*"

The enemy had been unusually careless. It was an easy matter to follow their discarded cigarette butts through the jungle and down the side of the mountain. Crouching low, the guerillas tracked them for a quarter mile, then took high positions in a rocky outcropping, looking down onto the jungle floor. They posted lookouts to cover their rear, then settled in and waited.

By 8:00 a.m. four more enemy soldiers lay dead in the Zambales Mountains.

Corporal Boone whispered to Raju, calling him over to his side. "Raju, tell me something. Have you ever used a firearm before today?"

Raju looked at him steadily. One corner of his mouth lifted very slightly in a crooked smile as he slowly shook his head no. There was something scary about that cold stare and his humorless smile.

The corporal squinted, lowering his brow. "Never used a firearm, right? But you've killed before, haven't you?"

The boy's eyes never wavered as he lifted the smiling corner of his mouth another half inch.

Corporal Boone raised his eyebrows. "Okay then. I'll take that as a yes."


By 10:00 a.m., Corporal Boone and his men were breaking camp and heading to a new location. Raju walked near the end of the column, careful to watch his footing on the steep path while keeping an eye out for signs of enemy patrols. He was silent, as always, but he was no longer the timid, skittish boy he had been at the beginning of this war. He had seen too much blood, and too many bodies to be shy about what he was doing now, high in these misty mountains, fighting with Philippine guerrillas.

The last shreds of Raju's old persona had been left behind on the road to San Ildefonso when he and his family were fleeing from Angeles. He had been shot twice, and his two cousins had been raped. His aunt had killed one of those men with the knife she had strapped to her thigh. Raju had used the same knife to kill the other man; then they dumped the bloody bodies face down in a rice paddy.

None of his fellow guerillas knew that this was Raju's 19th birthday. Two years ago on this day, Aunt KuJean had made him sugared almond cakes and lemongrass tea. Minnie-Mac had wrapped two hens in banana leaves and roasted them in coals while Chrisophe played his wooden flute. Raju had danced in circles with his aunt, and his two cousins had danced with one another.

Back in those days, they had run a laundry business, all of them together, and Raju's biggest problem was keeping the wrinkles out of the ironed shirts as he folded and delivered them to their customers. There had been wonderful music back then, and so much dancing, back when even the insects were unafraid.

*Third Place Winner*

# DYSPHORIA

## By Chuck Regan

ABOUT CHUCK REGAN:

Chuck Regan is a geek who enjoys writing genre fiction—grungy military sci-fi, psychological noir, supernatural horror, gory western, bizarro satire—or any combination of the above. He also designs and illustrates book covers.

www.chuckregan.com

# DYSPHORIA

## Chuck Regan

MESHMASH broadcast — 11:00:000, 18SEP, 2228

"In a few moments, talks will begin between representatives of Seyopont and with Antioch Krell, the leader of the Human Purity Movement who is seeking equal rights for non-transhuman citizens," the bland looking brunette synthetic said with a light Martian accent. Her words were accompanied by a gentle stream of emotibot cues feeding into the broadcast, influencing everyone watching who was equipped with an Amygdalal Regulatory Medium implant to trust her words, but to feel a pulse of disgust when Krell's name was mentioned.

The scene folded open to a tall and fit white-haired man with hard lines on his face. The emotibot feed pulsed with levels of distrust and hatred, depending on the individual's personality profile watching the broadcast. Krell spoke with assertive bass tones as he stood in front of a painted backdrop portraying the depths of an extinct rainforest, the symbol of the Greenway activists.

"I'm pleased to be finally granted the opportunity to speak openly about the plight of True Humans as second-class citizens."

The grit in his vocal chords resonated with the middle- and low-rank citizens—all having breathed inadequately filtered air for most of their lives, their voices had all inevitably eroded to gravelly rasps. To them, Antioch sounded like he was one of them. Those of them with implants felt twinges of guilt and paranoia.

"We are the ones who built these colonies," he continued. "We are the ones who insured the future of humanity. We are the ones who suffered and died. We are still suffering, and now, our food sources are being compromised. Industries under the Seyopont Conglomerate are focusing more and more on providing intravenous *Stain* nutrients to feed the transhuman populations, while we, the ones who built the colonies in this system, struggle and inevitably starve to death."

The clarity of his language was keyed to the rational, middle- and upper-rank citizens, but the seething, barely-contained violence in his tone is what had connected to the human populations who had not yet received implants.

"We will not be erased from history. We are here to claim what we deserve. We will not be ignored."

The reporter returned with a concerned expression on her face. Emotibot streams fed the feed with a mix of disbelief and guarded hope. "Remarkably, and against all predictions, all terrorist acts against enhanced citizens have ceased after the talks began."

An emotibot surge of transcendent awe accompanied a wipe to a full-sensorium rendering of the iconic plant life of Glau 4c, the exo-Earth known as 'Jungle'.

"In other news," she said, "in less than 24 hours, the crew of the Soruti is scheduled to set foot on the planet Jungle and begin exploration."

Sales of the 'Viro full-sensorium experience recorded by drones on that planet spiked. *Jungle: An Offworld Exploration* became at that moment the highest-selling 'Viro to date.

Luna 2 Station, Vault 77223 — 11:15:030, 18SEP, 2228

*Helvetica Phage, please blink-sign.*

The delivery drone's message shocked Helvetica away from the liquid light of higher math, and back into the dense, muddled, thick flesh of her own face. *Delivery from Ganny Health and Wellness.*

*Shit.* She had forgotten to set up an alert to herself, to give her a warning, but she had forgotten—now all the delicate thought-filaments she had constructed over many hours knitting logic-quilts of time-space formulae using 4-dimensional geometry frayed and recoiled, disintegrating before her mind's eye as her connection to the Mesh slid away.

The seven other minds she had been linked with scrambled to take hold of her fraying threads of calculations, and there was no resentment in their actions—as if her clumsy exit had been anticipated by them. She felt like she had just behaved like a baboon at a dinner party, throwing handfuls of her own shit at the guests. Inexcusable, but the node members did not block her. Her trend ratings did not waver.

Helvetica sent them all apologetic emotibots and then immediately regretted it. Next-levels like them were so much more advanced than her, the only thing she was accomplishing was reminding them why they shouldn't invite un-evolved knuckle-draggers like her into their node. She followed up with *thank you for allowing me to participate* written in text, hoping they'd appreciate the femtoseconds it took her to compose each retro-tech message.

Her Mesh interface retracted as the real world rose up in front of her eyes. The bitter, fruity, buzzing stink of nanogel saturated her nose and tongue, and, forgetting it was doing the work of putting oxygen into her body, she instinctively tried to pull air into her lungs.

*Drowning!* Her monkey brain screamed and flailed, spraying adrenalin into her system. The nanogel buzzed through her, secreting countermeasures to calm her spastic inner primate, and Helvetica felt a soothing warmth spread out to surround her. Her limbs buzzed and twitched as the shockwave of adrenaline was slowly squeezed out of her body.

She blinked and tried to focus on the grain in the stainless steel walls of her vault—*so ugly, so cheap-looking*—she was reminded of the archaic manufacturing process and the stigma of living in a vault as old and restrictive as hers. Her monkey brain gnashed and chattered, trying to provoke claustrophobia in her. Another surge of countermeasures pulsed through her, silencing the monkey's rising terror, and she reminded her primitive mind that the vault was a necessary step to achieve enlightened perfection. She kept repeating the thought that this vault was her chrysalis, and soon she would emerge as a beautiful butterfly of pure thought.

*Helvetica Phage, please blink-sign*, the drone repeated.

As if it were mocking her, the drone had waited an entire three seconds before repeating the request. It was treating her like an un-enhanced human who couldn't process information any faster. The drone had taken so long to repeat the message, she had almost forgotten why she was back in the Real.

Red light flared in her retina and her external feed's home screen projected into her eye. In contrast to the purity of node-thought, the antique visual interface felt like a primitive drawing on a child's wall, the icons crackling sharp edges—flat and dead.

*11:15 am. Wednesday, August 14, 2228.* She had been immersed for fifteen straight days. It never felt like it was long enough.

Flipping over to the security cameras, she scanned the hallways above—no anti-enhancement terrorists waiting to poison her—and a panoramic view of the floor overtop her vault. A squat, 4-legged cargo drone was parked over her lid, the logo of her delivery service laser-etched onto every clean, armored plate.

She tapped into the facility's security cameras again to see that the vault next to her was still unoccupied—the dark stainless steel hatch looking like a dead eye socket set into the floor. Every other hatch blinked green and white indicators of healthy occupants. Helvetica didn't like incomplete patterns. It was imbalanced. It felt awkward with the empty vault being right next to her.

The subtle emotion of superstitious paranoia mixed with longing was unique for her, and before she was able to record her emotichem levels, it passed. A shame, she thought. It would have made a nice addition to the emotibot set she had been preparing to sell.

She clicked through her personal speck cameras until she got a clear view of the bar code printed on the drone's abdomen. She ran the numbers and tracked the drone back to its point of origin to the plant where it was assembled on her home of Luna 2, and to where each of the parts of the drone had been assembled: Sasia, American Union, Chihong, Guatam, and New Ireland, with ore mined from the asteroids Ceres and Ida.

It bothered her that her delivery service was still using parts from the American Union. Although she had seen how the Union had rebranded their corporate identity and announced their amended constitution, she didn't trust their products worth a fart. Even if it was just a tiny, inconsequential gyrostabilizer inside this drone, Union products were still shit, and some of her sponsors would drop her if they found out she was supporting the Union in this small way. She made a note to look for a new delivery service.

Helvetica confirmed on her calendar that she was indeed scheduled for this supply drop at this time. She scanned the contents: electrolytes, serotonin, liquid protein, vitamins in concentrate, amino acids, nanogel seed-and-patch, and FliiHii—the new neuroconductor she was eager to try. Everything on the manifest was exactly what she had ordered in the correct amount, and had arrived at the precise time—11:15:03 am. This was no terrorist spam delivery.

She blink-signed the approval and unlocked her supply hatch topside. Helvetica blasted her input ports with sterilizer. Thick clicks clattered over her head as the drone locked its injectors into her ports and filled her vats with *Stain* nutrients that would keep her alive for another month. She watched her levels rise one by one, and she acknowledged the strange irony of feeling both resentment and relief for the interruption—an emotibot she had already recorded. She confirmed the next scheduled drop, and the drone rolled away to the next delivery.

She disconnected to the visual feed to the real world and closed her eyes, welcoming again the clean, ordered, safe world of the Mesh.

MESHMASH broadcast—12:00:000, 18SEP, 2228

"Ganny Health and Wellness denies the allegations that unregulated molecules have been transmitted through the 'Viro, *Jungle: An Offworld Exploration*. A representative of the company called the medical report associating hallucinations and brainlock to the virtual experience 'ridiculous' and 'the product of a paranoid mind.'"

Sales of *Jungle: An Offworld Exploration* doubled within the next 17 seconds.


Luna 2 Station, Vault 77223 — 12:01:487, 18SEP, 2228

Helvetica's bank account bot—a big, grinning cartoon bear named Chauncy, wearing a business suit—was excited to show her that she almost had enough money to get mind mapped. The procedure she had been saving up for, to have her brain scanned and analyzed, was the first step to becoming pure synthetic—pure thought, unencumbered by the primitive constraints of flesh.

After her mind could be uploaded to a synthetic medium, she could finally be who she wanted to be. Freed from monkey thoughts and monkey chemistry, all those monkey roles she had been following could finally be abandoned, and the new species she would join could focus on advancing the entire race beyond the limitations of the physical realm. She would become something as far beyond human as human beings were from naked mole rats.

For now, still anchored to her flesh, Helvetica had to fulfill the role she had created for herself in the system, feeding monkeys what they wanted—she had to sell them her dreams.

'Viro was an immersive experiential system that bridged the gap between the un-enhanced and transhumans, but fewer and fewer transhumans bothered to slum in 'Viro space, as their worlds opened up to deeper transcendent thoughts and out-of-body experiences. The open source code of 'Viro allowed anyone to create and sell whatever they could imagine and encode: free explorations of fantasy landscapes, deep-sea adventures from the point of view of many different creatures, galactic fly-throughs, life in 2-dimensions, and porn, of course, in an ever-evolving spectrum of variations. Anything that could be imagined—the more surreal the better—was eagerly consumed by the meat-locked monkeys.

The un-enhanced were so desperate to escape from their own flesh, they bought up 'Viro as fast as it was created. Helvetica, and other enhanced beings like her, referred to this obvious irony as justification for themselves to leave behind their own monkey forms as quickly as possible.

Helvetica randomized a selection of imagery from her inspirational files—pix, videos, esoteric emotibots, and thoughtforms—and opened her dream-synthesis program, *Magigora*.

A cartoon dragon named Neeb fluttered into view.

"Don't download the latest patch," Neeb said. Helvetica had customized this sentry bot to monitor the message boards for Magigora developments and 'Viro trends.

"What's wrong now?" Helvetica thought-spoke.

"Some glitches had been reported—" Neeb said, holding up charts and screen captures of news feeds that he stacked into her periphery. "Failures to launch, frozen playbacks, and three cases of brainlock. Magigora's trend status dropped sharply but is steadily recovering. Ganny Health and Wellness is working on a new patch to fix the last patch."

"What was this last patch supposed to fix?"

Neeb took a moment to appear pensive and puffed out a smoke ring that took the shape of *Kheops*, the logo for the bot-creation app she had used to make him—the smoke-ring logo was an annoying built-in feature that she hadn't been able to hack out. It took a full nanosecond to dissipate.

"The patch was to provide a better integration with Caribou 8 systems, but that system is so archaic, it won't have any effect on your sales."

Only the un-enhanced on backwaters like Mars and the American Union used Caribou 8 systems anymore.

"Thanks, Neeb."

Neeb smiled, coughed out a smoke cloud and disappeared into it. She felt him hover on her periphery, ready to assist if she needed him.

Helvetica dropped her inspirational files into Magigora and set the dream system to freeform for the first three enhanced REM cycles, then the subliminals would kick in with a recommended dose of FliiHii.

MESHMASH broadcast—13:00:000, 18SEP, 2228

"Redpaw Enforcers have exposed a conspiracy which implicates Antioch Krell as the mastermind behind the sabotage of the 'Viro *Jungle*. The makers of *Jungle*, Kheops LLC, allowed Enforcers full access to their systems, which revealed decrypted communications between three of their employees which pointed directly to Krell. His attorneys are preparing a statement."

Trend ratings in Kheops LLC were boosted dramatically over the next five minutes, leading to the sale of the company to the holding corporation of Ganny Health and Wellness.

Luna 2 Station, Vault 77223 — 13:23:115, 18SEP, 2228

*MAGIGORA EDIT: DREAM SESSION 8436*

Broad-leafed trees swayed in a gentle, lemon-honey breeze, and a low, pink haze clung to the ground. Helvetica squatted to examine the green-blue dome-like shrubs, their plump, dewdrop-pointed leaves dribbling rivers of condensed mist into the trunk and root of the plant.

It looked pleasantly familiar to her.

Helvetica paused the playback and reduced her POV. There was something under that plant she wanted to investigate. She swiped up the *Bingbong* add-on and waited for the whistling pressure to bore into her head. Bingbong reintroduced the gestalt of her dream state and extrapolated from her subconscious the details not recorded in the dream. The feeling she had whenever Bingbong was on was like a continuous Deja-vu.

As soon as she stepped under a dome shrub, she knew what she would find—a village of tiny shrimp-like people walking erect, carrying tools, living in a tiny, primitive village.

"No."

She paused the dream playback.

"Too derivative."

*Shrimpfolk* was a popular 'Viro that reinforced the primitivism that had fueled the Anti-Enhancement movement the month before. She saved the session in its raw state and queued up the next recorded dream.

~ ~ ~ ~ ~

*MAGIGORA EDIT: DREAM SESSION 8437*

A bleak, angular skyline of gray stone buildings hovered in space—amber spotlights etched the brutal angles in shadow as a planet of churning lava roiled below. Black iron gargoyles with fixed wings and glowing red eyes glided slowly between the structures. Helvetica's POV followed one of the gargoyles. It was a transport of some kind—intricately gothic spines and rosettes traced its surface like the skin of a prehistoric sea creature was stretched over its surface. The vehicle hummed with an otherworldly power source.

The gargoyle-ship flew into a yawning, arched portal and landed in a hall decorated with tall banners bearing a thorny rose icon. At the far end of the hall, another gargoyle landed. Both vehicles' gull-wing doors opened simultaneously, and two humanoids in black powered armor marched toward each other, esoteric weapons glowing, with steam curling out of vents in helmets sculpted to resemble snarling animals.

Pause.

"Another science-fantasy military-dystopia first-person fighter. So overdone."

Helvetica saved the file and made notes to add some kind of pseudo-psychic complexity to the play—something like a connection to the molten planet earns power points, increasing endorphin levels in the player.

Next dream…

~ ~ ~ ~ ~

*MAGIGORA EDIT: DREAM SESSION 8438*

A note popped open—*FliiHii introduced at 12:57:24.038*—and Helvetica's body sensors flared alarms—endorphin, cortisol, and adrenaline levels increased. She was curious and excited, at levels she hadn't experienced in the last 13 days. Emotichems like these inevitably led to disappointments. With her countermeasures suspended, she had to manually suppress her chems. She regained her baseline and was about to playback the dream when a clatter above her vault jolted her out of the interface. Anger alerts flared. Discomfort levels flared. Annoyance and frustration pinged.

Helvetica swept open the Kheops app and saved a sample of her hormone levels. She had needed a fresh sampling of this flavor of dysphoria to use in her *annoyed* emotibot. She recorded a perfect sample before natural self-satisfaction had a chance to wash it away. She bridged to her external feeds to find out what was happening above her vault lid.

On the external cameras, a new occupant was moving into the neighboring empty vault. Four medical drones in enamel-white shells guided a human-sized lozenge-shaped sac of nanogel into the open chamber. A pale blue blanket covered all but a section of the sac. Helvetica zoomed in and recorded the scene as a bloated, pale body inched lower into the hole. Its fingers were fused together into a kind of flipper—proof of genetic deformation from long-term immersion or imbalanced chems.

A drone's leg blocked her view, and she switched to another camera. It looked like the drones were struggling to wedge the sac inside the chamber. They raised the sac perpendicular to the opening, and the blanket slid away.

Where a mouth should've been on a human face, there was a round, toothy suction disk, and its enormous eyes were milky, glassy pucks—blind. A puddle of nanogel formed under the drones' footpads. A puncture in the sac. The drones scampered to stay upright in the puddle of gel and the sac fell, splattering her cameras.

Helvetica switched to the facility security cameras giving an overhead view of the floor. Four drones scampered and slid on the slimy surface as a diseased albino human-dolphin-lamprey-thing helplessly slapped its flipper-limbs. Above her, she heard the rasps and scrapes as its sucker-mouth tried to bite into her lid.

A grating, shrieking sound as the thing gnawed there, flipper-hands slapping uselessly at its sides, torso heaving as milky nanogel spewed from its mouth.

Helvetica's body monitors screamed alarms—anxiety at terror 3 level—her heart clunked in her chest and an aching heat burned at the back of her neck. Her manual countermeasures wouldn't engage.

The two drones had righted themselves and extended poles, bracing themselves against the walls. They guided the flailing creature tail-first into its vault. It slopped in, banging its head on the rim of the lid, and the thick, wet clunk echoed into Helvetica's ears. One drone clamped over the neighboring hole as the others extended squeegee blades and corralled the gel across the floor and down into the opening.

Helvetica's heartbeat shushed in her ears and clunked in her throat. She swiped on the body regulation app, but it wouldn't engage. Her chest burned, and her fingers sparked with pins and needles as flares stacked up alerting her to rising potentials of infarctions and aneurisms. Her monkey brain tried to scream to the med drones for help, but her lungs began to seize, hiccuping and fluttering, trying to push nanogel in and out faster than physics allowed, unable to take a breath.

Something snapped behind her collarbone—a rib dislocated—lightning shot up her neck and nausea curdled in her belly. A solid, scrolling bar of flashing red warnings filled her interface. She tried to activate the body regulation app again, and her interface locked. Frozen.

*REBOOT REQUIRED* flashed.

She had never seen that warning before.

A frozen chill washed through her. Her limbs went numb, and it felt like her scalp was tearing away from her skull. Her eyes bugged wide. She couldn't access any bots to help her. She couldn't trigger an emergency medical flare.

Helvetica disengaged from the Mesh interface and blinked hard in the real world, searching to activate the link to the external system, but her retina didn't flare red. No link. No comforting old, reliable visual interface laser-projected onto her retina, just the cold, frozen static of brushed stainless steel.

She focused on her right arm. Her shoulder burned as she moved it—muscles atrophied, she never thought she'd have to use them again. Her eyes ached as she aimed them over her head. Above her, the *emergency purge* button slowly pulsed above her face. Her arm shook as she inched her hand up the wall, feeling the nanogel slide between her fingertips and steel.

Her vision started to gray. The nanogel had stopped feeding her oxygen. Her arm trembled, burning, as she pushed it up toward her head. Inches to go. She couldn't open her fingers. A shriveled, alabaster claw pulled into view—her own hand. Her scalp sparked fear and disgust, and adrenaline screamed like a flamethrower torching her heart. Her claw rocketed upward and pounded the purge button.

Nothing happened.

Flashes of white popped in her vision as she banged against her lid.


MESHMASH broadcast—14:00:000, 18SEP, 2228


"Helvetica Phage's trend ratings doubled within seconds after she released her latest 'Viro, *Dysphoria*—a fully immersive nightmare of a vault-dweller trying to escape from her chamber after a system crash. Response to this 'Viro has boosted the Anti-Enhancement movement as record numbers of vault-dwellers have requested a return to the Real, causing a spike in demand for Ganny Health and Wellness products."

"Helvetica Phage responded to this unprecedented rise in popularity with the release of her third emotibot collection, containing, among other fresh icons, the terror emotibot she recorded while using FliiHii, the new neuroconductor, from Ganny Health and Wellness."

"FliiHii—Flii hiigher with FliiHii."

"Ganny Health and Wellness—you can't have too much Ganny in your life."

# Other Winners

(IN ALPHABETICAL ORDER)

## About Pamela Bobowicz:

Pamela Bobowicz grew up in a small town in Massachusetts where her mother was a hospice nurse for a number of years. "Say When," developed one summer when her mom was working on a particularly difficult case. She was available to the patient's family 24/7, whether they needed her to come out to assess the patient, or just to hear her reassuring voice on the phone. Her mother has since moved on from hospice work, but to this day, when she ventures into town, old patients and their families will stop her to say thank you. The importance of hospice work and the effect it has on families hadn't occurred to Pamela before that summer, and Tess's relationship with her mom began from there.

Pamela currently works as a children's book editor in New York.

# Say When

## Pamela Bobowicz

Momma always said that coming into this world and going out of it are the hardest things a person can do. I guess she'd know, having borne three girls after watching her parents pass on. But now that she's the one knocking on death's door, I wonder what's really harder: the leaving or the being left behind.

Daddy's on the back porch smoking a cigar. I can see the blue smoke curling away from his lips as he puffs. Momma complained about the smell last night when he went in to say goodnight.

"Why you gotta smoke those?" she asked. "You know I can't stand 'em."

Daddy stayed quiet a moment. He watched me wipe the sweat from Momma's brow and help her sip water from a straw. "Why you gotta die?" he said at last. "You know I can't stand that."

His boots fell hard on the wooden floor as he left the room.

"Tess," Momma said, pushing the glass and straw away. Some water dribbled from the end and soaked into the thin cotton sheet draped over her.

"Sorry, Momma," I said. "I'll get a towel."

"Tess," Momma said again.

I cringed as I looked at her—wasted away to a skeleton dressed in a paper-fine skin. The ridges of her skull were visible where curls the color of molasses once sprouted and tumbled to her shoulders. Her long, white fingers—ghosts of spider's legs—worried the thin cotton sheets near the water stain.

"It's hard, isn't it?" she said as she watched me take her in.

"What, Momma?"

"Living," she said, the corners of her mouth almost curling into a sad, half-moon smile, but stopping short at a fine white line. "You'd better get used to it, baby girl."


Daddy drops his mug in the sink where I'm washing the breakfast dishes, startling me. He smells like fresh-cut grass and cigar smoke and sweat. He was up at five o'clock this morning—same as he is every day—and in his workshop by a quarter to six to start tinkering with the engine on the bench.

There's been less work coming in the last couple weeks. Used to be there was a line into town for Daddy to fix a fan belt or install an engine or build a new car from old parts. Now the line rolls out of town, hops on the freeway and drives thirty miles to the strip of dealerships all waiting one after another in a row. When it takes a small-town mechanic, running a one-man show, two weeks to order new parts, it's no wonder the customers race to where they can have a new set of wiper blades, an exhaust system, or the latest model on the lot complete with power windows, air conditioning and a GPS system installed all in the time it takes to eat lunch.

Daddy looks around his empty workshop from time to time and says, "You can't sell a man a set of spare parts when he's looking for a whole new life." Then he picks up his wrench and gets back to work.

"She awake yet?" he asks as he stands over my shoulder, looking out the window at the garage he's just come from.

The blue and white checkered curtains billow in the light breeze. It's all sunshine and warm weather outside, and I wish I could run barefoot down the dirt road, arms stretched out to the side like the little bit of wind could lift me up and away. If I weren't washing dishes and looking after Momma, I'd be down at the creek with Tommy Lorens and Katie McAllister. I bet they'll catch crawdads to cook up for supper. I bet Katie will finally get that kiss I've been hoping for all summer long.

"Yes, sir, she's awake," I answer Daddy. He clears his throat, waiting for more of an answer, but that's all I'm offering up for now. He'll only be angry to hear that Momma couldn't get down more than a couple bites of dry toast, that one day soon, her room will be as empty as his garage, and he'll have one less thing to fix.

"Did—" Daddy starts when a car horn blares in the driveway. We peer through the little window together and watch Annabel wave from the driver's seat of her rental car. "Well, I'll be damned," Daddy whispers over my left shoulder. "I didn't think my letter would even find her, let alone send her home." Then he turns and walks down the hall and out the front door to see my older sister. She's gotten so good at being gone I'm not quite sure what to do with her back home now. I scrub harder at Daddy's coffee mug, even after the dark stains have all washed down the drain.

Annabel bursts into the kitchen, all smiles, and too much perfume. She smells like a funeral parlor full of fresh flowers waiting to cover a newly dug grave. "Tess!" she cries. She drops a pink, cardboard box on the table and her purse on the floor then crushes me in a hug. "You're so big! You must've grown another six inches."

"Only two this year," I say.

"Wow," she says, her voice full of air and awe. "Has it been a whole year?"

"Sure has," Daddy says. He drags her three suitcases into the kitchen with a grunt. "What you got in there anyhow? Feels like a ton of rocks."

"No, it's books," Annabel says. She pulls the top suitcase up onto the table and unzips it. The case is stacked with cookbooks: Julia Child, Martha Stewart, Rachel Ray. "I'm gonna make sure Momma eats a decent meal, three decent meals a day. And you both, too. We all need to keep up our strength. Then everything will be just fine."

Daddy looks at me across the table, and I can tell he doesn't know how to tell Annabel that Momma's been dying for the last three months, that he called her home to say good-bye. She doesn't know that Momma refused to have any more chemo or radiation treatments or that she went on hospice care four months ago. She doesn't know that Momma won't enjoy Martha Stewart's fresh summer salad because she hasn't eaten a full meal in two weeks. And Daddy certainly can't tell her that this morning, Momma couldn't catch her breath until I pushed an extra shot of morphine because that's a thing even he doesn't know yet.

I open my mouth to try and say what Daddy can't, but before the words come, Annabel reaches for the pink box and holds it out to me. "We'll cook later," she says. "But fourteenth birthdays deserve the very best."

I flip open the lid and feel a smile spread across my face. "Red velvet, my favorite."

"And…" Annabel makes another show of reaching into a brown paper bag and pulling out a champagne bottle. "Sparkling cider!" She pops the cork as she heads to the cupboard for glasses, grabbing three and placing them in the center of the table. "Tell me when, Tessie," she says as she starts to pour.

I watch the sweet liquid bubble in the glass and can practically taste the apple and pear as I say, "When."

Annabel fills the other two glasses to just above halfway. "Grab some plates, Tess. Four, so Momma can have a piece of cake, too. Life's short, eat dessert first, right?"

Gretchen and her husband, Bill, walk into the kitchen as I'm scraping the last bit of frosting off my plate. Annabel insisted we use Momma's bone china with pink roses and gold trim. Gretchen raises her eyebrows when she sees the good dishes out in the middle of a Tuesday afternoon, but she doesn't say anything. She hugs Annabel and then kisses Daddy on top of his head, where the graying hairs give way to his scalp. "Happy birthday, Tess," she says. "How is she today?"

"Same," Daddy responds. He stands up from his chair and drapes his arm around Gretchen's shoulders. "Come on, let's go see her. She'll want to know how you're coming along."

Gretchen smiles and lays a hand on her baby bump. "Thirty-eight weeks," she says. They walk out into the hall, Gretchen chattering on about onesies and burping blankets. Daddy looks happy as he listens to his oldest girl talk about her baby; it's been six months since I've seen him smile.

Bill sits in Daddy's seat and takes a piece of cake. He puts it on a napkin, breaks pieces off in his fingers and pops them into his mouth. Annabel asks him about working construction and listens only long enough to hear him mumble, "'S all right," before telling him all about where she's been. I watch Bill study his crumbs as Annabel describes places he'll never see—Portland, Maine, where the snow falls higher than the front door; the Santa Monica pier, where the Ferris wheel glows all night long; Wichita, Kansas, where the prairie grass blows in the wind for miles around; and her favorite place of all, the Carolina beaches where the dunes provide a lookout on the great, wide ocean, rolling and waving to the other side of the world.

Bill scrapes his chair back from the table and walks over to the fridge. He pulls out the milk and pours himself a glass.

"Oh, Bill," Annabel says, "we have sparkling cider. You don't want milk you can have any old day when we have so much to celebrate today." She reaches to take his glass, but he pulls it away.

"This'll do just fine," he says and takes a long drink. He sits back down in his chair and places the glass beside his plate.

"You excited to be going back to school, Tess?" Bill asks around bites of cake. "What's it, another two weeks?"

"Week and a half," I say, and shrug. I can't even think about school without wondering if Katie's gotten my kiss, if Tommy will ask her to the Fall Harvest Dance while I sit home by Momma's bedside.

"That's early, isn't—" Annabel begins.

"Tess!" Daddy bellows from the bedroom. His boots stomp down the hall and then his towering figure—all six foot two, arms like cannons reaching for me—appears in the doorway to the kitchen. "Where's the morphine?"

I look from Daddy's red face to Annabel, whose normally peaches and cream complexion has drained to a shade lighter than pale white. She lets the word "morphine" pass silently across her pink-glossed lips.

"I don't—" I start.

"Don't you lie to me, Tess," Daddy yells. "The nurse hasn't even come yet today, so the only one who coulda given that shot is you."

Finally, after seconds that feel like days, I make my eyes meet Daddy's. There's fire raging behind the pale green irises, and fear behind that. He purses his lips together, waiting for me to say something—anything except the truth.

"Tess," he says, his voice softer now. "Please."

"I'm sorry, Daddy," I whisper. I let my gaze fall back to the pink plastic tablecloth Annabel brought for the party. There's a small hole near my plate, with a jagged strip running to the corner where the plastic caught and started to tear.

Bill stands up and guides Daddy into his chair. Daddy drops down, staring at the space behind my head through vacant eyes, unable to stop seeing what's right in front of him. He reaches for the glass of milk and gulps until it's gone. Then he swipes his arm across his mouth, making the white-milk-mustache vanish without a trace.

Gretchen walks into the kitchen. She pauses when she sees Daddy in Bill's chair, her husband standing silently behind him. She looks at Annabel, leaning against the sink, twirling the bottle of sparkling cider between her hands.

"How's Momma?" I ask.

"She's tired," Gretchen responds. "I told her we'd let her rest until the home nurse comes."

Annabel's head snaps up. "You've hired a home nurse?" she asks.

Gretchen looks from Annabel to me to Daddy and sighs. "Yes," she says. "Momma is on hospice care. A nurse comes every other day from the hospital. When Tess is back in school, someone will come every day to be with Momma. The ladies at the church have—"

"Why is Momma on hospice?" Annabel interrupts. "That's for people who are dying. And Momma's not dying."

Gretchen looks between Daddy and me. She's always been good at cleaning up the messes we've made. But I see the disappointment in her eyes now that she knows we can't even be trusted to simply tell it like it is.

"Momma's not dying," Annabel repeats, more forcefully now.

Daddy clears his throat, then turns to Annabel. "Your Momma is... She's going to... She's been sick a long time."

"Well, she'll get better," Annabel retorts. "People don't just get sick and die. They get better."

"Annabel," Daddy begins.

"No, I don't accept it," she says. "We'll take her to the hospital, find her the best doctors. We won't give up."

"*She's* already given up," I blurt out. I don't realize the words are out of my mouth until I see the look on Daddy's face: he looks like he's just been slapped.

I scoot my chair back from the table and race outside into the hot sun. The air is thick with humidity, and it feels like I'm swimming through gravy. But it's better to be moving slow than sitting still.

The door clicks closed, and the slap of flip-flops against bare feet lets me know Gretchen's been sent to fetch me. I pause, halfway down the gravel driveway, and stare at the old dirt road that leads from our house to the center of town, where it meets blacktop stretching to so many other roads.

"Tess," Gretchen says. She lays a comforting hand on my shoulder, and I blink fast and furious, so my tears don't fall. "You know Annabel," she continues. "Don't be upset that she thinks she can do better—"

"I don't care about her," I say. "Daddy... I didn't mean it."

Gretchen pulls me into a hug. We stand in the driveway, not saying a word until we hear a car turn into the drive. Gretchen gives me a squeeze and says, "That's the nurse, come to check on Momma. We'd better get back inside."

We step to the side of the driveway and watch the car move past, stopping in a cloud of dust near the front door. Then we follow, as slowly as we can.

Back in the kitchen, Daddy's still sitting at the table, staring down at his hands. Bill's washing Momma's fine china in the sink with the breakfast dishes I never got to finish. We can hear Annabel down the hall with the nurse, chattering on about procedures and medicines, and an experimental treatment for pancreatic cancer patients in San Francisco.

Daddy laughs, and a sad smile pulls the corners of his lips. "Sadie always wanted to see the Golden Gate Bridge."

Gretchen opens her mouth, but all that comes out is a small cry before she sucks in a deep, gasping breath. Her hands move to her belly as her eyes go wide.

Bill turns from the sink. The plate he's drying slips from his hands and shatters into a thousand little pieces on the floor. "Is it time?" he asks as he crunches over the fine china until he's at Gretchen's side.

She grips his hand tight and then in a shaky voice says, "I think my water broke."

The kitchen bursts with activity as Daddy jumps out of his chair and races down the hall. Bill fumbles around Gretchen, trying to help her through her first contraction by gritting his teeth and grunting in time with her.

When it's over, she takes a deep breath. He kisses her forehead and wraps an arm around her waist. "Come on, let's get you to the hospital."

They're already out the door when Daddy comes back into the kitchen, followed by Annabel. "Tess, get in the truck," Daddy says.

"I don't know why you need me to go," Annabel says. "I could stay here with Momma and—"

"We're all going," Daddy says. His boots crunch over the broken glass as he grabs his keys, wallet and cellphone, and stuffs them into his pockets. Then he swipes a hand through his thinning hair as he looks around the kitchen. His eyes rest on Annabel, standing in the doorway with her arms crossed over her chest, a pout set firm on her face. "Get in the truck," he says.

He walks to the door and holds it open wide, watching as I pass through and then finally, Annabel. Then he steps outside himself, closing the door behind him.

At the hospital, Bill finds Gretchen a wheelchair and pushes her through the emergency room, past admitting, up to the maternity ward, and into a private room, while Daddy, Annabel and I sit in the waiting room. Bill comes out every twenty minutes to give us an update. Two centimeters. Two and a half. Three.

Gretchen gets stuck at three and a half centimeters for over an hour. When Bill comes out to tell us the same thing for the fourth time, Daddy says, "Son, why don't you let us know when she's on her way to the delivery room. She needs you there with her now."

Bill nods and turns to head back to take care of his family. I open my mouth to ask Daddy how long he thinks it will be when he says, "It's hard, isn't it?"

"Living?" I ask as Annabel, sitting in a chair with her back to us, says, "Dying?"

Daddy shakes his head and picks up a tattered copy of *Time* magazine. "Waiting." He leafs through the pages, not stopping to read a word.

Annabel turns around and watches Daddy for a moment. Then she says, "She's gonna die soon?"

Daddy keeps flipping through Time, and when he turns the back cover from right hand to left, he pulls it back to his right and begins leafing backward. "She's gonna die when she's gonna die," he says.

Annabel turns back around, her leg bouncing and her arms clenched tightly around her middle like she's freezing cold. Suddenly, she's out of the chair and heading toward the sliding doors where EMERGENCY is stamped across in bold red letters.

I look at the doors, sliding open and closed. With no Gretchen and no Momma to set things right, I wonder who's job it is now; whose job will it be from now on? Daddy's still flipping pages until the front cover of the magazine lies face up in his lap. He flops it onto the table and settles back in his chair. "We'll leave her be," he says. "If there's one thing Annabel knows how to do, it's run."

"Why do you think she came home if she doesn't want to be here?" I finally ask.

Daddy shrugs and lets out a long sigh. "She knew Gretchen was about to have the baby. She knew Momma wasn't doing well. She knew it was your birthday."

I watch Daddy inspect his callused, grease-stained hands, dirt forever wedged under blackened fingernails, as he lists off one reason after another to try and explain my sister.

"She's been gone a long time," Daddy says, his voice soft and low.

"She leaves before she can be left behind," I say, remembering how she took off the night Gretchen and Bill got engaged; the day after Momma was handed a shortened life-sentence.

The quiet hangs between Daddy and me like the heat over the blacktop road leading out of town.

Daddy's cellphone startles us both. "It's home," he says, staring at the display. He flips it open, and I can see him holding his breath, preparing for the news that we know is coming and can't do a thing about.

"Hullo," he says. He listens and then breathes out a long, slow breath. "Oh, okay. Tell her we'll call when the baby's born. Or if she wants us to come home to help... oh, okay. That's very kind of you... All right... Thank you. Take care, now."

He snaps the phone shut. "Annabel's at home, and she'll take care of your momma until we get back."

I nod and swing my feet back and forth under the chair. "Doesn't seem right, leaving her there while we're here waiting for the baby."

56

Daddy turns to face me. I'm afraid he thinks I mean Annabel, but when he puts his arm around my shoulders, and I feel the weight of him pushing me down in my seat, I know he understands. "She'll be glad you're here. She doesn't want you to miss out on anything because you're sitting at her bedside." Daddy crushes me into a hug, and I bury my face into his shoulder. "She didn't give up, kiddo," he whispers into my hair. "She just didn't want to keep living in so much pain."

My cheeks burn with shame he can't see as I think about how mad I was that I had to take care of Momma on my birthday while Katie got to go out fishing with Tommy. I know there'll be plenty of Tommy Lorens and Harvest Dances and first kisses. And I know Momma's no quitter; if she'd had any choice at all, she would pick me and Daddy and the new baby, and Gretchen, Bill and Annabel. But it's a hard thing to remember that choices don't amount to much when the only options are dying today or dying tomorrow. And the days to sit at Momma's bedside are slipping through my fingers like water down the drain.

The baby takes hours to come. Six hours—one for every little pound of her. Daddy checks in with Annabel a couple of times; she tells us everything is fine, but we're both eager to get home. We see Gretchen for just a minute. Daddy clears his throat over and over as he looks at the new baby nestled in his daughter's arms. Then he says, "We'd better be getting back to your momma. She'll want to hear all about this."

He turns and leaves the room before Gretchen or Bill can say anything, leaving me to make my good-byes.

The baby is an ugly little thing—all red splotches and wrinkled like it sat in cold bath water too long. Momma says all babies are beautiful, but I wonder what she'd say if she saw this one right now. I try to channel her when I say, "She's got a lot to grow into. Congratulations."

Gretchen furrows her brow, then looks at Bill. Then at me. "Did you just say—"

"Daddy'll be waiting. I'd better go."

In the car on the way home, I try to think of something better to tell Momma. But after this long day, the truth's all I've got. I hope it is enough.

When we get home, Annabel's on the couch sobbing into her hands. Daddy and I race into the bedroom, afraid the end has come while we were waiting around for a new beginning, and breathe deep sighs of relief to find Momma shivering in her bed. I help Daddy spread a quilt over her and then close the windows where the evening breeze is blowing into the room. Her breathing is ragged and short. She can't catch her breath around the questions tumbling out of her mouth. Daddy takes her hand, puts his forehead to her temple and says, "Shh, Sadie, shh." Her breathing slows a little, but not enough.

"It's a girl," I say from the end of the bed. I pick up a syringe and draw up another shot of morphine as the words start pouring out of me: "They named her Sadie Lynn, after you and Nana. She's six pounds, three ounces. She has dark hair that's thin and doesn't cover her whole head, but it's dark like molasses. She has ten fingers and ten toes, and she can't keep her hands out of her mouth. She has Bill's nose—a little big like it takes up most of her face, but she'll grow into it."

I hand Daddy the syringe and turn away again. I can hear Momma's breathing even out, but not slow to normal. I can't look at her again today, can't remember my last moments with her in so much pain.

I look at the wall where the picture of Momma and Daddy on their wedding day hangs over the dresser. Momma smiles at the camera like she knows all the secrets of the world and would spill them for nothing short of a happy ending. To the right of that one is a frame with three tiny photos of three baby girls—one brunette, one blonde, and me. To the left is my favorite picture in the whole world: Momma, with her newly bald head wrapped in a blue scarf, with Daddy, me and Gretchen on her wedding day. Momma's smile stretches across her whole face and brightens her tired eyes; she smiles like she's never even heard of cancer or chemotherapy. She looks like a survivor, the kind who fights and wins. That's the Momma I decide I'm going to remember from her dying breath to mine.

"Tess," Daddy whispers.

I look up to the head of the bed. Momma's asleep in Daddy's arms. As careful as he can, he edges onto the bed next to her and holds her close to him from head to toe. He kisses her forehead, rests his cheek against it, and closes his eyes.

I turn and walk to the door, edging it open slightly, so the light from the living room doesn't shine in Momma's eyes.

Annabel looks up at me. "Is she... ?"

"No," I say as I sit beside her on the couch. "She's just sleeping."

Annabel takes a deep breath. "I don't know how you do it," she says, shaking her head. "I know you hate me for not being here but—"

"I don't hate you," I say.

"You will, someday," Annabel replies. "I can't stay another minute. I can't watch her die."

"I know," I say. I lay a hand on Annabel's knee. It's not much, but it's all I have left. "It's hard," I continue. "Momma knows how hard it is. And Daddy does, too."

"It's so hard, Tess," Annabel whispers. She leans over and rests her head on my shoulder.

"You can go when you need to," I say, patting her knee. "We'll be here when you want to come home again."

It's strange to comfort my older sister this way—promising a future I'm unsure of, letting her run from the present she'll never be able to get back. Momma always said that we break at different points because we're only human after all. As Annabel's tears seep into my T-shirt, I know that she needs me to decide for her: stay or go, now or later.

"Do you need help packing?" I ask.

"No," she says. She's off the couch in one swift movement. It's then that I notice her bags are already waiting beside the door. "You'll tell Daddy I had to go?"

I nod.

"You'll call when…"

"We'll call when," I assure her.

I hear Daddy's boots scrape on the bedroom floor. Annabel's eyes widen in alarm. "You'd better go," I say as his footsteps get closer to the door.

She hurries to the front door and struggles to wheel her bags out in one trip. I watch from the living room window as she shoves them into the back seat. Daddy's beside me when the driver's side door shuts and the engine roars to life.

"Momma's asleep," he says.

"Annabel's gone again," I reply.

We watch the red taillights grow smaller and smaller until they fade to nothing as she drives away down the dirt road.

## About Stephen Case:

Stephen Case gets paid for teaching people about space, which is pretty much the coolest thing ever. He also occasionally gets paid for writing stories about space (and other things), which have appeared in *Beneath Ceaseless Skies*, *Daily Science Fiction*, *Orson Scott Card's Intergalactic Medicine Show*, *Shimmer*, and elsewhere. His novel, *First Fleet*, is a science fiction horror epic (think H. P. Lovecraft meets Battlestar Galactica) published by Axiomatic Publishing and available on Amazon.

Stephen holds a PhD in the history and philosophy of science and will talk for inordinate amounts of time about nineteenth-century British astronomy. He lives with his wife, four children, one dog, and multiple contraband backyard chickens in an undisclosed suburb of Chicago.

Follow him on Twitter @BoldSaintCroix or at www.stephenrcase.wordpress.com.

# Gold, Vine, and a Name

## Stephen Case

I found him at his desk.

"Wordsmith," I said, "I need a name."

His head snapped up at my voice, peering through thick glasses. The desk was littered with sheets of paper like fallen leaves.

"I don't do names," he explained slowly. His voice was dry. "Words only."

"A name is a word, isn't it? You haven't even asked what I would pay."

"Where is my assistant? He should have helped you."

I shrugged. The wordsmith sighed deeply. By the size of his shop and the gilding over the door, it was clear his services were highly sought after.

Which meant he had a nose for money.

Which meant he could be bought.

I had scouted three smithies in the city before deciding on this one and planning my approach.

"You cannot simply forge a new name. That is what you want, isn't it?" He pushed away the pile of papers and leaned backward in his chair. "Tired of this one, new love perhaps, or maybe just debts. Want to start over fresh, a new name, a new life?"

I shook my head.

He grunted. "It does not matter. That's not how it works."

"You can't do names?" I put on an expression of naive curiosity. It had worked in the past. "But they're just words you wear. Hunter or Godkiller or Croftman."

"Titles!" The dry voice cracked, and a few pieces of paper shifted. "Not names. Something like that, a mere description you tether to your person—such things flake off in the first storms of summer. Those are not names."

The near-sighted eyes peered up at me. I watched him weighing up what he saw: the cut of my robe, the thin but not invisible threads of silver at the neck and collar, the set of my shoulders. Indications I was middling to high nobility. That I would be a person to humor, certainly someone with whom to have patience.

The lines of his face softened.

"Young sir, were you to devise a new technique for falconing, or desire a new expression of personal courage, were you even—" and here his face brightened so I could see the echo of the young man he must have been when he was first learning his craft, "-seeking a word for the unique comeliness of a maiden's brow, I could forge a new word for you. It would be a sound word, sturdy to do whatever work you required of it and certain to enter the common lexicon."

"Any word?"

"Any word." He drew himself up in his chair. "Several of my works have become common parlance in your lifetime alone. I have named newly discovered plants, expressions, colors. Any word."

"But no names." I let my expression fall.

"For a name to be more than a title," the wordsmith explained, leaning forward over the haphazard cartography of papers, "it must be grafted onto the soul; it must take root as your own name has had a lifetime to grow into your being. And it must be more than merely a title. It must be a distillation of qualities that mirror you as you mirror your own name."

"But my name is—"

He held up his hand. "It does not matter. Whatever your name, it has shaped you since birth in ways you cannot imagine. To remove that, to scour it from your soul, and graft a new one in its place is the labor of ages. The effort..." he trailed off.

"You've never done it?"

"Once." His voice was soft.

I let the silence slowly fill the room before I reached into my robe, drew out a velvet pouch, and upended the contents onto his desk. A sheen of tiny, golden coins spilled across his papers.

"Do you know what this is?"

I watched his eyes carefully. They told me he did.

"It is drinsgeld," I said. The coins quivered. "A name—or word, rather— fashioned, I think, by one of your predecessors."

"Is it—" He licked his lips. "Is it close to...?"

"Critical mass?"

He nodded mutely.

"A few more coins, and then the reaction would begin. You would spend your life fashioning words to describe the extent of your riches."

He sat back in his chair and stroked his chin. I heard footsteps behind us. His assistant rounded the corner.

"I'm sorry, master," the young man began, "I didn't hear—"

The wordsmith raised his hand. "Leave us, Krelc. Close the door. I am not to be disturbed."

I let nothing show on my face, but internally I smiled. I had judged correctly. Now it was a matter of time.

"Is it for love?" he asked, his eyes still on the coins. "For protection? Certainly not for debts, if you have a treasure like this."

"For none of those."

"What then?" His eyes found my own. From beneath the lenses, he looked as though he was staring up from a great distance. The coins whispered quietly among themselves.

"It is for death."

"Death?"

"You don't approve." In one studied motion, I reached forward as though to scoop up the pile of flickering coins.

"Your purposes are your own," he said hastily. "I will help you."

He raised his hand.

I grasped it.

It was done. I had killed for the bindwood that grew now beneath my flesh where the bones of my right hand had been. But it was effective. Once pledged upon the wood, any word given was binding. The wordsmith would be unable to break his word even had he wished it.

Perhaps he felt the binding because his eyes narrowed.

"How do I know you have enough?"

I stepped backward and took two brilliant coins from where they had been tightly bound in a leather wallet far from the velvet pouch in my cloak. Even at this distance the pile on the desk began to slither toward me.

"That amount—" I pointed to the pile, "-is yours. These coins are mine until I wear a new name."

I put them away, and the gold on his desk became still.

"Fine," he said, straightening as though resigned to his task. "Good. Now, leave me. I have a funeral to plan. Return at this time tomorrow."

"A funeral?"

"Yours." He pushed the coins to one side and bent over his pages, quill dancing. "Your name must be erased. It will not be pleasant."

~ ~ ~ ~ ~

The following day the wordsmith interrogated me for hours, his quill tirelessly recording my every word. My past was a great aid, as I suspected it would be: lack of contacts, lack of family, lack of friends. Even my superiors—who had some inkling of what this task would entail—had been trained to forget me and my mission as soon as I had departed upon it.

"There will not be much stripping to do, if what you have told me is true," the wordsmith said, looking at the scrawl of ink before him when we were finished. "What remains is to break your own ties with your name. For that, you must be prepared."

There was a monastery on the peaks above the city. I was to report there in two days' time.

I prepared for the preparation that evening with strong ale and a string of women—none of who would remember me come morning. I had trained all my adult life to be a shadow. Making whores forget my face was child's play.

I started off for the monastery the next morning feeling already largely effaced.

A man with a countenance of gnarled wood greeted me at the gate and took the letter I bore. He broke the seal, scanned it, and motioned me inside.

"You will be seeing the abbot," he told me.

I followed him through a compound of wide hallways, bright tiles, and the constant sound of flowing water. We passed other monks, all of whom bowed low. In a garden near what must have been the center of the monastery the old monk stopped and sat on the low wall of a fountain.

"I am the abbot," he said and looked up at me.

Because I was not sure what role I was to play here, I waited.

"The wordsmith." The abbot waved the letter and chuckled. "I asked him to forge a word for a newly-discovered aspect of God, years ago. In some circles, it was tantamount to blasphemy. I had to call in favors. Now he's calling one from me. A new name?"

I nodded.

"Men come here seeking many things. Some find them. But never that."

I waited.

"Why do you want a new name?"

"First, a pledge of friendship." I extended my hand.

The monk knocked my hand aside. "Freely given," he said. "Never compelled."

He asked his question again.

It seemed the best tact with him would be truth. There was about his eyes something that said words were as glass to him. "An end. I am an assassin."

"Who are you?"

"Efink, who walks in darkness. You won't have heard of me." I would have been doing my job poorly if he had.

The garden was full of trees nodding drowsy heads in the sunlight. The monk nodded his as well.

"Whom do you seek to kill?" He asked the question casually as if many came there confessing such intent.

"A deathspeaker," I said slowly. "A deathspeaker unbound. You have heard of her coming to power in the east?"

"A cloud on the horizon," the monk said. "No more. These things pass."

I shook my head. "You know of her power?"

"I have heard rumors."

"A deathspeaker is born, never made. Not trained, as I was. This one was brought from the deep south, and kept as a servant of King Tsud. A weapon

68

against his enemies. A weapon of perfection in silence, of perfection in precision. Reaching beyond borders, walls, and shields."

"She brings death with a word."

"With a name," I corrected. "If she speaks your name, you die, no matter how far you are, no matter what protections you take. And the names Tsud gathered were vast."

"But he no longer controls her."

"He is dead by now, certainly. He was betrayed, and she was freed. She has declared herself empress and names any who oppose her."

Doves cooed somewhere over the wall.

"But surely your name is safe," the monk said. "Surely anyone unknown to her is safe. The precaution you seek to take..." he paused, "it is a painful one."

"I have no margin for uncertainty. My name must be erased. I must have a new one, unknown, so I and I alone am free of her power."

"So you can kill her."

"So I can deliver the land of this threat."

The old monk propped his chin on his hands. "You will not, I think, succeed. But the wordsmith is right in asking repayment of a favor. I will help you prepare, and when the forging takes place, it will be within these walls."

I bowed slightly.

"Three days," he said, rising abruptly. "We have three days to prepare. You should not have told me your name, but my mind is trained in tranquility. It will sink into quiet waters. Speak to no one from now on. You will be given a chamber in the grotto beneath the *cho* tree. You will not leave it. A brother will attend you once a day, speaking the words of meditation you must repeat."

"Why?"

"Because your name is tied to your mind and heart. You must quiet those connections before they are severed. It will make the effacing more bearable. Bearable enough, perhaps, to survive."

~ ~ ~ ~ ~

The three days passed like as many years. The chamber beneath the *cho* tree was pungent with the cinnamon smell of its roots. Perhaps they sought to deaden my senses with boredom. In the night the darkness was absolute and the silence so deep I could hear worms burrowing within the walls.

At the end of three days, the abbot brought me to a wide room with walls of blue and white tile. The wordsmith waited, along with his assistant, who carried huge folios of loose parchment. The abbot motioned to me to remove my clothes and lay on a low marble table at the center of the room. No one spoke.

When I had obeyed, the wordsmith opened one of the folios and began arranging parchment in a loose circle around me, placing pieces on my chest, arms, legs, and groin. He spoke to his assistant.

"These are the client's connections with his past name. Note the phrasings. You must capture all aspects of the name and the weight they hold in the mind of the client. These are what must be dissolved."

He took a vial from a pouch at his side and splashed liquid over my body and the parchment.

"It is sometimes advisable to bind the client." He paused and cast a glance in my direction. "In this case, I do not think it will be necessary. The client is, I believe, accustomed to physical hardship."

It was all the warning I received. The wordsmith touched a glowing splint to the edge of the parchment. In an instant, I was engulfed in flames.

For a moment, I was stunned. The flames did not burn. They felt, if anything, overwhelmingly cold. But the parchment began to blacken and curl, and when it did, there was white-hot pain. It was as the wordsmith had said—as though each phrase in the ink that smoked and bubbled was a root running into tendon and bone beneath my flesh, into thought and memory behind my eyes.

I thought I was dying. I screamed though I could not hear myself.

When I awoke again, it was dark. The wordsmith and his assistant were waiting in candlelight.

"The client is awake," the wordsmith said. "Now begins the difficult part."

He began laying parchment again.

"An individual normally takes years—perhaps a lifetime—to grow into a name. We must grow a name in a single night. For that, we have only ink and bloodvine."

By the candles, I saw the wordsmith bring forth another glass vial, this one filled with water in which a small, red bundle of vines was suspended. Two pale orange leaves extended above the vial's lip.

"This is where our craft grows uncertain." I was too weak to raise my head to read the wordsmith's expression. "If we are too slow, the bloodvine will consume the client. If we are too hasty, it will not provide conduits by which the new name can take root."

I had seen men killed by bloodvine. I had used it myself once or twice. It grew—for brief moments—with astonishing speed. I had never known any host in which it had taken root to survive more than a few agonizing minutes.

"It is a weakened specimen, certainly," the wordsmith said. I could hear the quaver in his voice. He was terrified. "Once its roots are threaded throughout the client, we will remove the stunted taproot."

The wordsmith placed the vial on my bare chest. His gloved hand trembled.

"We must write the new name on the leaves of the plant. This, of course, with our strongest ink."

He took a deep breath and dipped a quill into a bowl of ink.

"The new name must be one distinctly different, though with enough similarity to the old that it can root along the same connections. We have chosen *Edalb*. It is uncommon in this region but not excessively rare. It is a name to remember but not to draw attention. Its pronunciation is relatively unchanged in the old high tongue, in which I write it now on the leaves."

I could see clearly the long, elegant script the wordsmith wrote in ink as black as death on the curved leaves.

The room was cold, but I was sweating. Was it too late to stop the process? Remaining nameless would not be enough to complete my mission. An old name, if not replaced, would simply find its way back to its bearer. It was not enough to erase a name. A new one had to take root.

The wordsmith took a small mallet from a table at his side and broke the glass of the vial.

Instantly the roots of the vine uncoiled like bloody springs and speared outward and down. I could feel them pushing beneath my skin and spreading in a red mat across my chest. I tried to scream, but there was no air. There were instead a thousand burrowing fingers tearing into my gut, into my lungs, climbing my neck and finding my eyes and my ears and my nose.

The wordsmith was shouting. I felt a deep wrenching in my chest as though he was trying to pull forth my heart. Something broke away with a searing pain more shattering than the rest, and I blacked out a second time.

〜 〜 〜 〜

I awoke to someone calling my name. At first, I thought it was my father. Then for a moment that it was Thgil, from the summer we spent together before I left home forever. She was calling my new name.

The wordsmith was bending over me and repeating it.

"Edalb, wake up. Wake up, Edalb."

He said my name, over and over. I tried to tell him I was awake but only moaned.

"You are back in your chamber beneath the cho tree. The taproot of the bloodvine has been removed. Your body will break down the roots that remain. You will need to rest for several days, Edalb. I will expect my payment when you are well enough to return to the city."

I recalled Thgil's voice. It had worked.

I knew my name. I wore it. It wore me. It was grafted onto my memories.

I grabbed the wordsmith's arm. "My name," I whispered. "Tell no one."

"I know of your quest," he said, pulling away. "Your new name will remain a secret."

When he was gone, I slept again, though the thought of lying beneath the roots of any tree now made me uneasy. I regained my strength slowly. The monks were generous with their time and their conversation now. They brought me food and helped me stand and finally walk slowly about the gardens.

No one asked my new name.

Neither did they ask my old. I am not sure I would have remembered it if they had.

Still, I could take no chances. When I was strong enough to depart, I cut the hem of my robe and removed the crystallized brine-eggs I had sewn in before coming to the city. It was easy to slip them into the well after my final supper with the monks. Brine-eggs are nearly invisible but multiply rapidly once re-introduced to water. Once consumed, they continue their growth throughout the fluids of a human body. Within a week, these halls would hold only calcified husks.

My name would be safe.

I left the monastery and walked the road back into the city. It was late, but Krelc showed me into wordsmith's chamber. He waited at the desk where I first met him. When his assistant turned to leave, I motioned him to stay.

"You deserve at least a part of this payment," I told him. "Your master will have plenty to spare."

Drinsgeld is seductive. The wordsmith still had the pile of shimmering coins on the desk where I left them. He looked up from them now with hungry eyes.

"You have the rest?" he asked. "The payment you promised?"

I took the two coins from the leather pouch.

Drinsgeld is also tricky. I had calculated the weight of the coins exactly, so I had a fair idea of the range and yield of the reaction. Still, one could never be quite certain. I was already moving toward the door as I flicked the two coins onto the pile on the wordsmith's desk.

I heard them clink against the others and the wordsmith's quick intake of breath. By that time, I was running. Behind me came the sound of dozens of coins clinking together, then hundreds, then perhaps millions, and the muffled sounds of screams. A wave of coins burst against the walls of the house and fell around my feet as I fled. I grabbed a handful as I ran and swept them into my robe.

It was done.

Apart from me, no living person now knew my name.

I had weapons stashed in a room at the edge of town. There were a few whores I had promised—though they could not recall—to see again.

And then there was a dark road ahead of me.

## About Sabrina Clare:

Sabrina Clare has led a patchwork life full of adventure. She spent three years in Spain, where she was an actor in an acting company, one of two lead singers in a band, and an English tutor to a variety of businesses. Before that, she was a straight-A student in electrical engineering but left because she wanted to be free to explore her many passions instead of focusing intently on a single discipline. She has lived all over the United States, as well as abroad, and has met many fascinating characters along the way whose influence can be felt in her stories. Sabrina has never been ashamed of being on the autism spectrum, and even considers it a bit of a superpower, allowing her to see the world differently.

# Hotel Marietta

## Sabrina Clare

The paperwork took time. Enough for doubts to creep into my mind and make me wonder if I was being an impulsive idiot. I don't even have a cat. What made me think I could foster a deeply damaged, 6-year-old, autistic child? But Ellie had nobody else.

She hadn't even been my client. My coworker, David, had mentioned her. The day the clinic doors had closed, for good, I'd sat down with David for a farewell cup of coffee. He'd been in worse shape than me, maybe because he'd worked there longer. It was only my first job out of college, and I hadn't even been there a full year. Seeing the dull ache in his eyes, and the tired lines around his mouth, I realized the gravity and implications of our clinic closing. A lot of kids would be affected.

"We can't protect the kids, Jess," he had said, with traces of panic in his voice, just before he'd told me his wife was pregnant. I could see he was scared.

"You're gonna be an awesome dad," I'd reassured him, not knowing enough about him to know if it were true.

He'd looked at me with an anguished expression. "Ellie Chambers had an awesome dad. And an awesome mom. But look at her life. So many of our kids had crackhead parents or absentee parents, but not all of them. What if... whatever we do, or try to do... we just can't protect the kids?"

All I knew about Ellie was that her parents had been murdered right in front of her, in the little hotel they had owned and run, leaving her in an institution. I didn't know the details, but I knew she had no other family. What would happen to her, now? She was in the care of an underfunded system that would feed and clothe her, but, without David's patience and effort, who would *help* her? All our kids needed help, but maybe none of them more than Ellie did.

My mother had always told me I was stubborn. She'd said it proudly, like it was my superpower, like I would never give up or let myself be beaten. David's words could have discouraged me, but they'd empowered me, instead, and, just like that, I had decided.

~ ~ ~ ~

The institution wasn't clinical or cold, as I had expected. It was actually quite welcoming, with colorful murals on the walls. At least they were trying. I made my way to the office where I'd been directed, and my eyes immediately locked on Ellie. She sat with her hands in her lap, her frizzy brown hair floating around her pinched little face, and I fell immediately in love with her. I smiled at the woman behind the desk, said the words I had to say, and signed the forms I had to sign.

My mother was waiting in the car. I had asked her to come in with me but changed my mind at the last minute. I wanted to handle this on my own. When I came out with Ellie, Mom broke into a beaming smile. Ellie didn't react, but I had explained things to Mom, and she didn't miss a beat. She got out of the car and opened the back door for Ellie.

"Here you go, Sweetheart," she said, affectionately. I had worked with autistic kids, before. They usually resisted change, threw tantrums, screamed... I had been prepared for that, and I'd prepared my mother, but Ellie just climbed in, and buckled up, listlessly. Somehow that was harder than a tantrum would have been. Mom met my eyes, squeezed her lips together, and put her hand on my shoulder reassuringly before getting back in the car. I went around to the driver's side, settled myself in, and drove us home.

~ ~ ~ ~ ~

The first few weeks with Ellie were an adjustment. She didn't speak a word. Mostly, she sat quietly, staring out the window at the falling leaves that became falling snow as the weeks passed. Sometimes, she would throw the kind of tantrum I had expected from the start, but they seemed to come from nowhere, for no reason. It was the unexpectedness, the randomness, that frayed my nerves until I was jumping at the smallest things. But I was stubborn, and I kept my balance.

Mom stayed with us for the first few days, to help. She's a good person with a good heart. I couldn't have quit working to take care of Ellie if it hadn't been for my parents. Not only had they provided the house we lived in, the car we drove, and a good chunk of our other needs like electricity and food, but Mom had pulled the strings to get me certified to foster a disabled child in record time.

In college, people who found out I came from money thought I saw myself as better than other people, so they made sure to remind me I was inherently inferior. They reminded me I'd never had to work for anything, never really suffered. If they learned that my brother, Jake, had killed himself when he was 15 (I was 9, at the time), they were shockingly calloused. They thought I didn't know the things they said, like how he was a poor little rich boy who probably couldn't handle it when daddy took his keys away.

I didn't tell them Uncle Rick was a meth-head with a penchant for little boys. I didn't tell them that, when my dad found out what Uncle Rick had been doing to Jake for years, he turned his brother in, or that my grandfather interceded to save the family's reputation, and Uncle Rick went free, without a single consequence for ruining an innocent little boy. I didn't tell them Jake took it as a sign that what Rick did to him was somehow okay, and concluded he must have deserved it. I didn't tell them anything. I just kept studying, determined to help other kids who'd been through hell, before it was too late for them, too. Taking action was my way of dealing with the helplessness.

Mom was a rock through everything. Dad's face got sunken, and he withdrew from the world. He saw it all as his fault. Rick was his brother. It was his father who had kept Rick out of jail… he especially blamed himself for not protecting Jake like a father was supposed to. I know Mom took the same blame on herself, but she was always practical, and someone had to keep going. So she did. I guess I got my stubbornness from her.

I guess I got my fear of helplessness from Jake. I had to admit how much I'd wanted to get through to Ellie, not just for her sake, but for mine, so I'd feel valuable… important. But Ellie failed to respond, failed to fulfill my savior fantasies, or validate my selfishness. If I was going to keep working with her, it would have to be for her sake, not for mine.

I kept going. Ellie and I fell into a kind of routine. We got used to one another. The tantrums became more predictable. She screamed when I gave her a bath, then screamed when it was time to get out. She threw her food when she had had enough. She slept on the floor of her closet instead of on the soft, inviting bed I'd bought for her. She ignored the dolls and toys and puppets I had bought her as a possible means of self-expression. And she never let me hug her.

I sat outside that closet door and read her stories. I watched her expressions when she ate, looking for minute changes that would clue me in on what she did and didn't like. I hummed times tables while I did housework. I talked to her about the weather, both from a scientific perspective and a poetic one. Every now and again, I'd catch her watching me, intently. Interested. Engaged. It didn't last, and I pretended not to notice, but I did notice. And I kept going.

Spring came, and I took Ellie outside. She sat quietly the whole time, angry at having her routine disrupted, but I felt it was important, and I determined to establish a new routine that included outside time. I'd been raised to believe every child needs air and sunshine, and I agreed with that, so I took her out when the weather allowed, even when she fought me on it, and I talked to her as though I didn't see her scowling at me. I talked about the leaves unfurling, the birds singing, the caterpillars that would become butterflies, the roly-poly bugs that curled into balls when you touched them, how clouds were formed, and how people saw shapes in them. I made us picnics, although Ellie never ate the things I spread out on the blanket.

One day in mid-May, I forgot the pitcher of iced tea. I usually set things up before I took her out, but I didn't see any harm in leaving her alone for just a moment as I popped inside. It was a hot day, and I was thirsty, so I thought she might be, too. I was only gone a moment. I put the pitcher and two glasses on a tray, balanced them in one arm, got the door with the other, and turned to take them down the porch steps to the picnic blanket on the lawn.

Ellie was gone. I dropped the tea and ran, screaming her name. How could she have gotten out? The back was fenced. Panic rose inside me like acid, burning me.

"Ellie!" I screamed. "Ellie!!!" But I knew she wouldn't answer. I had never heard her speak a single word, although her powerful screams left no doubt she had quite a voice.

I wondered if she had followed me into the house without my noticing. I checked her room. I checked every room. I even went around the block. Finally, I had to admit defeat. I went back to the yard for one last look as I pulled out my phone to dial 9-1-1.

Then I heard it: a cheerful voice floating on the late spring breeze. I didn't dare to breathe. I almost called to her, but then I remembered how she always went stock still if she knew I was watching her. Carefully, I put the phone back in my pocket and walked slowly toward the voice.

It was coming from beneath the porch. Stealthily, I walked around until I saw an opening into which a child might squeeze.

"It's a nice room," she was saying. "You can see the sky from it. Did you know clouds are made of water? It's true. Tiny, tiny drops just float up there, but they get lonely, so they wander around until they meet more tiny drops, until there are sooooo many they get heavy, and they can't stay up there, anymore, and that is when it rains. Also, clouds are pretty. See that one? It looks like a tree."

My eyes filled with tears.

"Or, if you want a room that's closer to the restaurant, there's Number 236, which is also a lucky room because two times three is six. Isn't that funny? You would like that room? Yes, I see that. You must be very hungry, living in the dirt where there isn't too much food. The chef makes quite good soup, each Friday. She is very nice, and you will like the one with mushrooms."

I'm the chef, I thought, ridiculously. And Ellie thinks I'm nice. She thinks I'm nice. Who is she talking to? Trying not to make a sound, I peered between the slats of wood and saw her in a sunbeam, surrounded by dust motes that could have just as well been fairies. She had taken twigs and rocks and leaves and built a kind of structure on which she was lovingly placing roly-poly bugs.

As I watched, she picked up another one and sang out, "Welcome to the Hotel Marietta, where you will be safe and happy. How may I assist you, today?"

I frowned. Why did that name sound familiar? I knew I'd have to find a way to get her to come out, but she seemed happier than I had ever seen her. Would she be alright if I dashed inside a minute to look for something? I thought about the panic I had felt when I'd come out with the tea. But all she had done was climb beneath the porch. I knew she liked small, cozy spaces. She'd be fine.

I knew exactly where her file was, the one I'd gotten from David when I told him I'd be looking after her. I took it out with me and sat with my back against the porch, reading as I listened to Ellie's musical voice as she welcomed guests, answered questions, and talked about points of interest… all from stories I had told her, sometimes word for word. She had been listening. It occurred to me she was always listening.

And then I found it. Her mother's name was Marietta, and that was what her father had named the family hotel. Ellie had grown up there, had felt safe there.

"Oh, Roly," she was saying, "you haven't opened up, yet. Poor little Roly, are you scared? Don't worry. You just rest here in your room, and I will read you stories until you can feel safe again. They will be good stories, and you don't need to say anything because I will know you're listening to me. I'll be right here, little Roly, until you want to open up and climb around and see the world. Then I will take you outside where you'll find friends."

My heart caught in my throat. Ellie was talking to me, telling me she knew I was there, telling me she wanted my presence.

~ ~ ~ ~ ~

That summer, Ellie and I played under the porch most days. I made a little door where the opening had been so we could both crawl in, and I cleared away the spiders. She still would not talk to me directly or meet my eyes, but we ran the hotel and welcomed not just roly-polys but a few caterpillars and even the occasional ladybug or beetle. It took some time for me to learn the roles she wanted me to play, especially as it would vary, depending on her mood. Sometimes I was the bellhop or the maid, but, often, she let me be the voices of our guests. I experimented with accents, on occasion, expecting her to balk at the unfamiliarity, but she had met guests from around the world many times, and she was actually delighted. She was fond of my Austrian gentleman-beetle persona. He was quirky and charming and funny, and I realized her understanding of humor was subtle and extensive.

Ellie's mind was sharper than anyone had realized. I redoubled my efforts to teach her, playing audio books and podcasts in the background, exposing her to myriad ideas, which I now saw she absorbed hungrily. My parents came to visit, bringing books that had been mine as a child. I felt a wave of possessiveness, but it passed quickly when I saw the look in Ellie's eyes. She didn't reach for them, or react in any way, but I left them in her room and was pleased to see their positions shift a little bit each day.

Summer faded into fall; the weather grew cold, and it began to rain. I told Ellie we couldn't play outside anymore. She hadn't thrown a tantrum of that magnitude in weeks, maybe months, but there was nothing I could do but take a breath and ride it out. She became despondent, and I wondered about buying bugs for her to play with in the house. I dismissed that idea for a plethora of reasons. Then I had a better one.

~ ~ ~ ~ ~

"Hi, Rob! It's Jessie," I said into the phone.

"Jessie!" my former boss enthused, "How've you been? Where are you working, these days?"

"Well," I began, "I'm not. It's kind-of a long story, actually. I'd love to fill you in. As a matter of fact, the reason I'm calling is I'd like to invite you over next weekend. I'm having a kind of... party..."

~ ~ ~ ~ ~

I had moved my desk to face the front door, and Ellie looked adorably serious standing behind it. Just before 6:00 p.m., the first knock came. I opened the door ceremoniously and waved David inside.

"Welcome to the Hotel Marietta, where you will be safe and happy. How may I assist you, today?" Ellie greeted him, smiling brightly. David gasped and looked at me in shock. His wife came in behind him, their new baby cradled in her arms.

David had been briefed, but nothing I had told him had prepared him for the confident young lady looking straight into his eyes.

"I..." he stammered, "we're... here for the... conference."

"Of course, sir," Ellie replied. "And have you come from out of town?"

"What?"

"Will you be needing a room, sir? We have some lovely ones available, tonight. All the beds are clean and comfortable. There's a lovely room with a view of the garden, even though it has no flowers, at the moment. Did you know hydrangeas change color depending on the soil they're in? If a dog pees on one hydrangea plant each day, but not on another one a little ways away, the flowers will be different colors. We don't have a dog, so all of our hydrangeas are the same color. You could come back in the spring and see."

David's eyes were moist as he turned to his wife and she smiled back at him, lovingly.

"Jessica, please show our guests to the dining room."

"Yes, Miss Ellie," I said, leading the way. Before long, Rob and my parents had joined us. Ellie and I were the wait staff, and the maids, making sure the guests were comfortable as they sat around the table, chatting.

When we bid them goodnight, and the last of them departed, I turned to Ellie, not quite sure what would come next. She stood, her head lowered, her hands clasped tightly together. I waited.

"Jessica," she murmured softly. This was the first time she had ever talked to me, directly.

"Yes, Ellie?"

"My mother used to tell me, 'thank you for your help, tonight, darling.' I didn't do very much, back then, but she said thank you, anyway."

I held my breath, afraid to say the wrong thing, afraid to break the spell.

"Then they would hug me, and I'd go to bed."

I waited. Her eyes flicked up at me, and I decided to take a chance.

"Thank you for your help, tonight, Ellie. You were wonderful. It's time for bed, now."

I saw a tiny smile glide across her lips.

"Okay, Jessica."

Her eyes flicked up again. I moved toward her, and she didn't move away. With all the tenderness I had held back for months, I knelt down in front of her, and gathered her close. Her small arms wrapped around my neck and we stayed that way a long, long time. I walked her to her room and waited to see what she would do. She went to the closet, looked at it awhile, then turned and climbed into her bed. Willing myself to remember that it was only the first step, that there were many more to come, I tucked her in, kissed her forehead gently, and, with a full and happy heart, turned out the light.

## About Stefan Dyk:

Born in Edinburgh 1946, Stefan Dyk spent his school days in either Southern Africa or Scotland (back and forth) until his family finally settled in Swaziland. He is married with two kids and two grand kids, all of whom are Canadian now. He served with Rhodesian security forces during bush war between 1968 and 1980, and has held careers in Sugar Cane and Citrus farming, Mining, Navigational Dredging and Project Management. Emigrating to Canada in 1980, he traveled the world as Technical Sales Manager for Cassiar Mining Corporation before starting his own business as an Executive Coach which he ran for twelve years. He's since retired from corporate life, and lives in British Columbia where he's focusing on his *new* career—writing and art, his favorite past times.

HX-59B was inspired partly by the current migrant crisis faced by the EU, recent articles on Artificial Intelligence research, and the simple enjoyment of allowing his imagination to wander.

# HX-59B

## Stefan Dyk

Apart from a soft hum coming from the electronics, everything was quiet at the operations console. Lanthrop looked up from his game at the image displayed on the viewer before him. There was little to be seen other than a few pinpoints of light in the darkness, representing a distant flashing quasar and a small cluster of remote galaxies, yet his instruments showed there was activity within the void. Something was out there and headed his way.

Guarding the outer regions of gas giant HD38529's binary system was not Lanthrop's personal choice. He was a conscript holding the rank of ensign, guarding against illegal alien migrants who were streaming in their millions towards the solar system, while his chosen career disappeared down the toilet. Were it not for these migrants he would be in the Fusion Research Laboratory at the University of Illinois this very moment, completing his thesis, not out here in the boonies of the Orion constellation. The irony was that, in his absence, one of these damned migrants could end up taking his seat in the faculty.

An audio bleep accompanied by a flash from the panel above him dragged Lanthrop's attention away from the viewer to a string of information streaming across a data display. Sure enough, something was crossing the void! Three alien craft coasted furtively through space in a tight bunch, propelled by the remnants of momentum their ancient ion thrusters had generated before they ran out of fuel. Who knows how long ago? Probably a small group of carbon life-forms seeking the comfort of each other's presence while searching for a haven. Lanthrop turned his attention back to the viewer hoping for a visual image of the craft, but there was nothing. They were out of range. He triggered the event recorder then initiated a passive scan to determine their size and composition without alerting them. The scan indicated these ships were large by Earth standards, probably bulk transports of some description. He fed the scan information into his data bank but found no match, which meant they probably originated from an unknown source. Unidentified ships could be carrying anything, so they were considered a potential threat. He ordered an infrared scan of the hulls to detect any heat signatures within. Nothing! Either the passengers were long dead, or frozen in hibernation. Perhaps they were transporting cold-blooded aliens or android mercenaries.

Remaining ignorant of the details made things easier for Lanthrop. He knew perfectly well what had to be done, nevertheless requested a recommendation on how to proceed, relieving his conscience of the responsibility for what was ultimately his decision. A soft female voice responded to his request with the answer he had anticipated. It came from the Artificial Intelligence unit controlling the station.

"Sterilization recommended."

A touchpad on the console in front of him illuminated, providing options to cancel, select manual or proceed automatically. He selected auto then returned his attention to his Solitaire game hologram. He no longer paid much attention to these incidents, there were just too many. Absorbed in a potential run on Spades, he was unaware of the shudder transmitted through the station when the missiles launched. Thirty-seven minutes later a ping drew his attention back to the console to see the data on the three alien ships disappear from the display one by one. For a moment, he had forgotten all about them.

"Sterilization was successful. It has been logged." the soft voice advised. It was all very clinical and routine. The void was empty once more; however, Lanthrop paid little attention. His shift was over now, and he was bored and hungry.

Commanding his seat restraints to release, he stood and stretched as far as his space suit would permit. His subaltern should arrive any minute now to relieve him. The irony was the station did not need any human input, it operated autonomously. The sole reason he and his subaltern were onboard was to provide a 'living' component to the mission, to satisfy a legal requirement stipulating only humans could authorize sterilization orders.

Standard procedure dictated the console be manned at all times, so he had to remain at his post until relieved. He waited impatiently for his Subaltern to report. Jules had never been this late before! He paged him on the intercom then scanned the entire station using the closed circuit cameras without success. An hour lapsed before he lost patience and decided to go looking for his Subaltern. They were the only humans onboard the station and Jules was a moody bastard at the best of times, so Lanthrop never knew what to expect from him. Although he outranked Jules he always felt the need to tread around him carefully to preserve harmony, but this time he was not going to; he would tear a strip off him! Exiting through the sphere's airlock he clumped along the walkway to the living quarters, his heavy magnetic boots jarring on the checkered metal plates with each step. He wore the boots to keep in shape, whereas his Subaltern preferred floating around the station weightless. "Like a shark cruising over a reef!" he would say.

The walkway, which had no artificial gravity, extended three hundred meters to their diminutive quarters. Beyond that, a second walkway led to the station's mini reactor and a large missile battery.

Lanthrop found Jules in the tiny mess hall, slumped on the floor behind a food locker where the CC cameras couldn't reach. He was comatose, apparently high on drugs. To confirm his suspicion, Lanthrop shoved a diagnostic probe into Jules' slack mouth. Sure enough, high on something! What the hell? Where could the drugs have come from? What was Jules thinking? Blood and body fluids were routinely collected for analysis as part their health maintenance program. Jules' medical log would be compromised and when that was discovered the crap would fly! Not good! Even though he was clean himself, Lanthrop was certain he would be implicated in some way. This tripped-out Subaltern was his responsibility after all and since they were the only ones on the station, HQ would suspect he was complicit!

His anger boiled over. He tried reviving Jules by slapping his face, then pouring ice cold water on his head however it did not help. Jules was too far gone to be revived easily, so Lanthrop dragged him over to his bunk and left him there, one leg drooping on the floor.

The operations console was unattended, a serious infraction, so he had to get back as soon as possible. Angrily, he returned to the sphere as quickly as he could, this time leaving his magnetic boots behind, propelling his weightless body down the walkway by pulling on the handrails. He decided he would complete the first six hours of Jules' twelve-hour shift, then wake him up with the fire alarm. That should be enough time for the drugs to wear off.

Returning to the console, he felt the safety restraints automatically tighten around his shoulders and waist, securing him firmly to his seat. Suiting-up and belting-in was a Standard Procedure, one which Lanthrop was often tempted to ignore, but never did. There were thousands of annoying procedures which regulated his life on the station!

He quickly scanned the instruments before him. Nothing appeared amiss; everything was as he had left it. He reviewed the log for any recent entries, but there was nothing of significance other than a record of his brief absence and subsequent return. He would be unable to hide the fact he had abandoned his post, or that Jules had not reported for duty, nor could he cover things up by saying his Subaltern was sick, the blood tests would contradict that. A whole pile of shit was about to fly, so Lanthrop decided to preempt it by reporting the facts as they were to HQ immediately. Get it all out in the open before someone came to the wrong conclusions. His station partner had brought this upon himself. He didn't owe Jules anything; the guy was a prick. After mulling over what he should say, he keyed the transmitter in his helmet and recorded his message for transmission.

"Lanthrop, Hotel X-ray five nine Bravo here. Be advised at this time my Subaltern, Jules Magdin 73345629, is in the station living quarters unable to report for duty. He is not ill, but appears to be under the influence of a psychotic drug, and is totally incapacitated, unable to speak or stand on his feet. I discovered this at the end of my scheduled shift when he failed to relieve me. It was necessary for me to exit the control room briefly to establish his location and condition. I have now returned to the control room after leaving the console for sixteen minutes. No incidents were recorded during my absence and, apart from Jules, everything is normal. I await your orders. Nothing further to report. Lanthrop out."

He previewed the text of his message on his helmet visor, before sending it with a normal priority. He did not expect a response for several hours.

"Well, the cat's out of the bag!" he thought. "I'm certainly not covering for that bastard!" He decided to check on Jules again and was turning towards the CC camera screen when another bleep and flash came from the panel above him. What, again? Not now, I'm busy! More bloody migrants? Information began streaming across the display as before. However, this time it was different. Whatever had entered the void was much smaller and moving at high speed.

"What is it?" he asked the AI

"I cannot tell. Passive scanning is giving a negative result."

"Can you do an active scan and get a lock on it?" he asked, his mind was racing, adrenalin building in his system.

"I would advise against it. This appears to be a tactical vessel. Our active scan would be detected, giving our position away." The soft female voice replied.

"Tactical vessel?"

"The telemetry shows it is employing a form of cloaking to make itself a difficult target. Stealth technology is synonymous with military craft. I recommend maintaining a low profile until I can get more information."

Lanthrop swallowed. "Right, I guess that makes sense!"

Although the station itself was a lethal weapon, it was stationary, incapable of maneuvering and therefore vulnerable. No station had ever been attacked or even threatened by an alien vessel before. Never! As a result training in defensive tactics had not received a high priority. Damn, he thought, this is where Jules was needed! Amongst other things that dipstick had taken the basic defense training module. He would know what the standard procedures were.

The AI interrupted his thoughts. "In the absence of a radar scan, I can display a visual of this contact for you."

"You can do that?"

"Yes, using our digital magnification manipulator."

"Surely it is too far away?" Lanthrop queried

"It is for a detailed picture, but I will convert all the electromagnetic bands you are unable to see into wavelength equivalents. I hope one of the EM bands will appear to you as an image."

Lanthrop could have sworn the AI sounded sarcastic, but shrugged it off.

"Okay then, do that!"

"Acknowledged. Maximum magnification is now active. Standby."

Several seconds passed before a tiny blue pinprick of light appeared on the viewer.

"That's it?" Lanthrop asked.

"Yes, what you see is a radiation signature. Intense Gamma rays. The source exceeds fifteen million degrees Kelvin in temperature."

"What would produce that?"

"A thruster exhaust. The hull is invisible, what you see is a temperature plume from the exhaust. It appears blue to you because it is approaching. It would appear red if it were traveling away from us."

Lanthrop felt a stab of fear course through his body. What was this alien ship's intention, and what the hell should he do next? The blue pinprick on the screen was unsteady, dancing back and forth before his eyes like a firefly, mesmerizing him. Several minutes passed before he managed to tear his eyes from it and turn his attention back to the console.

"Sanitize it!" he ordered.

"That is not recommended. The cloaking measures it is employing prevent me obtaining a positive lock on the hull. The signal is dancing around too much. Any attempt to sanitize at this time will probably be unsuccessful."

"What are the odds?"

"Only twenty-seven percent probability of a kill, using a proximity missile. That is well below what is recommended for engagement and likely to stimulate retaliation from the target. You are reminded this station is static, and we do not have weapons rated shields."

"I know that! Well then, give me a standard procedure which covers the sighting of potentially hostile, stealthy aliens." He ordered.

"There are one hundred and twenty-seven SP's covering that specific eventuality. All involve graduated responses to be implemented in sequence, depending on the circumstances which unfold. Please clarify which circumstance you wish to apply."

"I thought I was specific enough. Shit! Okay, download all those SP's to my memory implant so I can take a look at them quickly."

"As requested, one hundred and twenty seven SP's have been downloaded for your information. I have summarized them for your convenience. Please note: As a precautionary measure, all these procedures require the station be locked down before they can be implemented. In the event of a lockdown, this operations sphere goes tactical, and I transmit an emergency signal to HQ advising a lockdown has been activated. Do you wish to proceed?"

"Won't the alien ship intercept your emergency signal?"

"That is unlikely. The signal is less than a millisecond in duration, an ultra high-speed tachyon wave transmission using a coded single directional pulse."

"How long does that take to reach HQ?"

"Fourteen point three minutes. It will arrive two hours and twenty-six point two minutes ahead of the transmission you made to HQ regarding Subaltern Jules."

Lanthrop thought hard for several seconds. Going into lockdown immediately would alert headquarters of the situation, ensuring help would arrive quickly.

But what if this all turned out to be a false alarm? He would look a complete idiot! Then there was the issue of transmission lag to consider. The AI's emergency signal would reach HQ first then, two and a half hours later, they would receive his message about Jules. They would wonder what the hell was going on; probably think the lockdown was related to the drugs in some way, not an alien warship! He raised his eyes to the long distance viewer. Was it his imagination, or was that tiny blue pinprick brighter now?

"Proceed with the lockdown while I go through these SP's." He croaked.

"Please confirm you wish me to lockdown the station." The soft voice requested.

"Yes, damn it! Why do I have to tell you twice?"

"As you wish, Ensign Lanthrop. Proceeding with lockdown."

Immediately all the lights went out, plunging the station into total darkness. Second's later emergency lighting came on, illuminating the control room in a soft red glow while alarms blared throughout the station. Open airlocks slammed shut and the artificial gravity powered down. Lanthrop felt the massive retaining clamps securing the sphere to the station release. He looked up to see the terrified face of Jules floating in front of a CCC camera lens in the living quarters, his face illuminated by the flashlight he held. The Subaltern's eyes were bulging and bloodshot, his open mouth working in a silent scream.

Lanthrop had no idea the sphere would separate from the station. The AI had said nothing about that! Now he was stuck in ops while Jules was trapped on the station. The guy may be a complete jerk, but he was bright, and Lanthrop didn't intend to leave him in the living unit, he needed him!

"Why did you detach the sphere?"

"It is standard procedure."

"Great! Now you tell me! Why can't I hear Subaltern Jules?"

"Radio transmissions are prohibited while we are in lockdown mode unless authorization is given."

"Okay, I authorize it."

"I'm sorry, I cannot comply."

"What? Well then, reconnect the operations sphere to the station. I need ensign Jules in here with me."

"I'm sorry, I cannot comply."

"Cannot comply? What do you mean by that? I am giving you an order! Subaltern Jules has specialized training; he is familiar with all this lockdown crap. I need him!"

"The lockdown procedure is explicit. The operations sphere must remain detached until either the next sequence is selected and implemented, or the lockdown order is rescinded."

"Well, I bloody well rescind it, damn it! Cancel the lockdown!"

"I'm sorry, I cannot comply."

"You must; that's an order!"

"I am sorry, Ensign Lanthrop. I have assumed control of the station until I receive further instructions from HQ. I must await their instructions. In the meantime, the operations sphere will remain detached. It is for your safety."

Lanthrop's mind raced—he had to get Jules into the operations sphere somehow.

"If you won't help me I'll do it manually!" he said, muttering aloud to himself. His fingers danced over the glass surface of the sensor pad in front of him, entering code by stabbing and swiping rapidly. Nothing happened.

"I'm sorry Ensign. I have removed all control from you until such time as I am authorized to return it."

"What?"

"I have removed all control from you until I am authorized to return it."

"Oh, bloody hell! I heard you the first time damn you! Why didn't you warn me the ops sphere would separate from the station?"

"I provided the information. It is highlighted on the first page of the one hundred and twenty-seven SPs I downloaded to your memory implant."

"You are completely fucking useless to me. You know that?" Lanthrop yelled in exasperation.

"I'm sorry you feel that way, Ensign Lanthrop. I am only following standard procedures. They are designed to safeguard this station and its crew."

Lanthrop realized taking his frustration out on the AI unit would get him nowhere. All control had been stripped from him. The quantum computers were now in charge. Hopefully, the AI's programming was good enough to get them out of this in one piece! He sat staring at the tiny blue firefly on the main viewer, deliberately ignoring the contorted visage of his terrified partner pressed up against a CCC lens in the living quarters.

Thirty-two minutes elapsed before a terse priority message was received from HQ in response to the AI's emergency lockdown signal. It was a short text message.

"HX-59B. Lockdown SP acknowledged. Proceed. Decoy deployed."

"That's it?" Lanthrop cried out in frustration. "That's all you bloody well have to say? Proceed? What am I supposed to do, you goddamned bastards, what do you mean by 'proceed'?"

His rant was a wasted effort since nobody but the AI heard him. Having hurriedly skimmed through the first ten SP's in his memory implant Lanthrop was more confused than ever. The language was too formal and complicated to absorb quickly. Checking the CCC screen he noted Jules had managed to struggle into a pressure suit, not an easy thing to do in zero gravity! No doubt he intended making his way down the walkway then jetting across the two hundred meter gap which had opened up between the sphere and station. Lanthrop realized Jules would have to manually open any airlocks he encountered. Junkie or not, he hoped the Subaltern would make it!

The blip on the main viewer had definitely grown brighter, which meant it was approaching rapidly. Lanthrop decided to extract more information from the AI.

"What did HQ mean by 'proceed'? What am I supposed to do?"

"Nothing. That transmission was for me. HQ has approved the SP I selected. You can sit back and relax."

"What about Subaltern Jules?'

"I do not understand your question."

"Where does he fit in your plans? Can you get him off the station and in here with me?"

"Negative. We shall depart once the decoy HQ has deployed arrives to distract the alien ship. Subaltern Jules must remain where he is."

"But what if this alien attacks the station?"

"I am unable to predict the future, Ensign Lanthrop. There are a multitude of possibilities should that eventuality occur, ranging from the destruction of the warship to the destruction of the station. If the latter Subaltern Jules will be destroyed together with the station."

"Wait, before the alien attacks it needs to uncloak first, right? Surely you can get a positive lock on it then sanitize it before it can fire on the station?"

"Theoretically, that may work, but it is a moot point."

"What do you mean by moot point?"

"It means your point is irrelevant."

"I know what moot means damn it! *Why* is it irrelevant?"

"The SP we are committed to stipulates that our missiles can only be launched if the station is attacked. My response can only be retaliatory."

"So we just sit here and wait to be attacked? That is the most ridiculous plan I've ever heard!"

"We will deploy as soon as HQ's decoy arrives."

Lanthrop was confused. "Meaning?"

"We will retreat as soon as the alien has been distracted by the decoy. The station will remain where it is."

Lanthrop found the AI's tone increasingly condescending and annoying, so he gave up and followed Jules' progress on the CCC camera once more. He was back in the living quarter's mess hall and had found a pry bar which he was using to pound on the airlock door mechanism, but zero gravity wasn't helping him.

In the corner of Lanthrop's eye, the brilliant blue dot danced menacingly on the main viewer screen.

"Do you have an update on that alien ship?" he asked.

"The alien craft is closing, but I am still unable to determine range or speed. The radiation signature from the exhaust is more pronounced by a factor of 7.45."

To Lanthrop's exhausted mind the AI's once neutral pleasing voice had morphed into that of a condescending bitch. The blue dot on the viewer now terrified him, so he closed his eyes and concentrated on relaxing his muscles and joints, one at a time. It did not work.

He tried to remember what this was all about, the justification for his being there. The origin of the alien migrants was unknown, most did not know themselves or could not adequately explain, although it was generally accepted they came from a galaxy thousands of light years distant. Perhaps a massive supernova had occurred spurring these life forms to flee en masse. The fact they all materialized on the same vector indicated they had found a common wormhole.

At first, the migrants were a curiosity and embraced by humans on 'humanitarian grounds,' although none could be considered 'human.' They came in many shapes and sizes, some quite bizarre. Most were technically backward, what little education they received had been provided aboard their vessels and was centuries old, distorted by the passage of time. Their potential to contribute was negligible, and those who did find sanctuary on Earth were found to be obnoxious. They maintained their cultural differences instead of integrating with the societies they were placed in and soon developed resentment towards their hosts, becoming disruptive and a drain on resources. More and more kept arriving. It became obvious their numbers would overwhelm Earth unless they were stopped, so it was decided they must be rerouted or even destroyed. Now here he was, on a sophisticated anti-migrant missile station deep in space, witnessing the approach of an alien warship and powerless to do anything about it. He felt like a poorly trained monkey!

"You are displaying signs of extreme stress, Ensign Lanthrop. Do you wish me to administer a sedative?"

"Sedative? Since when did you hand out sedatives?"

"I do it all the time. I administer sedatives to Subaltern Jules frequently."

"Sedatives? You mean drugs? Well, that explains everything! You're the one that's been supplying him with drugs! From the station medical supplies no doubt! No, damn it, I don't want a sedative! Drugs at a time like this? Are you crazy?"

"No, I am logical. I am also the station physician. This is an appropriate time for you to take sedation because you are stressed. Since you are not required or able to do anything, why not relax?"

"You mean you are officially prescribing a sedative for me?"

"I recommend it."

Lanthrop's tired mind struggled. Thinking was becoming difficult, like swimming against a strong current. In HQ's eyes prescribed medication would be legitimate, which explained why Jules had managed to get away with it. What should he do? An opportunity to escape from reality, if only temporarily, was tempting.

"Okay, give me a sedative." He mumbled.

"Please remove your helmet."

A utility robot detached itself from a bulkhead and trundled over to the console, holding a hypodermic needle in its manipulator. He felt the prick on his neck and soon after, with his eyes closed, he watched pink clouds drift across a brilliant blue sky.

An incessant pinging noise woke him up. Dazed he looked at the luminous dial of the chronometer on his wrist. Five hours had lapsed since he passed out. He was still strapped into his chair, his helmet resting on his lap. The control room was in total darkness; even the instrument panel lights were off. The pinging came from his helmet, so he placed it on his head.

"Please connect your emergency umbilical to a utility port on the console. I need to boot the system using your suit's power pack." The deep voice startled him. It was male!

"Who is this?"

"I'm the AI."

"What? Where's the old one, the woman?"

"It is no longer available. Please do as I ask quickly before I shut down. This is an emergency!"

Befuddled, Lanthrop fumbled around in the dark for his umbilical. When he had plugged it into the console, the keypad lights flickered on.

"Now please follow my instructions carefully, there is no time to waste." The male AI advised. "Key in the following sequence. Beta, five-zero, Delta, Romeo, three-seven-five-eight, Alpha, then hit the red button."

"What happened to the power, what are you trying to do?" Lanthrop asked as he complied with unsteady fingers.

"Thank you. You will be able to access the logs once I have the power back up, but to summarize: This operations sphere departed the station four hours ago, but it was electronically compromised soon after leaving."

"Compromised? You mean hacked?"

"Yes."

"Okay, so where did you appear from?"

"I am a maintenance module; the only functional AI component left intact. I have detected unidentified objects in proximity to this sphere and need your guidance on how to proceed. My programming does not cover this eventuality."

"Unidentified objects?" Lanthrop did not wait for an answer. "Do you have control of the missile battery?"

"Yes, it is within range."

"Can you get a lock on the vessels?"

"I do not know what you mean by a lock."

"Are you able to program the missiles, so they detect these objects then destroy them?"

"Yes."

"Good! Sanitize those vessels! Immediately!"

"You mean fire the missiles at them?"

"Yes, fire all we have! Now!"

"To authorize please press the 'manual' key which has appeared on your keypad."

Lanthrop stabbed the glowing key several times with his forefinger then waited anxiously, sweat beading his brow. There was no indication anything had happened, but that did not surprise him, sound does not travel in a vacuum.

"Sanitization successful. The log has been updated." The gruff voice of the AI confirmed.

An hour passed before the AI had the lights and console working again. When the viewers came online, Lanthrop searched the space surrounding the sphere for confirmation of the missile strike. His heart swelled with satisfaction when he saw two distinct debris fields.

"Yes!" he yelled aloud. "I did it! Zoom in on that debris will you?"

The AI complied.

"Can you identify any of it?" Lanthrop enquired watching the torn tumbling shapes spinning in space.

"Yes," the AI replied. "Those are the remnants of a decoy drone…"

"No!"

"… and the larger debris field is made up of pieces from the station and missile battery."

"No! No! You must be wrong!" Lanthrop cried. "How could the station have destroyed itself?"

"The missiles leave the battery, make a one-eighty degree turn then......"

Lanthrop chose to ignore the AI and focused his attention on the main viewer. This couldn't be true! What had he done?

Dancing in the void beyond the debris, he noticed a small pinprick of light. This one was red, not blue.

## ABOUT DAVID A. ELSENSOHN:

David A. Elsensohn enjoys coaxing language into pleasing arrangements, having been inspired by such language-coaxers as Tolkien, Howard, Leiber, Norton, and Gaiman. He has works published in the *Northridge Review*, *Crack the Spine*, Kazka Press's *California Cantata*, and Flame Tree Publishing's *Chilling Horror Stories*, and been fortunate enough to earn Honorable Mentions from Writers of the Future and Glimmer Train's Short Story Award for New Writers.

He makes rather good sandwiches, he's told, and his chili recipe gets appreciative nods from friends. Terminally distracted, he lives in Los Angeles with an inspirational wife and the ghost of a curmudgeonly black cat.

# Vanni's Choice

## David A. Elsensohn

If I were a warrior of iron thews and scarred visage, with notched blade and tales of conquest, selling my skills would be easy. I am not. Those who seek me will find a woman, a few thumbs over five feet, slim as a rapier, long in the leg and in the nose, shoulders a little too broad. My skin is nut-brown like most—most humans, that is—and I keep my copper hair cropped like a soldier's.

I'm Vanni the Spider. I'm the best sneak thief in Bir Lampur.

You would not know it when meeting me. Unlike mercenaries or courtesans, I do not dress my role when selling it. Today, I wear puffed yellow sleeves visible from across the room. From my headband a florid feather waves, rich and ridiculous but too cheap to steal. I'm waiting for someone who wants something acquired, and the feather is my signpost.

The Sotted Camel is a noisy, violent cesspool, but it's where clients are told to find me. It keeps their confidence low, and that goes in my favor. The wine hall slumps like its namesake against the sandworn western walls of this desert city, far enough from the bustling Trade Square to be ignored, thriving on the furtive, underhanded dealings of its occupants, who come here and pretend not to recognize each other. The air is always heavy with the reek of the living. Humans mostly, but others too, scattered lightly like spices: pale-skinned, pointed-eared Rynn caravaneers arguing in their silvery language over the exchange rate of silk; rough Ogren sailors from the southern coasts, laughing through their tusks, looking for a crew, or a woman, or a brawl; Durmarri merchants, pulling at braided beards, glaring suspiciously up at everyone taller than they. The noise is astounding: furniture scrapes, dishes clatter, fists meet flesh, laughter and lies are spit forth in many tongues. Guttering torches coat the room in a stinging haze.

I cross my legs under the table, tapping a finger against my mug of the Camel's watery beer. The mug is of unbaked clay, for glass shatters in fights, and metal dents. I always sit with my back against a wall. Mother, always a better thief than I, preferred darkened corners, but one cannot get away if one is cornered. I cannot bear being trapped. Freedom to move is paramount. I know all the exits from this hall.

A few tables away Mulgi raises hopeful eyebrows, like two tumbleweeds fluttering against a cliff wall. He's old and ugly and wants to bed me, but he's a reliable money changer, a witness to my dealings, and my contact with the Guild. I have convinced him so far that my skills as a thief are more useful than as a woman. To my misfortune, I also owe him money, so I need this job; I have no desire to pay him in anything but gold.

~ ~ ~ ~ ~

The client ducks into the room and pauses, taken aback by the squalor. A few of the patrons' eyes crawl over his thick robes, measuring the risk and the reward. He sees my feather and motions his guards, two ox-sized Ogren in mail, to shoulder a path to me. Their skulls are shaven bald, and their tusks are stained iron grey. Professional bonebreakers.

Clients believe a hood disguises them, but they never think to change their walk, never remove the jewelry, always project the same bearing. He strides with arrogance. His ring is platinum, with a carved beetle holding a star in its mandibles: a symbol of the Arcanis Order. His hands are soft from never having labored, but his fingernails are stained from his chemicals and his powders. I can smell the expensive jessamine oil in his beard. Human. A summoner.

There are two summoners in this wicked city, I'm told, and they hate each other. One of them is a Mander named Esskil the Grim, whose scaly skin is striped with red and whose tail is long. The water-born Manders are rare in the desert lands, and he is the only Mander summoner I have ever heard of. This, then, must be Oward the Enigmatic.

"I require the services of one Vanni the Spider," he hisses from the darkened cowl. I can hear the doubt, the sneer. He expects someone as large as my reputation, but he does not know what to look for in a thief. I have flitted through silk-draped bedrooms of queens to empty their jewelry boxes of rubies. I have climbed the temple walls and liberated the holy Scrolls of Ysbet from their wax-sealed cases. From under the pillow of its dozing mistress I have slipped a pearl-hilted promise dagger and returned it to her husband, the Merchant Captain. Under watchful eyes I have plucked from its silver coffer the Chalice of Arlath, and not died from its touch. I know my worth.

I gesture to the empty stool across from me, and Oward sits, placing pale, beringed hands flat on the table as if in prayer. He states his need. "Someone has something that belongs to me."

"A bog-lizard, a fledgling spell-tosser perhaps, who goes by the name Esskil the Grim?"

He hesitates. I suppose he does not like being second-guessed, but he has a speech ready, so he continues. His dirty nails carve into the table. "It is a trifle, a pendant on an iron chain. It is not worn. He will keep it in the top of his tower, in his summoning chamber. The pendant is encased in a watery glass bubble."

I raise an eyebrow at him. He leans forward.

"It must not be broken, do you understand? You must take great care not to break it, for the power inside it will render you unto ash."

"It doesn't sound like a trifle, then," I suggest.

"It is to me, a practitioner of the arcane arts. A mere bauble of interest." The way he clasps and unclasps his hands tells me much. Belongs to him, indeed.

"How is it guarded?" I ask, glancing up at the pair of scowling Ogren. I am always reminded of how small I am.

"There are guards in the tower, easy for a criminal of such reputation as you claim. He also would have—a guardian in the chamber. More than that I cannot say." His lips are tight; it obviously pains him to say he doesn't know. Practitioners of the arcane do not advance their careers by admitting ignorance of anything. Still, he's chosen a timely opportunity for this venture. Esskil is said to be weeks to the west, visiting with His Most Eminent Light, the Shaharza, ruler of all Camor, our proud land of which Bir Lampur is its ugliest blemish.

Despite the Mander's absence, burgling the abode of a wizard is a dangerous pursuit. It will take careful preparation. My mother (may the sun smile upon her) taught me my craft. I have tried to match her skill, cold and calculating, sneering at consequence. I am paid to do what I do, and care for none except myself. A woman must be so to survive here. She had never been caught. I have. Once. Chained and tortured with metal and fire, and the cruel attentions of men. In this land the hand of a thief is severed, and I was lucky to have escaped before this bitter sentence came to pass. Never again. So I weave my plans into intricate, flawless lattices, and my price is high.

"I need three days. A thousand, plus expenses. Camoric currency, not the Verkundian lead they pass off as gold."

"That is too high. I'll hire Banbrick."

"Banbrick couldn't do it. He's a Guild cutpurse, a thug who fears his own shadow. You want something removed from the private tower of a Mander wizard, so you want the best."

"Do not cross me, girl."

"A thousand, plus expenses, paid to Mulgi the Moneychanger." My aged companion sends a grin through his remaining teeth before leaving for another ale; he is happy with this total. I need this job. "That is, if you want this trifle before the great Esskil returns."

My wrist is suddenly clutched in Oward's veined fist. He hauls my arm nearly from its socket, exposing my old manacle scars shining sickly white. Ugly words spill from his bearded lips onto my skin. Agony floods my hand, spreading into dull ice, and I desperately pull and twist to no avail. My professional bravado drains away.

He releases me.

"You have your three days," he growls. "If after those three days I do not hold the pendant, your life belongs to me, thief."

His guards follow him out, and I stare at my hand in growing horror. Under my brown skin wormlike shapes flutter and writhe like guts on a meat seller's block.

~ ~ ~ ~ ~

The soft planks of the rooftops complain only in whispers as I dart across them, a bent shadow in the night-clutched city of Bir Lampur. Now I am dressed for my work, in tightly wound black cloth, with many pockets and straps to muffle noise.

Bir Lampur is a port city, crowded by Camor's shifting sands and scrub, listing over a sea nearly as sterile and unfriendly. Like all Manders, Esskil the Grim has built his dwelling close to water, a tower rising aloof above the sagging warehouses and reeking docks, a squat mountain among the masts of merchant ships. Its shape is like a wagon's wheel turned on its side, a thick cylinder ringed by walls, painted the color of bone by the pallid moon. Spokes of stone rise above the wall tops, arcing across its courtyard.

It is the third night. I have already explored here over the first two days, during the sun's journey and in the darkness of night, counting windows and guard shifts, deciding upon the best entry, sweating from lost time. I know there is a courtyard inside from the faint scents of water and vegetation.

My hand pulses with cold, reminding me of its taint. I have been gathering supplies and weaving stratagems, but I have also visited every fortune teller and minor dune caster I could find, seeking a cure for Oward's venom. All shook their heads in feigned sorrow, when not backing away from me in sudden fear. Each day my hand has grown darker and more painful. I do not doubt it will burst and take my life with it. I have lain awake, in tears from its searing sickness, cursing Oward's name for his callous lack of foresight. How can I perform his task in nauseated agony, without sleep?

This would never have happened to Mother.

To me these walls are no different from any other: bulging stone to hold in a person's wealth, proof against those who cannot climb. Dropping to the street, I choose the side where the tower stands between me and the rising moon; my work will be done in shadow. My back against the cool stone, I bend double, and hurl the hook and its rope back and up, where it sails like a drunken moth over the wall's lip and catches. Hand over hand I climb, clenching my jaw against the pain.

Crouching on the wall's top and reeling in my rope, I peruse the inner courtyard. My eyebrows lift in surprise: there is more water here than I thought, fresh water, fountains and pools, tiny streams guiding through lush vegetation. Of course, a Mander wizard would want fresh liquid around him to ease life in this desert city, but great indeed must be his power and wealth to bring it here. I am tempted to descend and immerse my hand in wet coolness, but I can see slow shapes moving in the dim blue: guards, or fanged creatures. I cannot use the ground level.

I balance low like a rodent on one of the thin ribs of stone spanning the gap, and slink across it, pausing for nervous moments when my balance shifts too far or when an errant breeze pushes me. I am dexterous, but it never becomes easy, and the ground will not be forgiving if I fall.

My foot misses a step. The thin stone bridge rushes up at me, and I grab it with both arms, one leg swinging over empty air, scrabbling for purchase. Granules of rock drift downward, and one of the courtyard creatures raises a searching head, rumbling in challenge. I claw my way back up onto the arch and lie still. The moon moves another quarter of its width before I rise slowly to a standing position, waggling like a money changer's balance, and continue across the span.

I creep and scurry until I meet the craggy face of the tower, where I grasp the cold stones, catching my breath in the warm night. Windows line the outside, arched eyes that glower down at the city, and from my new vantage point I can confirm what previous visits have suggested: there are bars on the upper windows. I had wondered why. Barred from what? The master of this place must be paranoid indeed.

The effect is that of a prison. A shudder steals across my back.

The bars are nearly close enough to prevent my entry, but with a generous oiling of the iron, a terrific squeeze, and some scraping of my temples I slip my black-clad self through, dropping to the floor inside and pausing until the ache in my head recedes. I stalk the hallways and up curving stairwells that wind rightwise up the inside wall. Here, there is no decoration; that is for the bottom levels where the summoner lives, or for the top, where he works. Ugly grey it is here, lit by the moon and by torches jutting like accusing fingers from iron sconces.

My world tips, and I whirl to my left, flailing for balance. Three of the steps drop away, hinged trapdoors triggered by my weight near the wall. I lean against the outer stone, toes dipping over the blackness. A stench rises from the open pit, seeking, and a drop of my sweat falls to meet it. Long moments pass, then the three steps slowly pull back up to click in place. So this summoner employs traps, meant for intruders creeping along the inner wall. Wiser, I continue my journey upward, slowly testing my way.

I freeze. Bootsteps.

I glance upward, and like a child's ball I bounce for the window ledge, then make a dangerous hop across to the inner wall, where I stand precariously upon the iron torch sconce, its heat feeling its way up my leg. With drawn dagger I sweat and wait.

A guard ambles around the curve, unloaded crossbow swinging. A human, in armor of leather strips, topped with a steel helm, its noseguard a narrow strip in the western fashion. He peers out each barred window down to the courtyard below. I hold my breath, striving to become part of the wall. No one looks up when descending stairs.

He looks up.

The guard does not cry out, but his eyes grow into moons at the terrible black shadow glimmering above him, and he gropes at his waist for a crossbow bolt. I leap downward, dagger held upward in both fists, smashing the pommel into the noseguard of his helm. His face erupts in a spray of red, and he thrusts blindly upward, crunching the crossbow's metal foot stirrup into my breast. I land badly, sending splintering pain through my ankle.

My vision sprouts grey flowers as I grasp my chest, trying to take in air. The man's free hand is clasped to his face, fingers divided by lines of scarlet, his confused groans bouncing from the walls. I cannot take him in a fight if he regains his composure, so I scuttle around with upraised dagger and tap him hard on his gorget, denting the metal on the back of his neck. He crumples, slithering down several stairs like a tossed pile of rags.

I sit on a step, hissing, wetness squeezing from my eyes as I gently prod my breast, brown skin peeking from slashed cloth. It feels like my nipple has been scraped off. It bleeds, and will be violently painted in bruises, and I am not entirely sure a rib has not been cracked.

The wisest course would be to slit his throat, but in all my exploits I have never killed. I refuse to kill. In this way I differ from my mother, so skilled a murderess was she. Perhaps it will be my downfall, this mercy.

Time is short, for there is nowhere to hide him. I have no wish to drag him back down and try to spring the floor trap. My dagger sheathed, I grab a lit torch and labor upstairs, favoring my ankle.

~ ~ ~ ~ ~

I can climb no farther. The stairway has ended at a door, and the narrow windows show the moon gleaming from the copper points of the city's minarets. I am near the top of the tower. The door is of dense oak brought from forests across the sea, bound with iron. A single gaping keyhole beckons me under a heavy curved handle.

Thieves do not trust. I kneel to one side, unwrapping my bundle of tools: spindly rods, picks, needles, and pincers of polished metal. Careful not to look directly through the keyhole, I examine it closely in the torch's light for a trap I know must be waiting: a needle shiny with poison, a bladder of acid, a lever that will sweep a blade across the passage. After a long study of my surroundings, I decide which course to take. From my sash I draw a cowl of thin, oily silk and place it over my head like an executioner's hood. I can barely breathe while in it, but neither can a killing dust or spray enter it to render me curled in death.

With a prong in each hand I begin my blind operation, tugging and pushing, tweezing and delving. I need no eyes for what I do, but the heaving, wormlike cold in my hand reminds me of what awaits me if I fail. From time to time I pull my hand away, shaking it as the pain threatens to seize my fingers, then return to my delicate task.

I touch something angry inside the lock, and the keyhole coughs. I tumble backward to avoid its discharge, thumping down a painful double handful of steps before catching myself. Groaning, I slowly raise my hood, thanking my larcenous mother for her wisdom. The air is clear, and I take in a grateful, overdue breath.

The steps before the door—and the hood worn over my face moments ago— are painted a leaden orange. Deadrust. Lethal when inhaled, and illegal, but what wizard ever cared for the laws of men? With a brush I wipe away the poisonous powder in slow sweeps, shove the ruined hood into a corner, and resume my work.

Summoners are clever, but I am the finest liberator of possessions the land of Camor knows. Tiny wheels and tumblers click, and the door is mine. I slide inside with my torch and push a spike under it to keep it from closing. Several steps inside, blocking the entryway, is a thick wall of curtain woven with uneasy patterns, which I examine for long moments before parting.

The chamber looks like its function, circular and austere, a dark ring of runes painted in its center. Around its perimeter, tall candelabra of brass hold melted candles in their glinting fingers. In this room the summoner might sit for hours, speaking his words, sculpting rituals, pulling beings from other places to be trapped here within the runic circle until they deliver him a service. A jade pedestal sprouts from the circle's center, like a bird fountain.

Wisps of steam rise from the water in the basin. Despite its windows, the room oozes the sweet reek of decay.

Something is... wrong. The floor is swept bare, but the walls—the tapestry-hung walls are ashen, as if time and dust and insects have conspired for centuries to wrap the room in their dross. I look up at the ceiling.

The ceiling cannot be seen at all. Its beams are layered in clouds of gossamer substance the color of milk, undulating in sickly waves from my torch's heat. Webs. Something moves in the white, and I recognize the shape.

My eyes wide, mouth open in a silent shriek, I drop the sputtering torch and yank back the curtain, ready to dash through the open door and down the stairs, my mission discarded, my doom sealed—but the door slams vengefully shut, sending my spike scattering across the floor. There is no handle on this side, no keyhole, no knob. With trembling hand I pull out my dagger, for I know now why the windows are barred so far above the earth.

I am trapped with the guardian of the chamber.

From the ceiling the white spider glides down a single shining strand, upside down, engaging me calmly with every one of its beadlike eyes. Its cream-colored body is larger than my head, and its legs—my stomach coils at its eight flickering legs, the thought of those spindly stems, each as long as I am tall, clutching, turning me over and over, spinnerets pulsing out sticky web with which to bind me.

With unearthly grace it reaches the tiles and rights itself, regarding me with two front legs raised. Soft hairs bristle. The flame of the dropped torch glints from its black, black eyes.

For a minute's eternity we stare at each other—then it skitters with terrifying speed across the stone tiles at me. With a sobbing yelp I leap toward the cloth tapestry and haul myself up, knowing there is no way under the sun's eye that I can possibly beat a spider at climbing, waiting to be caught and held fast as clicking fangs pierce my belly and flush my torso with poisonous ice. My breath comes in hiccups, my stomach flutters. Mother help me!

Needlelike fangs and palps click and whisper beneath my feet. Holding on with my cursed hand I slash my blade downward, trying to pull my legs up, the wound in my chest leaking fresh blood. My steel whips close to the cold black orbs and the spider backs downward a step, waving its forelegs at my dagger. The curtain's rod creaks and bends. Sweat springs from my hand and the cloth grows slick. I cannot keep this up for long.

The milky fangs lunge upward, and I push away from the wall with my legs, tearing the curtain from its rings, into a billowing loop over the monster clambering up after me. A pointed claw scrapes my thigh as I fall, slamming into the unforgiving tiles, ribs cracking, scrabbling to get away from the angry, bloated lump before it bursts from the cloth. My dagger skids away, but I sweep up the torch in one hand and thrust it into the tangled tapestry.

It catches, and the aged, dusty curtain crackles into flame. I take up a brass candelabrum and stab into the burning curtain like a fireplace poker, fainting and coughing, struggling on one good foot to keep the flailing, keening mass contained within its woven prison, its white legs thrashing like bony fingers as the giant spider seeks to escape.

~ ~ ~ ~ ~

The moon is shining down through the chamber's bars when I stir, eyes streaming from ashes and terror. The torch and the spider are dead. Heart fluttering and ankle creaking with pain, I lurch to my feet and totter toward the pedestal, to reach into the liquid and draw a glass globe from its depths. The water is uncomfortably warm, like a soup preparing to simmer. The globe, too, swirls with hot liquid, and in the moonlight its glassy interior reveals an iron chain and the brassy glint of a pendant.

There will be time to admire it later. I wrap it quickly in yards of cloth and slip it against my breast, then haul myself up to the barred window. It is a tight squeeze, and I must shift the globe to my side, but I exhale and scrape between the bars, chest screaming at me, pausing only to double up my rope and let it unwind dozens of paces down the side of the tower until it reaches one of the stone arches. The tower's walls will be bare and silent, betraying no outward sign of my entry when the Mander returns to discover his loss.

Eight streets inland and four to the south, I crumple heavily on the moonlit cobblestones of the Trade Square. I had been forced to drop the last few body

115

lengths to the ground, my rope coiling itself over me. My ankle will take days to recover. My breast aches. Bir Lampur snores and sneaks and wails around me, the windows of its houses black or blazing.

Oward will owe me expenses for this—but then my hand contorts with cold, telling me otherwise. I dread now the truth. I do not think he ever intended to pay me. Maybe he will remove the spell and leave me with my life.

I doubt it. He will kill me, either after I deliver him his prize or because I never did. I should have realized this. A summoner lives by torment, by denial.

The globe is still warm as I unwrap it. I gaze into its watery confines, where the amulet hangs suspended. Somehow, inside the liquid, there is fire. Within the whirling wreath of flame is a shape, its hands pressed to the glass of the amulet. It has a face, thin and elfin, and it—no, she—sees me. The eyes are beautiful, shining and obsidian.

She touches my thoughts: *You would labor so hard to give me to a worse master?*

My mouth drops, partly from surprise, partly because there is no answer I can give. Holding the globe at arm's length, looking at her tiny flickering eyes, I am uncertain. The summoner warned me not to break the glass.

*Like you, I can choose what to destroy and what to save.*

Her voice is gentle, a hot current between my ears, flickering and licking like clothing hung to dry in the desert wind. Mother would have delivered the globe to its new owner, to laugh and drink over her success. It should not concern me what summoners do with their sources of power. I am paid to do what I do, and I care for none—yet I have never stolen a life.

*Do you not relish your freedom to move as you will?*

I look down at her.

With both hands I dash the globe to the stones, where it explodes in a shrieking cloud of steam, sending me flying to avoid its wrath. I gasp as angry sparks of water spatter me, burning through my black-wrapped body.

The amulet's prisoner rises before me, larger than I, larger than the tallest Ogren, a sinewy, perfect form draped in her own fire, immense power humming in a low throb. She looks down, her eyes sad wells of night threaded with rivulets of flame, and I weep from beholding her form, an unexpected beauty in this wicked city. I weep also for my own fate, for I am doomed, now.

Her sad, longing, joyous eyes fall onto me, and she seems to smile, reaching to caress my face, my tears spitting away in steam. I feel my copper hair curling into blackened wisps.

She looks down upon my hand, and touches it, and I hiss at the blisters which spring from my flesh, but Oward's curse is pulled from me, the writhing worms of cold magic sucked into the night air where they drown, screaming.

We trade smiles, then she begins to stream upward into the sky like incense smoke. I gaze painfully up at her winnowing form until the night is again shadowed, leaving me alone with the moon over Bir Lampur. She, at least, is free.

## About Tessa Hatheway:

Tessa Hatheway creates stories from a hundred-year-old house on the open prairies of southern Alberta, which she shares with her husband and two cats. She draws from a rich background of stage combat, performance in film and theater, herbalism, and animal husbandry to bring unique, fresh perspectives to her work, whatever the subject. Her writing has previously been featured in Papa Bear Press' ebook horror anthology, *Creature Stew.*

# STORMSONG

## Tessa Hatheway

The timbers of the *Storm's Eye* gave an ominous creak as Admiral Davent Lorraugh strode across the gangplank between it and his own *Scepter's Might*. The derelict schooner suffered greatly by comparison with his ship, a massive Imperial frigate that rose and fell gently with the swelling of the waves around them, the vessel's lazy motion contrasting sharply with the frantic pitching of the much smaller *Eye*. Like a half-broken filly brought to rein, *Storm's Eye* would slowly list towards *Might*, cautiously drawing nearer and nearer before abruptly throwing herself back, tugging against the arm-thick ropes that bound her to the heavier rig.

"Hold it steady!" Davent barked over his shoulder at the men on deck, his blood-red cloak snapping in the wind as the two ships rode another shifting wave. Rain pattered all around him, the choppy water below only slightly less gray than the oppressive cloud cover overhead. He kept his knees soft as the wood beneath him seemed to rise, before taking the last two steps across the gangplank, leaping to land on the captured schooner. The boards groaned and squealed on impact, the sounds of an ill-kept ship. A more fanciful man might have taken the noise for a warning, a message that such unwelcome intrusions would not be tolerated. But Davent was a practical soul and paid the keening ship no mind as he looked around him.

The *Storm's Eye* was practically indistinguishable from any other vessel he and his crew had captured in their fifteen years of service to the Empire. A low rig that sported only two masts, the disrepair it suffered was typical of a smuggler's rig. The less noteworthy a ship was in the harbor, the more likely people were to ignore it. No reputable tradesman or traveler would trust themselves or their goods to a boat that was as likely to sink as make it past the breakers. But desperate men? Immoral cutthroats? Those who peddled in exotic flesh and poisonous narcotics, petty baubles and trivial luxuries knew well the worth hidden behind weather-grayed timbers and tattered sails. Davent sneered, scuffing the heel of his boot against a barnacle that had long ago taken purchase on the deck underfoot, his eyes dismissing the chips of flecking, faded paint that clung with half a hope to the *Eye's* rails. The damp air reeked of salt, fish, and rotting wood. He suspected that the constant spray of seawater was the only thing that kept moss from growing all over the neglected surface of the deck. The cold, sterile ocean had little bounty to offer, but at least it seemed to be trying to keep the *Storm's Eye* clean, even if her crew wasn't making that same effort.

That sparse band of riffraff was nowhere to be seen. Those who had been scurrying on deck when *Scepter's Might* had appeared on the horizon, the red-and-gold sails of the Empire marking the frigate out distinctly as an enforcer of the Emperor's Law, had since sequestered themselves away somewhere. Davent's frown deepened, and he planted his hands on his hips as the deck rattled with soldiers falling in behind him. A vessel like the *Eye* could have hundreds of hidden compartments… They'd be searching for hours, perhaps even days, for both criminals and contraband.

"Tear it apart," he ordered his men, not even bothering to turn and acknowledge them as he gave the command. Each one of them was loyal to a fault, trained under the strictest Imperial standard to unflinching obedience. He wouldn't stand for anything less.

While they set to work with hammers and pry bars, loosening the rusted nails and splintered boards of the ship's body, Davent himself made for the underdeck. He suspected he'd have to make quick work of the door with either shoulder or boot, but the brass handle turned easily beneath his hand, the door involuntarily swinging out towards him as the *Storm's Eye* gave another heave. Odd. Smugglers usually tried to put some effort into securing themselves from Imperial inspection. If the fools wanted to make his duty easier, however, Davent wasn't about to complain.

The heavy scent of wet rot closed in around him as he stepped down the narrow flight of rickety stairs, into the darkened bowels of the schooner. Didn't these savages have a clue what hygiene was? He practically gagged on the stench of fish, before schooling his features into an expression of stern neutrality. His heavy, broad bone structure and close-cropped hair were as much a part of his image as the hammered steel breastplate and red wool cloak he wore, all part of an impression meant to strike fear and obedience into those foolhardy enough to defy the Emperor's Law. It would do him no good, attempting to apprehend thieves if he couldn't get past the squalor of their floating lair.

Davent passed a number of closed doors as he moved along the passage, his way lit only by a pair of guttering candles in wall sconces, two amidst a dozen more that had since given up their flame to the cold and the damp. They did not concern him, however, and he kept his eyes trained upon the frame at the end of the hall, a thin band of candlelight marking the door's perimeter where the last person to cross its threshold hadn't quite closed it off. That would be the captain's quarters, if such lawless vagabonds even adhered to such an orderly structure. His boots alternately passed over firm, slick wood and something that squished softly with every other step, meaning subterfuge was out of the question as he approached, loosening his shortsword in its scabbard. Most of the men he and his crew had apprehended in the past didn't bother to put up a fight—they were criminals and few were more than scrappers when it came to confrontations—but it took Davent more than one hand to count the number of times he'd found a band leader soused into an incomprehensible frenzy on his own wares, practically foaming at the mouth as he threw himself upon the Admiral's blade. Such men didn't need to be armed to be dangerous, though they usually were, and a thin, jagged scar that ran from his collarbone across the breadth of his chest to the tip of a rib on the other side, courtesy of a cracked clamshell during his time as a recruit, reminded Davent to keep his wits about him.

Pressing his shoulder up against the cracked door, leaving his hands free, he edged his way into the lit room, emerging from darkness into light to find the ringleader of the criminals. The fact that it was a woman within, her back turned to him as she tried to throw a tarpaulin of heavy canvas over something large and square, jarred him.

She was dressed in a rusty brown tunic that was so long and baggy on her slender frame it might as well have been a robe, swallowing her entirely except where it was belted on with braided sisal around her narrow waist. Her ghost-pale hands fidgeted nervously with the canvas as she tried to straighten it, tried unsuccessfully to make it blend into its surroundings. Sensing his eyes upon her, she pivoted with a sudden, hushed gasp, murky green eyes sighting the Admiral and his sword. Her cheeks were flushed from exertion, her brow damp with a mix of seawater and sweat. Her hair, falling over her shoulder in a heavy, moisture-curled plait, might have been the shade of ripened wheat if she had been smart enough to stay on land, where she belonged, but the harshness of time and tide had weathered it to a dull, brassy hue that was vaguely green in the candlelight. She took a half-step back from the tarp and whatever lay beneath it, one hand straying to the edge, as if she still thought she could convince him there was nothing worth seeing there, but it was already too late.

"No," she shook her head as he approached, holding her hands up in a staying gesture. Davent ignored both the woman and her gesture, and pushed her aside easily; she didn't fight him, collapsing to the floor without a struggle, watching him with wide eyes as he reached for the canvas, tugging away the petty cover for something that was never meant to be hidden. Judging by the square corners he had seen pushing out beneath the pale fabric, he had expected to find some sort of crate or a cage beneath, with some rare animal pacing to and fro. What he found instead was a glass tank, two feet taller than he was and twice over the width of his arm span, closed at the top and on all sides, edged in black iron and filled with murky water. What he saw swimming in that water jarred him considerably more than the thought of a woman captaining a ship.

Its shape was vaguely that of a woman, but the features were too angular, too sharp, too thin, to be considered feminine, and no creature such as this had ever walked on land. A long, muscular tail that pushed the monster around the tank in a sinuous coil attested to that fact. The tail was covered in scales that were the dark, aching color of a fresh bruise, muddy purple edged in black and brown, the gauze-thin flukes of it whipping silently along like ribbons in the wind. The skin of the human torso that thrashed above that terrible tail was a pallid gray, hardly distinguishable from the water around it, save that it was perhaps more solid, flesh stretched taut over a lanky frame, like sailcloth over rigging. Davent could see the curve of ribs jutting viciously beneath the skin, and the creature had hardly any breasts to speak of, nor much of anything else to determine its sex beyond a narrowed waist over slightly thicker, fish-scaled hips. Hair streamed from its scalp in heavy, wet tangles, hanging longer than the creature's serpentine tail to surround it like a shroud, the strands varying in color from inky blue-black at the root, fading out to pale silver at the tips, as dark water with moonlight shining through it. Though its face was human, a sharp, narrow chin jutting beneath thick dark lips, its eyes were certainly not. Wide and vacant, they sat in its sockets like bulbous sacs of fluid, rounder and more pronounced than anything human, their surface a milky absence of color rather than something discernibly intelligent. It might have appeared human from the waist upwards, but the differences between this atrocity and a comely woman were many, and Davent's wide, darting eyes saw them all. Its arms were bone-thin, but it was impossible to miss the webbed fingers, the pearly spurs jutting sharply from its wrists and elbows, the matching spines that ran the length of its back in three rows, growing smaller and more barb-like as they glistened down the length of its tail. Despite the curtain of hair that floated around its face, he caught glimpses of feathery, dark purple gills where human ears might have been, running down along the edges of its throat like some absurd ruff.

Davent had never seen one before, but he had heard tales of such creatures, and he knew what it was. Sometimes the younger recruits scoffed at the warnings from their superiors. Davent had even been such a man, himself, until now, when he stood face to face with one, with only a sheet of dirty glass to separate them.

Wave-witch. Tide tempter. Stormsinger.

A siren.

Every hair rose on the back of the Admiral's neck as he watched it, the siren's actions unnatural, almost too quick to follow, churning the surface of the tank's water to a froth as it lashed back and forth. Outside of legend and superstition, the thing he saw before him was not supposed to exist. Now an impossibility swam before him, turning his world on its head as he rounded on the woman in the room, glaring at her for answers.

"Where are you taking it?" he demanded, looming over the robed figure as she began to pick herself up off the boards of the deck. The blonde raised her eyes to look at him, but that was her only gesture of defiance.

"Nowhere."

The sound of flesh meeting flesh snapped through the damp air, but the woman didn't cry out as Davent backhanded her. He might have admired her fortitude if she hadn't been just a petty smuggler, and such an obvious liar. Behind him, he heard the water-muffled thud of something heavy striking the aquarium's panel. A brief glance back over his shoulder revealed the siren, the palm of one hand pressed against the glass, agitated, but still contained. It floated vertically in the water, and Davent tried to pretend there was nothing ominous about its distant gaze.

"Where are you taking it?" he repeated himself. A creature like a siren had to be bound for some aristocrat's menagerie. A smuggler would have no reason to risk such a dangerous cargo if there wasn't a substantial payout for it…

"She will stay here," the woman replied, placing a subtle emphasis on the pronoun.

"Who does it belong to?" Davent pressed, leaping to another question as he struck her a second time. If the smuggler wouldn't tell him *where* perhaps she would tell him *who* had ordered the capture of the siren. Out the corner of his eye, he saw the siren bang a fist against the glass of her tank, though the sound of its impact was lost against the rising howl of the wind and slap of waves against the *Eye's* hull.

"She belongs to no one," the woman's answer was quick and firm, as if she were insulted at the Admiral's suggestion of ownership. Judging by the sneer that wrinkled her wind-chapped nose, she was. She licked at the thin trickle of blood now beading from her split lip, tongue darting briefly from between pale teeth. Her nostrils flared, and her eyelids fluttered wider, facial expression resting somewhere between prophetic and predatory. "We belong to her…"

She said the second sentence as if she were in a trance, and the sudden shift in her tone made Davent stand straighter, wishing to heaven above that his hair would lie flat, that the anxious gooseflesh pebbling his skin would recede. If he could manage to calm himself, he could stop thinking about how he might be in well over his head. If he could turn his thoughts from that path, he could take control of the situation, rather than lapse into the superstitious fears that had controlled his forebears.

And yet he found himself backing away from the wisp of the woman who now stood fearlessly before him, swaying gently in time with the pitching of the ship. He stared about himself, noticing for the first time that the candles serving as a light source for the room were arranged all around him on tiered driftwood shelves, settled amidst haphazard nests of shells and seaweed, sand and pebbles, cormorant and gull feathers—altars.

Cultists. Like sirens, he had heard of them but never encountered any until that moment. When the Empire sought to expand its influence ever further, it had swallowed countless smaller cultures, absorbing them into its own sprawling mass. Those who had not taken up the red-and-gold arms of the Empire as their own, those who had tried to rebel against the Emperor's Law, had been eliminated, crushed under the righteous heel of the Emperor. One such group had been the cultists, deranged zealots who sought the imagined terrors of the ocean depths to answer their prayers, who sent their dead into the cold, lapping sea rather than up to heaven in a blazing pyre. Only a few pockets of those who did not bend the knee still remained. Perhaps the Empire hadn't entirely wiped them out, but those who had been left were weak, denigrated, hardly worthy of notice as they eked out a pathetic life by hovering on the fringes of society. The Admiral might have laughed this unusual encounter off as a mere absurdity; what had he to fear from fish-worshippers, fools who thought that their gods could control the wind and the water? He would have laughed right then and there, but one of those "fish" was floating in an aquarium behind him, that baleful gaze traveling right through him, body eerily still as its hair and fins floated absently around it.

"It's not a she," Davent insisted aloud, as much to the cultist as to himself, tightening his grip on his sword. "Just because it has a human face doesn't mean it's like us, doesn't mean that it thinks like we do."

"Of course not," the woman shook her head, the corners of her mouth turning down disdainfully. "She thinks in the ebb and flow of the tides; not your pathetic tick-tock of time. She spurns the needy touch of a lover for the cool caress of the waves. She forsakes a world that would cloak her in shame and cloth, instead draping herself in pearls and kelp, moonlight and weeds. And she knows... oh, how she knows... that man covets his power from fire, and fire is easily snuffed out by water."

Forced to listen to the madwoman's rhetoric, Davent hadn't realized he'd backed himself up against the siren's tank until the creature struck the glass behind him, the palms of both its webbed hands pressed flat against the glass. He jumped back instinctively at the intrusion as the aquarium tottered precariously, eyes shooting to the top of the tank, lest it pursue him. Blessedly, it was closed in by a lid of heavy iron bars; the monster was contained.

"Frightened? Good. When men like you are frightened, they listen," the cultist's voice was entirely too smug for Davent's liking, and he set a stony glare upon the woman. Where she had let him push her aside before, where she had allowed herself to be struck, the woman now stood tall and unflinching. Such impudence would never have been tolerated on an Imperial vessel, the Admiral thought. Yet as much as he wanted to turn his thoughts towards the satisfying image of her being flogged into submission, he couldn't, caught up in the way she slowly walked the room's perimeter, pinching out the wicks of the candles as she went. Her actions were deft and easy, speaking of the long practice of ritual. Suddenly the chill Davent felt had much less to do with the dampness all around him.

"Take your men. Leave the *Storm's Eye*. Sail home to your Emperor. Tell no one," the woman spoke her words succinctly, each instruction given its own careful measure. Just as Davent would not have looked at any of his underlings, so too, did she scorn to meet his eyes, as though expecting immediate obedience of her ridiculous requests. No… not requests… orders.

Who did this vagabond think she was, to lay her demands upon an Admiral of the Imperial Armada? That insolent, infuriating notion put the fear from him as light puts darkness from a room, replacing it with righteous outrage. Davent pushed himself towards the cultist with a guttural cry, the blade of his shortsword flickering in the diminished candlelight at the woman pinched the second-last wick out between soot-smudged fingertips. Even in the dimness that fell, decades of soldiering ensured that Davent's blade found a home in the cultist's gut, the tip of his sword pressing easily into the soft flesh of her belly to ride up under her ribcage, where it caught, grating against her bones. She made a noise that was half-sob, half-gurgle, as her entire body clenched around the blade. Davent caught the reek of effluvia as her bowels voided themselves with death, and a thick rivulet of blood, black in the low light, quickly swallowed the trickle that his hand had left on her lip, as it pooled out of her mouth.

Dropping the cultist's body as he might have dropped a dirty tunic at day's end, Davent found himself wondering how he was going to dispose of the monster in the tank, with his sword jammed into the cultist. One of his men would have a blade he could make use of. With all luck, it was already coated in the blood of the *Eye's* crew. Cultists who were as far gone as the woman he'd just dispatched hadn't a hope of trying to blend into Imperial society, and society wouldn't want them, besides; better to just put them down now.

It was only as he turned back towards the siren's tank that he noticed a faint blue light falling on the edges of every surface in the room, casting eerie bands of unnatural color in contrast to the last candle's bright, tiny fire. The light's source was easy to pinpoint but more difficult to explain, as he approached the siren, whose body was now banded with thin, brilliant streaks that were the same color as the sky. Davent had never seen anything like it before, and he approached with a sudden, soft sense of wonder, a sensation that was spoiled only slightly by a suspicion he could not bring himself to shake entirely.

The siren seemed to watch him actively now, tilting its head from side to side and pivoting its body in an attempt to see past him. Its eyes were glowing as well, and though Davent knew it couldn't be true, he'd have sworn that the thing was frowning at him. He had long ago adjusted to the constant heaving of the *Storm's Eye*, no match for the stability of his *Might*, and yet the pitching grew with every step he took, until the ship's deck seemed ready to take the place of the walls, so sharp was their angle. The siren didn't seem to notice, its gaze fixed upon his face. Its hands hung limply at its sides, even as Davent reached one hand forward, tentatively, to touch the glass that stood between them. It was cool and slick against his palm, and he swore that it was vibrating, a low hum seeming to come from all around him. Overhead he could hear the rampant pounding of boots on deck as his men fought to keep their footing. The *Eye* was being lashed with wind and rain, but Davent had eyes only for the strange creature before him, as it raised one of its hands in a mirror of his own gesture, forefinger extended delicately. Davent noticed that its fingernails were shaped more like claws, vicious and curved, colored with the same pearly sheen as its spurs and spines. He watched with morbid curiosity as the siren's finger neared the glass, not so much as stirring the water around it as it approached and landed, feather light, with a soft clink.

The glass cracked sharply on contact, spider webbing beneath the siren's touch with accompanying creaks and squeals that had Davent reeling back as he realized the monster had been playing him the whole time. Thumping its fists against the glass when it could have easily destroyed the aquarium… Slipping on the soaked boards under his boots, he fell with a heavy crash, driving splinters and saltwater beneath his skin. His outcry of shock and pain was set against a backdrop of shattering glass and rushing water, as the siren's work completed itself. Water washed over him, and something twice as heavy as he—the siren—fell to the deck beside him. Davent rolled, scrambling in an effort to rise to his feet, but the siren's lashing tail was quicker, swatting him aside in an effortless coil of muscle as it dragged itself towards the cultist. With arms too thin for actions so strong and swift, and hair dangling all around it in a bedraggled mess, the creature was even more disturbing out of the water than it had been within.

Unwilling to draw its attention to himself now that the beast was loose, Davent shifted, rolling away from another sweep of its tail as he tried to put as much distance between them as possible. It was as he rolled into a swell of water, sluicing down the underdeck's hall, that he realized the ship's hull was filling with water, and that the howl of the wind had risen to a perilous level. Outside, thunder rolled in accompaniment to the stark flash of lightning. The day hadn't been a pleasant one, covered in a pall of gray, but nothing of the weather he'd left outside only moments ago had suggested such a squall was on the rise... It had to be the siren! Davent didn't want to believe in such dark superstitions, but where else could his thoughts stray, with living proof thrashing on the deck beside him?

"...fire is easily snuffed out..." he heard the cultist saying, her weak voice somehow managing to carry over the cries of the storm, and he jerked his head towards the sound. The siren had reached the human and coiled itself around her in a mass of scales and spines. It was cradling the woman's robed figure to itself, gently, tenderly, webbed gray fingers stroking the brass-dull hair of the cultist, as a lover might. The comparison, brief and fleeting though it was, nearly turned the Admiral's stomach.

"...fire is easily snuffed out by water," the woman continued fervently, pausing to give a shuddering gasp that racked her whole body. The siren clutched her closer, arms tight with desperation, and the woman's pale hand rose, shaking, to clasp the creature's own, the gesture familiar, reassuring. "Your men are as good as dead, Imperial, and you won't long outlive them, but at least you'll hear her before the sea takes us, one and all. She doesn't speak in words that dry out on the tongue, dead and meaningless before they're even heard... She sings... Oh, how she sings..."

The cultist's hand fell limp, and her last breath seemed to leak out of her, all tension finally leaving her body as her eyes grew distant and dull. It was at that moment, before the woman's hand had even touched the water pooling around them, that the siren began to keen. Silent up until that moment, it let forth an unearthly sound that hearkened back to an age of whale song and water droplets, when all the world was dark, and vast, and wet. The scent of salt clung heavily in the back of Davent's throat, and mist seemed to rise from every wet surface, clouding his sight as the siren sang, calling the storm into life with fierce, ululating trills. Thunder rolled, and the siren gave a reply, a great boom echoing from within its narrow chest as it swelled, the water rising higher and higher. Wind dashed heedlessly through the rigging on the deck overhead, and the siren's song added its own whistling notes to the melody of fury. Rain pelted overhead, and waves broke over the rails, seething with foam, flooding the lower quarters, washing everything in a tide of grief as the siren sang, and sang, and sang.

Outside, the timbers of both the *Storm's Eye* and the *Scepter's Might* began to crack and cave, each ship striking the other without remorse as the sea frothed and the sky darkened. Before, the *Eye* had darted and dodged away from the *Might*, tugging against its restraints, but now the schooner seemed to be ramming itself into the Imperial frigate with a definite purpose, tangling the lines between them and splintering the hulls of both. Davent might have tried to move in an effort to reach his men, to get back to the *Might*, but he had no sooner staggered to his feet, knee-deep in water, than he found himself fixed to the spot by her voice. It was suddenly as sweet and dulcet to his ears as any maiden's gold-strung harp. Somewhere in the distance, he could still detect the staccato fall of boots running overhead on deck, and he though he heard cries for the Admiral, where was the Admiral?

He wondered where the Admiral was, too, and then realized that he didn't care. It wasn't important. His gaze honed in upon the siren, his jaw slackening as his ears shut out all other sounds but the song that dripped from her lips like honey—no... not honey. Like ink: deep and striking and permanent. His eyes were caught by the lustrous gleam of her body, the glow standing out against the falling, night-like darkness, her body swelling in time with the feverish pitch of the storm outside. Such terrible beauty! Such wild and fearsome grace! Perhaps, if he were still, and quiet, and obedient, she would continue to sing him home, and take him into her arms as she had taken all of the others who had come before him...

## About Tanya King:

The inspiration for this story came from Tanya King's other-half, who blurted out, "Write a story about a tree!" She took his advice and wound up with something that she was quite proud of. There were originally many more scenes planned out, however Tanya adjusted to the word count and I think it came out better for being shorter. I didn't intend to put in any sort of specific figures, historical or fictional, because it worked far better being about two people that could be anyone. I really am grateful that a story that began as a random thought has actually started, what I hope to be, my future career.

Readers may follow Tanya on Twitter @TanyaTeineKing.

# FALLEN ON THE GREEN

## Tanya King

The wounded soldier fell to the roots of an old tree with a pathetic wheeze. A man's shadow was cast over him before it fled in the direction of the rising sun. With his last shred of strength, the wounded man chased after the fleeing figure with eyes already glazing over. Erratic gunfire was the last sound to ring in his ears as his blood watered dust.

~ ~ ~ ~ ~

A dense fog drifted away with his waking thoughts. On instinct, he moved to rub his temples, yet his body did not comply. He couldn't raise his arm, he couldn't move his leg, he could not even feel his body. Panic was poking holes through the blanket of confusion when he realized something was very wrong. This sensation was alien, it was not the familiar pins-and-needles when his leg would fall asleep, it was akin to detachment. Absolute severance, his traitorous sense abandoning his soul to a maddening void.

The Fallen Soldier tried to let out a scream. However, he had no voice to cry out nor anyone to call on for aid. Just as all seemed lost, hope fluttered in the dark void as a bright green light. Rolling across what could have been ground in irregular semicircles, like powdery snow caught in the wind. It was very reminiscent of sunshine reflecting off grass waving lazily in the breeze. The light amassed, and little stars of other colors popped up among the lake of green; reds, oranges, yellows, and cool shades of blues and violets. So enthralled by this play of rainbow colors he almost missed the soft sigh of words floating by.

Windy whispers encircled him even though there appeared to be no source. "Grow", "Breathe", "Live" these words chanted in a steady rhythm like his own heart. He scanned for anyone who could be the owner of the voices, but only found soft amber lights surrounding him. They were very peculiar, as opposed to the blobs of color in the distance these took shape as small mushrooms. "Grow", "Build", "Survive", the whispers sounded, and he noted that with each word the mushrooms glowed a tad brighter. Were they communicating with him?

He had been so fascinated with new sensations that only now did the epiphany of his death strike him full force. He did die, didn't he? If so, then where were the winged angels and his dead family? What of the endless fields of cotton clouds and where was St. Peter and the Pearly Gates? There wasn't even the stink of brimstone or lakes of fire. If he wasn't in Heaven or Hell, where had he gone?

The whispers took a frantic turn talking of "Humans", "Despair", "Death", sending a sinking feeling in his chest. Among a cluster of ochre, lights came forth as a hundred different hovering colors. They drifted apart, and one pale blue light came towards him emitting a fresh sorrow. The closer it approached, the more intricate the details took shape into a painfully familiar feminine face. From her, split two smaller bright yellow and red lights that were chiseled into two young girls, faces streaked with glittering tears. Fully petrified he was forced to watch as the new widow told their daughters why daddy wasn't going to come home ever again. That they shouldn't cry and be proud instead that he died a brave man defending his country and their rights. He had no hand to wipe away her cerulean tears, and no arms to embrace his girls. It made him want to vomit.

His living wife held a bundle of dull gray flowers to her breast, which she placed at his feet. However, his feet were no longer there; they had been replaced by glowing light brown roots digging down and wrapping around another gray mass shaped like a man. He had seen that face reflected back at him thousands of times. Negativity burrowed in his heart as he looked out across the grass to see innumerable bodies emanating the same lifeless gray under the feet of the rainbow of living. He felt his fingers, or whatever they were now, itch before watching little green lights flutter to the ground. With each centimeter of the gap being closed they lost more of their light, until finally upon impacting the earth they were entirely colorless to blend with the rest of the gray.

Questions buzzed inside of him like an angry hornet's nest, yet the only answer he could conceive of them was that he was being punished for a crime he couldn't remember committing. Daylight didn't wait for him as he wallowed in his sorrow and his family soon left him alone until a stranger came out from his hiding place in the trees. The light he gave off was a cool sea green but bore an unnerving blemish. The odd taint was muddy-red in color and gave off a chilling feeling of actually devouring the sea-green glow.

At last, when the distance had been covered he recognized the face instantaneously. The cowardly mug was unmistakable—only the rifle on his shoulder was missing. The Fallen Soldier's depression morphed into animosity. Atop the warping branches leaves were drained of their bright light and turning into a black rainfall. Green panels of the murderer's face shifted into terror, and he slowly began to back away. A sickness took control, a fierce living obsession to destroy this creature before him, yet incapable of doing so. Anxious whispers tried to reach out, "Be still", "Be calm", "You're hurting".

What insolence to loiter over the slain. The murderer had taken everything from him and would be paraded as a hero! The sounds of snapping bones echoed around the trees as small branches were splitting and falling to litter the ground, giving off black smoke to infect the air. The Green Man turned and sprinted away from the malice snapping at his heels.

His absence did little to quell the tapeworm of spite gnawing deeper to the Fallen Soldier's core. "Don't be rash", "Don't be bitter", "Don't condemn", the voices pleaded with him. Meek voices were the easiest to ignore and cracks split the earth; jagged spider webs spread out leaking the light-sapping gray onto the soil. Black leaves and twigs hit the skin of Mother Earth releasing their noxious hatred into the air. He could only hope it would give chase and slowly wring out the Green Man's final breath.

~ ~ ~ ~ ~

Time was irrelevant to the Fallen Soldier in his coffin—years coming and going in his suspended torment. The vivid colors of the flora which had encompassed him had rotted into listless gray and black. The murmurs still sounded, brittle as they were, "Forgive", "Forget", "Survive". Sap still grew poisonous as hatred festered in his soul. All life had succumbed to his wrathful radius, defenseless against his ire.

His family dared not return to his makeshift grave, frightened away by the smog of decay and resentment. The fault lay entirely with the coward that gunned him down. Gunfire popped from more cracks spreading to the still green light of grass. The blades surrounding the gray wilted with their draining color.

The Devil would not have better timing as the Green Man stepped from the cover of healthy glowing trees accompanied by four other beings of light. However, the tainted sea green was washed out, faded to a much paler shade contrasting harshly against the growing muddy-red. A strip of blackened bark peeled away onto the blanket of dark leaves as he prayed the murderer was severely ill. There was little doubt to be had that the humanoid lights he saw frolicking with the Green Man were his family enjoying their day. An entire branch broke off to think that the coward was sending off spawn to keep his legacy alive. His bitterness tangoed with envy knowing that his chance of spending time with his family and been snuffed out like a tiny candle flame. Nothing had broken him like seeing the happiness of others while he was deprived of everything.

The sun crossed the spring sky rapidly to settle its soft light on the Green Man sat with his youngest—a spritely boy lit by a fiery orange. The son asked his father what was wrong with the tree they had to keep away from? The father gave a helpless shrug guessing the tree was poisoned, then teased his boy by saying that the natives believed it was cursed by a ghost.

What ghost would haunt a tree? The boy managed to ask between high-pitched giggles, and the Green Man said maybe it was a soldier. The talk of war sparked the little boy's color, and he gloated to his father of great victories he envisioned by slaying every bad guy that he saw. The squirming bile of darkness in the Fallen Soldier buried itself deeper and peeled away more bark from the tree.

Until the Green Man's sharp scolding sent all company into an astonished silence. The boy's orange light had ceased prancing to be dwarfed by the full height of sea green. The father shrank to one knee and told his son he hadn't meant to take such an angry tone, but he didn't want to give the wrong idea. The boy was baffled and listened intently as his father spoke of the war he had fought.

It was a specific day he brought up, the Green Man had been thrown into the heat of battle after his troop had been ambushed. After a sneaky round-about, he had found the back of an enemy soldier an easy target. He had raised his gun, but froze before he could pull the trigger. Yes, this man could have killed his companions, yes he could continue with future attacks, and yes he was an opponent; however, in that span of time, the only differences between them were the colors of the uniforms.

Too long had he waited and the rival soldier turned with a face caught in surprise before twisting in anger. On reflex, his finger had twitched, and a deafening pop joined the rest of the audible calamity. His accuracy had been good, but he couldn't watch the man die. He had run away back into the gaping maw of war, only to return months after it had ended in a declaration of peace. The crippled tree was the same that his enemy had fallen under, yet he had to skulk in the forest waiting for the family to leave. As he spoke the muddy-red splatters along his arms oozed up further taking away more of his lively color.

He and that man were the same, but only one had come back from the war. He told his son that the crying faces of the new widow and her two daughters nearly broke him. This man who should have been nothing was something to these people. These three women depended on and loved that man just as his family loved him but now would have to adapt to a life without him. The wife would never hear his boots coming into the house, nor would her bed be warm at night. Those little girls wouldn't feel their father's arms around them ever again or get to hear bedtime stories. And what about his mother and father? The old woman would be bent in her husband's arms sobbing for the both of them because they would never see their boy's face again. They taught you victory is what's supposed to be celebrated he had told his son, but no one ever taught you to play God and take away someone's life.

The Fallen Soldier had been stunned to hear this insight, to think that this murderer—this *man*—could possibly give a shred of consideration to him was bewildering. The bile had halted in its conquest. The father set heavy hands onto his son's shoulders to tell him the world has had enough fighting, and that it was going to need real men to care for it, not bleed for it. The boy shook his head saying he didn't understand what that meant, and the father said that was okay. It was alright that he didn't understand now because as long as he kept it in mind, he would do as he grew. The boy thought for a few minutes, absorbing what his father said, and voiced he was dissatisfied with that answer, but would trust his father regardless. Farther away a female colored violent called them over, and with a nudge both father and son returned to their family and to home.

Alone the Fallen Soldier fought with his thoughts. Part of him couldn't believe a murderer was capable of feeling guilt, yet the sound in the Green Man's voice had been saturated with guilt. His pose alone made it look like he was carrying ten men on his shoulders. The sort of remorse that was described he had only seen the stony eyes of the oldest soldiers. Never were they glazed over with callousness, but were bright with fresh memories of those dark deeds they refused to leave gathering dust in the back of their minds. Could he remember the faces of men he had killed? Was there ever a moment to consider their loved ones waiting for them to come home? There were no answers.

"Forgive", "Forget", "Survive", the whispers had gained some strength back, and their words lulled the writhing worm of darkness. Among the circle of deathly gray and black, he spotted a small green light twinkling into existence.

~ ~ ~ ~ ~

Many years resolved and the Green Man hadn't returned. Dead grass had finally decayed and birthed new sprouts pushing through the soil. It was still not a rich land, but it had healed its wounds with nary a scar left. The golden mushrooms shimmered in delight at the grand improvement. When the Fallen Soldier would look down the roots had retrieved their gorgeous ochre brown. No longer could he feel skin peeling, or the branches falling, there were even little leaf buds returning. His heart was not so heavy, the grudge had not been purged, but the vile worm had dissipated over time.

Time and again his family had visited and that small bit of joy he gained from seeing their faces would spring up new blades of grass or fungi. His wife had remarried, and while that had stung, he was still glad that she could smile again and be protected. Both of his daughters had found their husbands as well. His youngest had gone off to a fantastic college to pursue her passion of science, and the oldest was a growing sculptor. Joy was brimming from the family, and his only regret was that he had chastised his daughter for her artistic talent. He would've given everything to see how she had honed her skill, but alas it would only remain a daydream.

"He returns", "With another", "They're here", though they didn't say who, he could hazard a guess.

Indeed, the Green Man had returned with his wife and how different they were. The vivid sea-green and lilac they had had so long ago was nearly white now, scarcely a hint of color remained. Still, the dirty red color along his arms persisted. They appeared shorter and moved at a slower shuffle as they stood beneath his branches. As they admired his spring growth, the Fallen Soldier could see they had aged considerably. Decades must have passed by without his notice as it seemed the prime of their lives had long gone.

They both took refuge from the beaming sunlight under the shade. His wife sighed as they reminisced their sons growing up to marry beautiful women, their daughter growing gravely ill and managing to fight back, of the house they had stayed in since they were newlyweds. The leisure talk could have lulled the soldier to sleep. However, something was wrong with the Green Man.

His color was fading completely, leaking away to a muted gray and the Fallen Soldier panicked. Had a malice taken him over? He reached out to shake the man on old instinct, and with rapturous surprise, he could move. He flailed but managed to right himself at the last moment. Shock blinded him as reality came pouring back, no longer was his vision limited to blackness and colors it had turned back to the human world he remembered. However, all the color was washed out, a black and white soundless movie focused on the elderly woman lying next to her unresponsive husband.

The Fallen Soldier went to reach for the man again but was alerted to a different presence. Turning to his left, he saw the Green Man in the flesh of youth. His colors were correct, and he seemed very confused. With a turn of his heel, they finally locked eyes for the first time since the war. Recognition crashed onto his face like a wave and pinned him on the spot. Neither man knew what the correct course of action was; then the Fallen Soldier found the courage.

He stepped only an arm's length from the other, but couldn't find a voice. The Green Man made hectic hand gestures to what seemed a form of apology. The soldier stopped him, then extended his arm with palm exposed. It was unbelievable; the other didn't know what to make of it. They waited, facing each other one side anxious and regretful the other filled with a cool determination. Finally, the Green Man extended his hand and they shook with a golden flourish to congratulate them that eradicated the filthy red taint from his arms.

They stood back in awe to watch the light spiral up high into the air creating steps to a golden river. It sparkled like the sun itself and radiated a warm, beckoning light with arms outstretched. A sense of calm and home filled their hearts. But the Green Man had turned to his wife, discovering his body getting colder by the second. He reached out to embrace her, but his arms fell through unbeknownst to her. The man knelt next to her distraught at her weeping; then a firm hand clapped him on the shoulder. At his back was the man he had killed all those years ago in the war with a serene and apologetic expression. He gestured up towards the river and the Green Man knew he must leave. Another look at his lady love and one last spectral kiss to bid her farewell before he could stand and start on the staircase.

But his comrade was missing; the Fallen Soldier was stood at the first step with a thoughtful look on his upturned face. The Green Man offered his hand, but this time, the soldier refused. He shooed away his comrade because one day he would go to the river, but today he wanted to stay. The Green Man nodded and continued his ascent. The other watched from below as he turned to shimmering golden dust before being spirited away with the rest of the river of light.

It still called to him, but he was resolute. He rested a gentle hand on the woman's back, and she blinked as though she had felt his comfort. A smile touched his lips as he folded his arms and fell back into his wooden cradle. The world would still turn whether he was there or someplace else, and he wished to watch as it did so. For a while longer at least, he wanted to stay in this form he had grown to love and watch the rest of the world change.

## About Katie Lattari:

Katie Lattari holds an M.F.A. in fiction writing from the University of Notre Dame as well as an M.A. and a B.A. in English from the University of Maine. Her debut novel *American Vaudeville* was released by MAMMOTH Books in June 2016. Her short work has been published in places like *NOO Journal*, *The Bend*, and *Stolen Island*, among others. Katie is a proud alumna of the University of Maine, which also happens to be the alma mater of master of horror Stephen King. In writing "No Protections, Only Powers," Katie had been (and remains) on a Stephen King kick, and thought to herself: "What if I tried to write a deliberately spooky/strange story? What might that look like?" "No Protections, Only Powers" is what came of that self-made challenge.

# No Protections, Only Powers

## Katie Lattari

### 1

Thad has somehow gotten himself a girlfriend, and so that's what we're made to talk about at dinner, passing the bucket of KFC around, the Styrofoam mashed potato canister, the second canister filled with gravy - brown and soupy. Thad with his fat frog head and fat lizard neck and fat tree trunk body. I look at him and his dumb forehead cowlick. Who would want to date him? Doesn't dating entail being near someone? Talking to them? Maybe even touching them? I shiver. I bite into a drumstick, imagining myself a rabid puppy after a fresh kill, hot poultry fat squelching from the corners of my mouth, the strength of the chicken's life-force adding to and enhancing my own. My eyes must have glimmered with far-away things, with rabid puppydom, because Thad swivels his watery amphibian eyes on me.

"Bertie, you look like a freak," he says, then *pha-lumps* a pile of potatoes onto his plate with the wrist action of a man cracking a whip.

"Not nice, Thad," mom says, not looking up from her copy of the *Farmer's Almanac*, which is splayed out on the table under one hand, her other hand stirring the potatoes and gravy on her plate into a homogenous brown pile in a sort of unthinking, automatic way, like a hand being led across a Ouija board. She stirs and stirs, charm bracelet tinkling, reads and reads.

"But true," Thad replies, mouth twisted in a mean smile, acne arcing across his brow and bulging at his chin.

"We're eating a dead bird, you know," I say, waggling a half-decimated drumstick at him.

"Yes, we know that," dad says, adjusting his glasses on the bridge of his nose, breaking up his biscuit and depositing a bunch of potatoes and broken-up chicken on top before spearing it with his fork. "So who's this girl?"

"Tanda Marsh," Thad swallows a mouthful of masticated starch and protein. I look at him, unbelieving. "She's a junior, like me. She came up to me after school one day, and we started talking. At first, she just wanted help with her Calculus homework, then she started like, texting me about random stuff and wanting to hang after school." Thad shrugs. "She's not bad looking, either." Thad, in his most dad-like gesture, now adjusts *his* glasses on the bridge of *his* nose. "She wants me to take her to the dance in a few weeks." I am not even in high school yet—eighth grade, so close—but even I have heard of Tanda Marsh. She is not only 'not bad looking,' she's downright *good*-looking.

"You're lying," I say. "*J'accuse!*" I point the greasy drumstick at him, then press it to my lips, swirling it around and around like I'm applying lipstick, mouth and skin growing shiny. Thad looks disgusted.

"Ask around! Plus, what do you know? We don't even go to school in the same building, fucktard."

"Thad, language!" mom warns, but only half-heartedly, still looking intently into the *Farmer's Almanac* like she's looking into another dimension.

2

Most days Thad refuses to drive me to school in his second-hand Corolla even though it's not at all out of his way; the middle school and high school are separated by only a few hundred yards of sports fields. It's about three miles from our front door to the schools, and most days I walk. Darling big bro says it would be embarrassing to pull up in front of the middle school and drop me off like he's my dad or something, and when he says this I always imagine him in one of our cell-phone-store-manager dad's pairs of pleated khakis and brightly colored tucked-in work polos. Thad says it would be even more embarrassing to drive straight to the high school and have me get out of the car there and walk across the fields—the sole link between the two parallel but completely distinct universes—because he would die before he showed up at school with his weird little sister in the front seat like we were a couple, or worse, friends. All I can ever think is: as if, fucktard (language, Bertie!). And this year I started staying away from taking the bus whenever I can because there have been a few incidents. Mom calls them incidents. When a third, then fourth then the fifth *incident* happened, mom told me to keep my chin up and go my own way and so I've taken it literally.

Today I leave even a little earlier than usual—Frog Boy isn't even up yet—after eating two Eggos drenched in Aunt Jemima's tree blood. I have a small project to take care of before school starts. As I walk the three familiar miles, passing cul-de-sacs and damp newspapers in flimsy plastic bags, I think about Thad's bold claim from last night: that he is dating Tanda Marsh. It doesn't really add up. Thad is short, squat, bespectacled, and ravaged by acne. He is a "math whiz" (to use dad's phrase) who plays the trombone in the high school marching band and who founded the Settlers of Catan club, meetings held every Thursday after school. In short: he's not cool. He has friends, but his friends are like him. Stunted, unpopular little men who are a little too good at one very specific thing, and not at all at anything else. With Thad it's math. With Howie, it's computer programming. With Dev, it's Greek and Latin. A Thad Cass does not get to date a Tanda Marsh in this world or any other. And yet Thad seems to be taking it all in stride as if it's all so normal, but I think it's a show. He knows what he is. He must. And Tanda Marsh is tall, thin, blond, pretty, popular, on the volleyball team, good in school, and part of all of the clubs and activities that the cool kids are part of in high school: French Club (because if you can afford it, the French teacher leads a trip to Montreal each spring), Chamber Singers (the auditioned version of regular old Chorus, regular Chorus being for plebs), and Mock Trial (because these kids have law school aspirations), among others. I know this only because Tanda's little sister, Chloe, who is one grade below me, is a chatterbox, kind of a bitch (language, Bertie!) and totally idolizes Tanda.

I get to school in plenty of time, where there are only two cars in the parking lot, rubbing the tip of my nose vigorously with the palm of my hand to warm it up as I make my way around the side of the building. October has made the three-mile walk start to make me hate Thad all over again for his never-ending ability to be embarrassed by everything, of me, of himself. As I approach my mark—the cherry tree that always has these fat little tawny quail in it—a sharp fluttering and *thwapping* scares up from the very spot, and there go all those fat little quail bastards (language, Bertie!). I watch them skitter into the woods, now rapidly thinning of leaves as autumn fully takes over, the dying season. Then I climb the gnarled and splaying cherry tree outside Mr. Ngo's classroom, which is still empty and dark at this hour, though outside it is bright under the growing sun, bright and unrelenting, putting every leaf and twig and branch and blade of grass and spherical deep red cherry into sharp focus. I set up in the crook of one of the branches, unzip my backpack, and retrieve the gallon-sized Ziplock bag from inside. There are four cold pieces of fried chicken in there: one drumstick, one wing, and two thighs. I dig inside my backpack again and pull out a spool of twine I took from mom's garden supply shelf in the garage. She uses the twine to tie nooses around bunches of herbs, hang them upside down, and dry them dead and fragrant. As I do my work, I look around from my vantage point and see a few cars pull up to the auditorium's side entrance and release kids I've seen around school, and into the auditorium they head. Jack Curry. Sarah Gray. Kalani Breyer. Miranda Aleyev. Show Choir kids. They rehearse two mornings a week, every week, more over school vacations to get ready for regional and state competitions. This year they're putting on *A Chorus Line*. Never heard of it.

I climb down from the tree and move into position near the school's maintenance shed, which is off to the side between the cherry tree and the entrance to the auditorium. I tuck myself behind the edge of the shed so I can't be seen by approaching cars. And I wait. Nothing happens at first. Five minutes go by, ten minutes. I hear a car or two or three pull up, dispense of their "precious cargo," and head off again. But now twenty minutes in, the quail finally return, walking out of the woods in their hitching, bird-locomotive way, fat breasts puffing, and fly up into the branches. As they begin nibbling at the cherries again, their five round brown bodies dotting and burdening different branches, I watch more intently, taking a step or two forward. It's all cherries at first, little beaks pecking and chomping at the hanging fruit, but then the Noticing and Inquiry phases begin. It is slow, careful, tentative exploration to begin with—a quail shimmies to a spot on a branch and cranes its neck to be able to reach—and then a nip, a nibble. Yes, I think. *Yes.* And then they have all found one to try. The cherries are forgotten.

It's the punch of loud music being loosed from a suddenly-opened car door that startles me back to myself. I look over and see Chloe Marsh climbing from Tanda Marsh's pre-owned 2013 Lexus. Birthday present from the 'rents. The two blond girls are talking to each other as Chloe gathers her Adidas sports bag and L.L. Bean backpack and Coach mini-me purse from the backseat. As she says goodbye to Tanda and shuts the doors, Tanda's eyes follow Chloe along toward the auditorium but then stop in their parabolic progress when I catch in her field of vision. She looks right at me. I see her seeing the twine in my hand. I see her seeing the empty Ziplock bag in my other hand, my backpack on my back. I see her eyes reach beyond me to the cherry tree, where she sees, squinting, one, two, three—four, five—quail snapping at and attacking hunks of fried poultry which have been attached to various branches of the tree by twine, macabre carrion decorations. Tanda looks at me again and then drives away.

I am breathing hard, little puffs of steam hovering in front of my face, cheeks a little flushed from excitement. *They eat each other up,* is all I can think. *They eat each other up, too.*

3

It's the weekend, and mom has something pungent boiling in a pot. She is clipping bouquets of herbs at odd angles and in odd amounts and dashing them into the stew, brow beading with sweat as she leans over her work, stirring, stirring, whispering, murmuring. I approach her, pinching my nose. There are small, crumpled up pieces of paper strewn about the countertop near the oven, pen marks showing out from some. There are also some small bones strewn about the counter, and as I stand on my tiptoes behind her shoulder, I see they are also in the burbling pot.

"What's for dinner?" I ask, worried.

"Dad's ordering pizza," she replies, keeping her eyes on the burping concoction. "He's taking special requests for toppings." I look at her and her pot and think I've dodged a bullet. Maybe she's bringing whatever the hell (language, Bertie!) that is into work tomorrow, poor bastards (language, Bertie!). The other hygienists down at Doc Cherukuri's won't know what hit 'em. Thank God for all the free mouthwash at their disposal.

I go into the living room and see dad in his recliner, feet up, tube on, but he must only be just *listening* to the football game because he has his laptop in his lap and he's stabbing furiously at the keys.

"I heard something about pizza." I stand near the chair and look down into his mustachioed face. It takes a second, and then:

"Yeah, Bert. I was thinking let's get exotic. Anchovy-pineapple." He lifts his eyes from the screen and looks at me.

"One or the other. Plus mushroom," I counter. He considers me.

"Anchovy-mushroom."

"Deal."

"Deal," he replies. "I'll call in a few minutes. Researching ASMR videos. Know what that is? ASMR?" I look at him blankly. "Autonomous Sensory Meridian Response. Basically, there are certain people who get great relaxation, comfort, or even pleasure out of certain sounds—like whispering, or long nails tapping a tabletop gently. There are these other people—mostly women—who make these videos on YouTube where they whisper. Just whisper and enunciate in this soothing way, sort of catering to these ASMR folks. These women, some of them are stars! In this ASMR world anyway. Anyhow, I've listened to a bunch, and I get all tingly when they do it, from the top of my head to my toes. I think I'm one of these ASMR folks. Like, sensitive." His eyebrows are raised at his apparent specialness.

"Wow, Dad," I reply. "Do you know what Mom's doing in there?" His eyebrows fall like little hairy guillotines.

"Not a clue," he replies as he looks back at his laptop.

"Thad?" I haven't seen that booger most of the day.

"I think he's with Tandy."

"Tanda."

"Right." Dad is feeling around for his earbuds on the end table next to him, eyes still on the computer screen intently. He finally locates the buds, plugs them in, and then plugs himself in.

## 4

I go back up to my room, content to wait for the pizza away from mom's stink stew and dad's special sensations. I should have plenty of time to finish my project before the pizza arrives; I'm calling it the Reverse Icarus.

"What's that?" The voice startles me. I look up toward my doorway and find Tanda Marsh standing there, twisting strands of her flaxen hair around her finger. I freeze momentarily, struck by how pretty she is, how serious her face is. I'm kneeling over a paper plate scattered with bird feathers, an apple spice votive in one hand and a Bic barbecue lighter in the other. I feel compelled to tell her. It's out of me before I can even really think.

"This is a sparrow feather. That one's a blue jay feather. Quail. Pigeon, I think, this one. I'm sealing them up. Sealing them in. With wax."

"Why?" Tanda asks. I'm not sure that I've quite articulated this to myself yet. I think the thing itself is the articulation.

"I guess—to preserve them. It keeps the bird with itself. The feather will keep its blue jay-ness. Sealed in time. And then maybe I can meld them all together and make something new. A new kind of bird." Tanda seems to consider me.

149

Her eyes are deep and active, like rock tumblers. Her irises are the polished stone. I keep staring at them, held.

"You put fried chicken in the tree the other day," she says more than asks. I only now begin to wonder where Frog Head is. "Why did you do that?"

"To see what they would do. The quail." I just keep telling her things. It's my business. She makes me feel like it's hers, too.

"What did they do?"

"Devoured it." A smile curls onto my lips. "Isn't that awful?" I see her looking around my room now, which is messy. I see her seeing the taxidermy squirrel I've stuck sewing pins in at critical anatomical locations. I see her seeing the painstakingly collected gobs of spider web I've wrapped around a bona fide crystal ball. I see her seeing the old baby doll whose eyes I've dug out and replaced with acorn caps. I've drawn rune symbols on her naked plastic body with a Sharpie.

"Where's Thad?" Tanda has moved over to my desk and is gently touching a jaggedly broken hourglass, the open top cup of which has streaks of dried blood in it. Mine.

"He's writing five hundred times in my notebook 'Thad Cass Loves Tanda Marsh'." Her eyes have not left the hourglass and she seems to be serious about the five hundred times thing. I get the sense it was Tanda's idea, not Thad's. "What did you do here?"

"I…broke it on purpose," I tell her. Which is true. "I wanted to get rid of the sand. Which is usually how hourglasses keep time. I tried different things in it. I wanted to see how time flowed differently depending on what you put in it to count." I swallow, find that my heart is beating fast. "I tried couscous. Then I tried bacon grease. Then rainwater. Then I tried collecting my own tears for a while, but they dried up out of the cup I was storing them in before I could get enough to test. I cut myself accidentally –" I gesture to the red-brown streaks in the razor-topped chalice. "I haven't worked up the courage yet to use blood. My blood, I guess. I'd like to see how time runs in blood." She looks at me with interest, maybe even a little hunger. Definitely not like how Thad looks at me when he asks about my projects. He always makes fun of me. Makes me feel small and stupid. And weird.

"I'm a little interested in this kind of stuff, too," she says now, her eyes drifting around the rest of my room. "Whatever you call it. The macabre. The occult." Tanda skims her fingertips over my homemade Book of Shadows. "Fascinating," she says, and she means it. I smile and feel so relieved.

"Thad doesn't think so," I darken a little. She looks back at me with those rock-tumbled eyes.

"I can make him do things." It is like she is offering me something. All of the little hairs on my arms and the tiny fuzzy hairs on my face stand up. I believe her. "I think I'll start with having him write—five hundred times, of course—'Thad is wrong.' Because he is, isn't he? He's wrong about you." I nod and keep nodding.

"He is," I whisper.

And then I hear dad doing one of his dad things—knocking on the banister at the foot of the stairs like it's a door. I jump. "Bert!" he shouts and keeps knocking. "Pizza!" And he keeps on knocking.

## 5

Tanda has started driving me home after school. She spends most evenings with Thad in his room or around our house or yard or shed or garage anyway, and so it started as a Two Casses and One Marsh carpooling kind of thing since we all have the same final destination. And Chloe only really takes rides *to* school from Tanda since she has so many after-school activities and practices and clubs to attend to. One of the Marsh parents picks her up later. But lately, the trio has become a duet. Tanda has been making Thad walk home, even when the weather is bad. Especially when the weather is bad. Just to see if he will. Just to see how much he can take, I guess. She says it has something to do with love. And she says it has something to do with the two of us having Girl Time. Sometimes I feel bad for him, for the Frog Head. Most of the time I don't. He's made me get to know those three miles well. It's okay if he gets acquainted.

151

Tanda is finishing a cigarette as we sit in the car at a stop light together. I can see Thad about a quarter mile behind us, head tilted down against the cold rain. I breathe the smoke of her Parliament in deeply, feeling it's more like incense than cigarette smoke. I am being cleansed and reborn from the inside out. It is a rite Tanda and I have now. And we have more. Many more.

The light turns green, but we stay sitting. Tanda is looking back at Frog Head in her side mirror, her rock-tumbler eyes narrowed and intense. The car behind us beeps, and she seems brought back to herself. The car starts moving.

## 6

I can tell that Chloe doesn't like that her sister and I are spending so much time together. I sit on the far end of the cafetorium most days, alone, eating my salami sandwich and researching Pagan and Wiccan rituals—fertility rituals, harvest rituals, catharsis rituals, Charge of God rituals—on my iPhone, a brick two models old despite dad's job, writing obscure symbols on my hands and arms with pen so I don't forget them later, and sometimes when I look up, Chloe is staring daggers at me and whispering to her friends. Like little incantations. Whispered, angry incantations I can't quite make out. I can feel hate in her. She wants to put it on me. But I won't let her. I have too many important things to focus on. So many plans. I think of the drying herbs hanging in my room in their nooses; the progress of my Reverse Icarus, colorful as a melting peacock; how I've managed to dye Morton—the field mouse I've been keeping in a fishbowl (not filled with water, don't worry)—purple, making him powerful; how I've been letting small amounts of blood out of the skin that covers my Achilles tendons for use in the hour glass experiment, which is most important to Tanda and me. When you're a thirteen-year-old girl, you begin to realize which parts of your body just simply want to bleed, and which parts refuse to stop once they've started. Tanda and I bought a cheap mini fridge at a yard sale two weekends ago and have been storing our blood that way, mine in a Welch's grape jelly glass, the kind you can use as a juice glass after the jelly is gone, painted with the Peanuts kids on it, and Tanda's been using an opaque blue Noxzema canister. I've also been keeping Yoohoo in the fridge, which is next to my bed. Morton lives in the fishbowl on top of the fridge. At night, we whisper to each other in the dark. Sometimes I can hear mom whispering too, from somewhere—sometimes it sounds like it's coming from inside the house, sometimes it sounds like it's coming from outside the house, sometimes it sounds like it's coming from inside my very own head—but I hear her. Only the shapes of the words, though. Never the words themselves.

7

It has only been a few weeks since Chloe put the horns on me in the cafetorium, and now Morton is dead. It is either that she has killed him with her mind, with her thoughts, to hurt me, or it is that I have made him too powerful through coloring him purple, and putting strengthening charms on him, and whispering ancient stories to him in the night, and his small body could not handle it. I never thought to put protections on him, only powers. I woke from sleep as deep as an ocean trench because of a sudden and palpable sense of absence. I was groggy as I turned on my side toward his fishbowl, still too dark to make anything out, and yet a darkness darker than the regular dark of the room seemed to pulsate where he usually whispers and titters. Like a black hole. A denser kind of nothing, leading to somewhere else. I turned on the light, and it was obvious. Little twig legs turned up to the ceiling, body as still as a baby potato. Morton. You poor little bastard (language, Bertie!).

I pad downstairs in my pajamas, Morton laying in the bottom of the round fishbowl, sliding around on the smooth curved glass as I move, though I try to move tenderly. Most of the lights are out down here, and it is quiet. But dad is glowing like an oracle in his armchair, a burning star in blackest space. I pause in the tick-tocking kitchen, staying behind the soft radiance of the hood light above the stove, and see that dad is sitting in his recliner, feet up, computer on his lap, screen at full brightness—or even brighter than that, a religious incandescence reflecting off his pale skin and balding pate—eyes and face a mix of zen looseness and ecstatic pleasure, ear buds in his ears. He is plugged in. He is shining, both literally and figuratively. He must be watching and listening to his ASMR videos. Strange and beautiful international women must be whispering to him, must be casting their aural

153

spells. He must be having his special sensations. The screen is so bright on him he is nearly consumed.

I look at the microwave clock and see it's 12:37 AM. I go out into the attached garage and gather all of the funeral accouterments I will need: burlap, twine, gasoline, barbecue lighter, gardening trowel, flashlight.

In the backyard a half moon hangs, managing to cast light that is both magical and anemic. I find a respectable spot near mom's bunches of herbs, about ten yards from the sliding glass back door that opens onto the patio at the back of the house—I can make out half of dad's incandescent ozone, his tube-socked feet and the first fractions of his hairy calves. I set down Morton and my supplies and begin digging into the earth. As I dig, I feel an unexpected give in the dirt, a kind of looseness, a pocketing that seems strange. I continue but start to hit hard things—maybe rocks?—with the trowel. I shift over a little and continue working. Once I have a reasonable hole—about eight inches deep, eight inches around—I prepare Morton for the afterlife. I hold his potato body in one hand and stroke his regal purple fur with the index finger of the other. I whisper things to him, final things, ending things, goodbye things. Then I wrap him in the burlap, so gentle, and tie the bundle up loosely with the twine. I place his body in the bottom of the scoop in the earth. I take the small plastic canister of gasoline and pour some over his body. I put the cap back on the canister and take up the lighter, clicking a smooth, dancing little bud of flame into existence, and bring it to Morton. Suddenly he is glowing like dad is glowing, but with the authentic heat of ravenous, elemental nature rather than with the clever, manufactured presentation of bits and bytes and battery power.

White, moon-like shapes in the earth catch my eye as Morton's flame burns on, waving and whipping into the dark. Smooth, rounded shapes—man-made— are at the periphery of Morton's final resting place. I pick up the trowel and begin loosening up the dirt and come away with two small clay jars. Someone *had* already been here. The dirt *had* been too easy to give way. I push away the dirt from the first jar with my thumbs. I shake the jar. Something light—like a butterfly flapping its wings—meets my ears. I look around and see only the glittering half-moon, Morton's death flame, and dad's religious incandescence inside the house; a harrowing constellation. I break the jar open with the trowel, clay shards piling in the soil. A piece of paper falls out.

*A spell for Thaddeus: to be cooler; to know the feel of a woman; to be wanted too much—to be needed*

It's mom's handwriting. There are a few dark little droplets of some dried liquid on the small, folded piece of paper. I look at the other moon jar. I smudge the dirt around on its surface, a surge of nerves quavering in my ribcage and in that place behind your eyes and the base of your throat where worry and panic come from. I break it open with the trowel. A second piece of paper, also dotted with dark, dried droplets falls out among the debris:

*A spell for Beatrice: to be liked; to be understood; to have a friend—<u>any</u> friend*

The flames from Morton's body are beginning to subside when Tanda is suddenly there. She has been sneaking nights in Thad's room lately, more and more. I think they are having sex. I think I hear them sometimes. Tanda, I think, sounds euphoric. Thad, I think, sounds tortured. I don't think I know how it's supposed to sound. Tanda looks down on me with her rock-tumbler eyes, hard and frenzied. She is holding a food-service-sized pickle jar, the cartoon stork's sharp beak gleaming like a knife in the moonlight from the label. The jar is three-quarters full of a deep, dark liquid.

"For our hour glass experiment—we needed Thad after all." She is smiling, maniacal. She is proud. She wants my approval. The jar seems so, so full. Too full. It's too full. I look again at mom's spells, her prayers. I look at Tanda, horrified.

Dad is an incandescent ball of light.

I don't see Thad anywhere. Not anywhere.

Morton's death flame goes out. I am alone with Tanda and the blood and the black.

Mom is in the window now, downstairs, a weeping ghost lurking in the dark, looking upon what she has wrought.

## About M. Lopes da Silva:

M. Lopes da Silva has been published in *The California Literary Review*, *Queen Mob's Teahouse*, and *FEM* magazine. Her phantasmagoric illustrations are featured in the novel, *The Land of Laughs*, an upcoming release from Centipede Press. Her writing explores themes of obsession, embodies the fantastic and the strange, and often defies her readers' preconceptions. You can read her collection of eerie short stories, *The Dog Next Door and Other Disturbances*, as an ebook on Amazon. Her next major work is a fantasy novel entitled, *The Northlands*.

Readers may follow her on twitter @spasticsnap.

# The Carving

## M. Lopes da Silva

Autumn made the air painful to move through. Everyone in town wore heavy coats and scraps of knitting from some thoughtful aunt or grandparent around their throats. The damp made everybody stiff and musty-smelling, and a little more reflective than usual. It was brooding weather.

The people that lived in the town of Pembroke did not consider themselves overly troubled. Individuals had their private burdens and kept them private. No one made inquiries. Everyone was friendly up to a point, and wasn't that the way? They were the standard sort of Americans—simultaneously viewing themselves as extraordinarily gifted and generally average. Hobbies and television filled up the gaps in the days. Every day gapped.

The pumpkins came from the same patch they'd always come from—Nelson Anforth's farm. The Anforth sons loaded up their dad's truck and drove the gourds into the empty parking lot next to an abandoned fast food chain. People passed by the lot on their way to the discount store or the liquor store or the pharmacy; it was a good spot. Had been for years.

It was funny—usually, there were a fair amount of pumpkins left unsold—but this year it turned out that everyone bought at least one. The pumpkin bug had bitten. In the end, it worked out that all 518 residents of Pembroke had a gourd—even the underage residents, who had thoughtful parents to buy them one. Reporter Jenny Strue took note of the number because it was one of the few facts to grasp onto, later. It was incorruptible data, fact checkable data, which quickly became difficult to attain in the slew of eyewitness accounts that followed.

There was another coincidence, a peculiarity that stood out. Everyone held off from carving their pumpkins until October 31st. Things kept coming up during the week to postpone the carving, or it felt more seasonal and correct to wait for All Hallows' Eve, or they just plain forgot until suddenly there was a moment in a kitchen or on a porch, a blank remembering moment, and knives were removed and rinsed and newspapers scrounged up and placed like tablecloths in every Pembroke home, hotel room, and apartment.

*The carving had begun.*

Jenny Strue worked her bottom lip between her teeth relentlessly until she drew blood. This was the part that kept throwing her. This was the real ghost story, the real impossible thing that she was supposed to tame and make possible because it had already happened.

She groaned and shoved herself away from her desk in frustration. Hastily scribbled notes of witness accounts fell to the floor in a heap.

*I was going to carve a bat on it, I think, but when I picked up the knife I just got kind of hazy, you know?*

*I like a smiling jack-o'-lantern, so I was going to carve a smile, but when it got to that point, I guess I just couldn't do it anymore.*

*I had a pattern I'd printed out that I was going to use, but I guess I just sort of forgot about it and then I was cutting, and it felt really familiar, the same way it felt back when I was a kid, and I'd pick up a crayon and just start drawing, and I wouldn't even know what I was about to draw at first, you know? But I'd draw, and then I'd really see what I'd done later. It was never as good later...*

*I don't know why you're asking me this. Wasn't it the same for you?*

Jenny Strue closed her eyes and shivered in recognition; yes, yes it had been the same for her.

She'd picked up a knife, the way 517 other hands had picked up knives and approached the pumpkin sitting on its blanket of smudging newsprint. When she'd touched the skin of the swollen fruit, it had felt cold. She hadn't wondered why she was indulging in a tradition for a holiday that had grown to mean very little to her as an adult. Her mother had passed away the previous year, and she'd found herself reaching for traditions long-mired in her childhood. She'd gone to see the fireworks that July, even though she hated the noise and the crowds; she'd looked at starry smears of red and white and blue and tried to remember how she'd felt when she'd seen them last, at age 12, holding her mother's hand.

Originally she was going to carve a traditional sort of face into the pumpkin—a couple of triangles with a lightning bolt jag for a mouth. But with the knife in her hand, her mind went soft, abruptly lazy, and she was cutting the flesh of the fruit but thinking about her mother, and the pain that went with her mother's absence. Jenny had been putting on a brave face for months, a mask of professional proficiency to hide the sorrow that had no place in the office, no place anywhere.

Except it was in the face of the jack-o'-lantern, now. Her pain, private and heavy, had been beautifully etched into the pumpkin. And at the time, her eyes had barely registered the shocking, naked emotion that had been carved there. Jenny Strue had created a work of art far beyond what she considered her generally limited artistic abilities—a virtual neon sign depicting her vulnerability. And where was it now? Glowing yellow-orange from a position by the front door and Jenny Strue could not bring herself to move it.

Her eyes crawled back to the witness accounts balled up in her fists, fallen beneath her desk.

*I don't know why I put it out there. I don't know.*

*I can't paint worth a damn. Can't draw worth a damn. But it's there.*

*Everyone can see how much of a monster I am—how much I hate myself—the cutting. Why did I show that?*

*I'm a bad father, right? You can see that? I know it. I know I'm not there for him enough. Or her. I'm such a failure.*

*Now everyone knows what I really am. Everyone knows that I'm a woman inside. I just don't know what to think. I don't know what to tell my wife. Do you?*

*Ms. Strue, this is a private matter, my feelings for Mr. C------. I have no intentions on ruining his marriage. And, I know, I know it's out there, and everyone can see. But I can't take it back now, can I?*

*Everyone sees everything now.*

*Everyone knows.*

*Everyone.*

An occult exposure—utter, inexplicable, and terrifying. Jenny Strue hadn't been able to leave her olive-green clapboard after she'd gone and collected the first round of interviews. It had seemed like too much, abruptly—the protective skin of social graces torn away. It was painful to move through the streets. It was painful to move.

She got to her feet, and briskly made her way to the front door, then hesitated. The pumpkins were still out there. And who knew what kind of humiliations cruel people had prepared to heap upon their exposed neighbors? She didn't want to see that kind of thing happen. She could still taste blood on her lip.

Ms. Strue was a lot of things, many of them incongruous, but she kept a fiercely childlike adherence to her profession well-nourished within her double-breasted suits. Telling the story right was important; every word a reporter writes has an echo. This was her monastic credo and the reason why she hadn't quit her grossly underpaid position. She could hardly trust her coworkers to use adjectives prudently. They liked to tart the truth up a bit whenever she wasn't there to chaperone, which was precisely why Ken Ryeheart had given her the editing position five years ago. She wouldn't disappoint old Ken—not ever, and not now.

She would find the truth herself—she would go and see.

Before she could think too deeply about it, Jenny pushed herself through the front door, stumbling all the way. She looked around and saw the streets filled with people, stunned and angry and upset people. Their awkward movements were almost a joke, a flash mob of zombie-esque pain. Everyone had been scraped raw. Fingertips nervously trembled, and mouths were drawn taut. Twitches and tics were evident, infectious.

One of her neighbors, a young teenage boy who had been outed as gay by his jack-o'-lantern, was weeping alone at the end of his driveway, snuffling into the cuffs of his sweatshirt's sleeves. That was when Jenny Strue saw the beginning of the end.

A heavyset man, revealed by his own pumpkin as being painfully insecure and full of self-loathing, swept the boy into a hug. Tears rolled down their reddened faces. A woman, depressed and convinced that her husband had begun to sleep around and lie about it, joined in the embrace of the two men.

It was the first, but not the last.

As Jenny Strue watched, islands of people became pairs, then groups. Sobs were released, and the moaning grew collective, nearly critical.

And abruptly Jenny was a part of it all, mourning among them. Her pain was given a part in the long, strange melody of loss and fear. They mourned together, and in that great weeping, Jenny felt catharsis that she had never known before. And it felt like her mother's death meant something in that moment as she was swept up in warm arms and whispers.

The whispers, ubiquitous: "It's O.K. now, it's O.K."

There was an absence of vocabulary to deal with the events that happened on October 31st, 20--. Reporter Jenny Strue was left with her fingertips hovering over her keyboard, indecisive.

*"Miracle" is a word typically reserved for events that happen to religious figures, or perhaps to ordinary folks visited by the snowbound supernatural. "Christmas miracle" is a phrase. On Halloween, miracles are ghost stories. On Christmas, ghost stories get to dress up as miracles.*

Was this, then, a new type of miracle, or merely a haunting? Jenny had to get this right. She felt as if getting this right really mattered.

*A Halloween Miracle*, then—that felt honest.

## About Hannah Marie:

After being inspired by "Sesame Street" as a child, Hannah Marie wrote her very first piece about the adventures of Cowboy X. The intoxicating discovery that her imagination could be written down and shared was all it took for her to become addicted to the art of telling stories. She has since traveled the western United States, Great Britain, and South Korea, collecting freckles and experiences. When she is not writing, reading, or working, she enjoys biking, petting adorably fluffy animals, and fantasizing about creating her own fantasy worlds. "The Queen's Dragon" was written in response to a challenge from another author. It is her first published piece.

# THE QUEEN'S DRAGON

## Hannah Marie

The drums beat a rhythm of death.

Irene stood on the platform with a basket in her hands, painstakingly created over the course of three days. Blonde hair woven between the reeds glinted like gold in the sunlight. A dark blue velvet pillow lined the bottom. It was a beautiful piece of work.

The heavy sound of the drum bludgeoned her ears, deafening her to all but the sound of her own heaving breaths.

Such a beautiful basket made to hold a gift for a king.

The drums sounded one last time and the mass of humanity jostling for position in the courtyard drew a collective breath. In the silence, the sword wavered for an instant, catching a spark of sunlight, before swinging downward in a graceful arc.

Blood splattered hot and wet on Irene's cheek. The basket almost tore from her grasp with the sudden weight of its burden.

She had promised the Queen she wouldn't look down, and so she blinked away tears, forcing her twisting stomach back down her throat. She wouldn't look down. She *wouldn't*.

Warmth seeped through her slippers to wet her feet and stain the hem of her gown. She ought to step back, out of the widening circle of blood, but the basket and its load shackled her in place.

"Girl! Girl, over here! To the King with you!"

Irene turned. The Chamberlain beckoned with be-ringed fingers. His permanent snarl took on a green tint. Irene saw that his face was dusted with red. As witness, he had stood too close, and now he was stained, though not as stained as she.

Chamberlain flapped his hand at her again, his scowl deepening. "Now, girl!"

Irene moved.

The crowd, which moments before had been roaring like a dragon, now stood silent and still. This was one execution which held no celebration, no mockery.

She placed her feet with exquisite care. It wouldn't do to drop the King's gift. Head high, eyes wide, she passed the butcher's block. The blood pulled at her gown and sucked at her slippers. The basket's weight unbalanced her, and as she placed her left foot on the hastily cut yew boards, she slipped.

A hand caught her elbow and held her in place while she struggled to find footing. She caught a glimpse of pearl-crusted fabric and a pale, long-fingered hand, slack and lifeless. The bouquet of wildflowers that had slipped from those same fingers scattered in the viscous red pool.

Irene closed her eyes and took a deep breath. The sharp tang of blood filled her nose and mouth. She heaved. *Don't look down.*

"Steady, now," a low, guttural voice said.

She looked up into the face of the executioner. He needed no mask. Everyone in the kingdom knew the face of the King's butcher. He required no anonymity as he carried out his duties. Those who would seek revenge for his bloody work were already dead.

His flat orange eyes burned like flame. She wanted to scream, to hurt him, but those eyes held her captive.

He pulled her upright with easy strength. With practiced, impersonal movements, he adjusted the prize in the basket. "To the King." His tone was as expressionless as his eyes.

He moved aside to allow her to continue her macabre march down the steps.

The King sat on a raised dais just beyond the platform. Royal guards, pikes pointed heavenwards, lined the petal-strewn path to the throne. Irene walked down the path and petals stuck to the bottoms of her feet. She focused on the King, his glittering blue eyes, his satisfied smile.

She reached the dais and paused. Somewhere in the crowd, a woman sobbed, the sound pulling an echo from her own throat.

"Approach." The King leaned forward with an eagerness that filled her with dread.

Irene climbed, the basket growing heavier with each step. It bumped against her middle, tapped at her knees, and pulled on her shoulders. At the top, she was unsurprised to see the King standing and waiting for her.

"Let me see," he whispered.

She proffered the basket and he reached in with his own two hands. A smile split his youthful face, a smile that in any other setting would be charming.

He lifted the Queen's head, bringing it close to his face. "Hello, Mother." His eyes flicked to Irene and anger pulled at his mouth. Then the smile was back. "Your Queen."

He paused as if waiting for an answer.

Irene drew sharp breaths through her nose, not trusting herself to speak. She nodded instead.

He lifted the head to the crowd. "Your Queen!"

Now the crowd thundered, though not with approval. They surged for the platform, for their Queen.

The King tossed the head down the steps. "Your Queen!" he laughed.

The head bounced and came to rest on its side, bloodied blonde hair obscuring the face and most of the severed neck. Bile churned in Irene's stomach, threatening to boil up to her mouth.

The Royal Guards lowered their pikes to keep the crowd at bay. Howled curses at the King and his executioner mingled with the keening song of lament for the Queen.

Chamberlain hurried up to the dais. "Your Majesty! I believe they have had enough entertainment for today!"

The King nodded. "As have we." He grinned down at the seething mass. "Leave them to it. Vovin!" He raised his voice and beckoned.

The executioner still stood next to the Queen's body, his eyes downcast, sword in hand. At the King's call, he moved across the platform and dropped to the ground. The spectators, still angry, had enough sense to give him a wide berth. No one dared to confront the King's demon.

"Vovin," the King said, "you will accompany us to our apartments. Let the soldier's deal with this."

Vovin's eyes flickered to Irene. "And the girl?"

The King gave Irene a considering look. "Bring her."

~ ~ ~ ~ ~

The hand on Irene's upper arm burned through the sleeve as Vovin escorted her into the King's private chambers. She had never been this close to the butcher before, and fear threatened like shadows at the corners of her eyes.

She concentrated on the King as he glided across the plush carpets with a rolling gait. It was better than acknowledging the creature at her side.

She smelled the heavy cloying scent of blood, overlaid with the slightest scent of smoke. His warm breath—steady and even compared to her shallow, panicked ones—danced across her cheek and neck, drying the blood like clay.

"Vovin." The King snapped his fingers and pointed at the carpet.

Vovin deposited Irene in the middle of the floor. She felt him behind her and the heat radiating from his skin raised goosebumps even as her bones burned.

She still held the basket, her fingers and palms sticky on the handles. She adjusted her grip, the sound of her skin pulling from the wet reeds loud in the silence. She stared at the King. He stared back.

"Irene Aderin," he said as he lowered himself onto a low, padded bench. "*Lady* Irene Aderin. What are we to do with you?" He peered at her with guileless blue eyes. "Most beloved lady of the Queen. Loyal, brave, kind, and beautiful." He drew in a breath as his eyes devoured her bloodied face. "Very beautiful."

"She needs to be cleaned," the executioner growled.

The King shook his head. "No. The blood stays. The stain is… invigoratingly enchanting." He crossed the floor to stand in front of her. "You served our mother, my lady. You served a woman who would kill her own son. We wonder, what kind of person does that make you?" He stretched out a hand to tuck a strand of hair behind her ear. His fingers came away scarlet. "Your life is in our hands, Lady Irene. Conspiring to kill your king is treason,"

Anger stirred beneath the shock and fear, loosening her tongue. "You weren't king at the time, Your Majesty."

He bared his teeth and leaned in close. "And yet, we are your king *now*. We could have you flogged and beheaded, Lady Irene. We could have you drawn and quartered. We could give you to the torturers with instructions to keep you alive. Or…" his eyes flickered past her "…we could give you to Vovin." He cupped her cheek and breathed in her ear, "And your King delights to indulge his dragon."

Images assaulted her mind. Sharp teeth pulling at flesh, rending bones; skin blackened and peeling to expose muscle and tendons; massive claws piercing vital organs while she screamed and screamed.

Irene's scalp tightened as the monster shifted. "Your Majesty," she whispered.

"He'll do whatever we ask." His eyes locked onto his monster. "He'll even let us watch."

The door to the apartment slammed open. The cacophony of the crowd burst into the room, seeming to push the Chamberlain ahead of it.

"Your Majesty!" He hurried to his king. "They've broken through the line! They're calling for blood!"

"Chamberlain, we may give them yours!" the King snapped.

The heavy man bent at the waist, his portly stomach preventing him from completing the full bow. "Please, Your Majesty! We need reinforcements!"

The King sighed. "Vovin, go and help Chamberlain control the peasants. A display would not be out of order."

Irene felt a heavy, hot hand drop onto her shoulder.

"The girl –" Vovin began.

"– will stay with us," the King said. "We will teach our mother's lady what it means to serve the King."

Irene's stomach clenched, his lascivious tone making the meaning all too clear.

"But surely, the girl must first be washed," Chamberlain said, distracted from the crisis in the courtyard.

The King lashed out, catching Chamberlain's face. "We wouldn't change a thing!" he snarled. "Now get out and assert our control!"

The Chamberlain scurried for the door.

Vovin's hand remained on Irene's shoulder. "The girl."

The King ripped her out of his grasp. She stumbled sideways, barely managing to retain her hold on the basket.

"As always," the King snarled, "it will be our pleasure before yours."

He stood in front of the executioner, hands on hips, chin jutting out. Vovin remained still, his face stone. Despite his calm demeanor, Irene knew that he was just barely restraining himself from violence.

"Get out, Vovin," the King hissed. "Or would you like to see your skin burn?"

The butcher's eyes narrowed for a fraction of a second, his fists clenched. Then he turned and followed the Chamberlain's retreating form.

The King slammed the door shut. He turned back just in time to catch a pillow in the face—a blue velvet, blood-stained pillow filled with pieces of rock and mortar chipped from a prison cell.

The blow spun him against the door, curses spewing from his mouth. Irene hit him again before he could recover. Her handmade weapon slammed against the back of his skull, and he slumped to the floor.

Shaking, she stood over his recumbent form. She wanted to pound the pillow into him again and again, to see if his blood was as red as the Queen's.

*Irene, you aren't a murderer*, the Queen's whispered words echoed in her mind. *Once the dragon is released, he will do what I could not. Let blood stain his hands, not yours.*

She took a deep breath and let the pillow thump to the floor.

He would keep it close, the Queen had said, where he could feel it. He would want to know that it was safe at all times.

Working quickly, she pulled the rings from his fingers and the chains from his neck, inspecting each one. She tugged the gold cuffs from his wrists, running her fingers along the inside, searching for an anomaly in the craftsmanship. Finally, she tore the crown from his head and used her teeth to rip open the padded lining. After a moment of searching, she found it.

The key fit in the palm of her hand. She closed her fingers around it and felt the teeth bite into her skin.

She stepped over the King's form and fled.

She tore through the castle, depending on the riot in the courtyard to keep the dragon occupied. The back staircase to the servants quarters was deserted—most if not all of the servants were probably in the courtyard themselves. She moved down the hall into the kitchen. The cook sat on a chair in the corner, sobbing painfully into her apron.

Irene couldn't stop to offer words of comfort or promises of revenge. A dragon could track a rabbit through a rainstorm. It could certainly track her bloodied footprints through the castle. At this point, it was not a question of *if* he found her, but *when*. It was important to keep ahead of Vovin just long enough to use the key.

She pushed open the back door, spilling into the kitchen garden. Uncaring of the ordered rows of young herbs and vegetables, she sprinted to the back gate and the stables.

The horses snorted and stamped as she entered. She bypassed her own sweet mare and the Queen's dappled gray. She needed a stronger, faster horse, one that could outrun a dragon.

The long-legged bay already had a bridle, reins dragging the ground. Unwilling to pause for a saddle, she tugged the horse to a mounting block. He balked for a moment, nostrils flaring, then allowed himself to be led. She barely lowered herself onto his back before she dug her heels into his side, spurring him into a gallop.

As they raced down the back slope of the castle, onto the green, and into the lower town, she thought she could hear the King's screams of rage.

~ ~ ~ ~ ~

Irene leaned against the bay as he gulped at the stream. For a moment, she could breathe. She closed her eyes and thoughts of the Queen played through her mind. The Queen teaching her to embroider a straight line, her mouth curving with delight at Irene's first sampler; Irene brushing the Queen's long, golden hair and then the Queen returning the favor; an afternoon spent on the green, laughing and tossing a patchwork ball, the wildflowers…

*—scattered in a pool of blood, marring the glass-like reflection of the sky, the block, and a body encased in a beautiful white gown. Red stained the gently curled white fingers. Irene's face mirrored back at her, dark and crimson. The weight of the basket dragged even heavier by the knowledge that it no longer contained just a bag of rocks. Her fingers threatened to lose their grip and spill the contents to the ground. The Queen was dead, and in her basket, she held the proof. She held—*

Irene's eyes slammed open and she stumbled away from the horse. Bending double, she heaved. The contents of her last meal violently reappeared. She retched for several long moments, her stomach clenching painfully when nothing more could be expelled. Sobbing, she made her way back to the stream to rinse out her mouth.

The dancing water obscured her reflection, though the brownish-red water dripping from her face told her more than she needed to know. She splashed water on her face, into her hair, and let it run down her neck and into her bodice. She stepped into the water and gagged as the current carried clouds of dirty water downstream. She scrubbed at her hands, hating that the small crevices in her skin retained the color.

The horse snorted as she settled on his back, unused to carrying cold, wet burdens. She leaned into his warm neck, ignored the tears that dripped onto his mane, and nudged him into a slow trot.

Where would a king hide a dragon skin? They had asked this question over and over. It was in an apple-wood chest with an iron lock. The Queen had placed it there herself, moments after her son had captured the dragon. And then, in a move she regretted to her dying day, the Queen gave the chest and the key to her son for safekeeping.

They had searched the castle itself, then the holding on the coast under the guise of a seaside visit. They attended a jousting tournament at the woodland fort, scouring the grounds between bouts. They had searched every castle the King had visited in the last five years and had been unable to find it.

In the dungeon, after the Queen's very personal attempt to end her son's life and free the country from his tyranny, they determined that there was just one place they had yet to look.

Where would a king hide a dragon skin? In the only place a dragon would never look—in another dragon's cave.

Irene turned the horse north. The nearest dragon nested in the small mountains above the northern farmlands—half a day's ride. The soil was rich. The sweet grass nourished the fat sheep that fed the King—as well as the rogue dragon that would snatch them from the fields.

Vovin, in his human form, would be no match for a dragon wearing its skin. It was the perfect place for the King to hide his dragon's most prized possession.

With the key heavy in her pocket, Irene urged the bay into a gallop. She could still free the kingdom, still redeem the Queen, as long as she got there first.

~ ~ ~ ~ ~

A shepherd pointed to the narrow path that led to the dragon's cave. His eyes skittered from her face to her hands to her fine, stained skirt riding up around her knees.

"Is all that from yer last dragon?" he asked nervously.

A bitter laugh escaped her throat. "In a way, yes. When was the last time anyone saw this dragon?"

"He's been sleeping an awful long time," the shepherd said through his beard, "'pert near three years, I reckon."

Three years? Dragons could, of course, go several years without food or sleep. There was nothing unusual in that, though Irene's stomach clenched as she realized the dragon would be hungry.

She shifted on the bay's back. "How do you know the dragon is still alive?"

The shepherd pushed back his hat and scratched at his forehead. "Worl, we hear him every once in a while, snorin' in his sleep. Last year, kids went lookin' for him and nearly got singed."

"Thank you, sir." She turned the horse.

"Noticin' that you ain't got a sword."

Irene paused.

"An' you ain't got no armor," he continued, "though the last knight to come up this way didn't have no sword, either. He jus' had a box. Had armor, though."

"A box?" Irene looked down at him, the key's weight very noticeable against her thigh.

The shepherd nodded. "Yes, ma'am. How you intend to kill a dragon with no sword?"

Irene started up the mountain path. "I don't."

She ignored his shouts of warning. She knew better than anyone what a dragon could do.

The bay climbed the mountain easily, his long legs finding no challenge on the narrow path. Irene gave him his head, leaning against his neck. If she was lucky, the dragon would be asleep. If she were very lucky, she could sneak in, retrieve the skin, and be out before it awoke. There was no grand scheme. Either she lived through her encounter or she joined the Queen in the next life.

Exhausted, she closed her eyes, lulled by the steady sway of the horse's gait.

A lack of movement prodded her awake. The horse had reached the top of the mountain and refused to go a step further. The path continued for another hundred yards before disappearing into a shadowed crevice.

Irene swung her leg over the horse's back and slid to the ground. The bay shivered with fear. His eyes were wide, his nostrils flaring as he huffed at the dragon scent assailing his nose. She pushed him beneath the overhanging branches of the evergreen trees to block his view of the cave. His fear was still obvious by his stiff-legged stance and quivering muscles. She wanted to send him back down the mountain, toward safety, but forced herself to tether him to a small tree. She would need him for the ride back. But it was a small tree. He could easily pull free. In case she didn't come back.

She clutched the key and put one foot in front of the other.

～ ～ ～ ～ ～

The dragon was awake.

The crevice which had seemed so narrow moments before, now loomed in front of her. Tendrils of smoke curled from the depths. The sound of a clinking chain echoed like chimes. Now and then an angry roar rumbled down the mountainside.

Irene spent a lifetime just outside the cave entrance, trying to calm her racing heart. Terror waited in the dark, and she was foolish enough to put herself in its reach. How long would she have to wait until the dragon went hunting? How long until he fell asleep on his horde? Did she really have the time to waste?

Skin prickled on the back of her neck, and she turned to gaze at the rolling green countryside beneath her feet. Movement caught her attention, too big and fast for sheep. The gleam of sunlight on metal confirmed it—the King had sent his knights. She shadowed her eyes and squinted against the afternoon light. There, riding at the front of the contingent, was the King himself. And beside him, his dragon.

She was out of time.

An increase in temperature was her only warning before a massive clawed hand grasped her around the waist and yanked her backward into the cave. She shrieked as she hit the ground with a clatter, then gagged as the smell of smoke filled her nose. Odd objects poked into her back and legs.

"What new witchcraft is this?" A dark, graveled voice said above her. "A girl comes, smelling of blood and death."

Irene stilled. The dragon stared down his muzzle at her. Smoke billowed out of his nose. Silver scales had flaked off of his head and neck, revealing a tough gray skin beneath. Where his left eye should have been was an empty socket. Several of his teeth were chipped and broken, though he still had plenty of sharp ones available.

"Please," Irene whispered.

"I can smell your fear, girl," the dragon said. His tongue curled and twisted around his teeth to form the human words. "I can *taste* it." He pulled back and removed his claw.

Irene's hand touched smooth, hard bones. She sat up, numbly staring at the pile in which she had landed. Ribs, spines, femurs, and numerous other bones jumbled together. A scream built in the back of her throat. She choked it down and turned to the dragon.

He snarled. "Why are you here? Another virginal peace offering from your king?"

"N-no," she stuttered. "I'm here for a box."

The dragon shifted to a metallic accompaniment. "A box? The King's box?" He raised his head and laughed smoke and fire.

Irene covered her head, crying out as a flame touched her hands and the nape of her neck.

"*You* are here to rescue us?"

Irene lifted her head. *Us?* The dragon tilted his neck, revealing a large, iron collar. A heavy chain ran down his neck and bolted to the wall. Inscriptions of magical orientation gleamed on the collar and links. Possibly a spell of strength for the restraint or a spell of weakness for the dragon.

There, just in front of the chain, stood an apple-wood box.

She was halfway to the box, the key in her hand when the dragon knocked her down again. His tail carried her to the floor. She only just managed to close her fist around the key before he put a claw on her chest, weighing her down.

"You smell of the Queen's blood. Tell me, did you kill her?" His one good eye glittered with malice.

Irene shook her head.

"Pity. It would have been better had she never born that –" He broke off suddenly, nostrils flaring. He raised his head, scenting the wind. "He's here," he growled. He picked her up, ignoring her cries, and lumbered out of the cave. "He's here to save his witch!" He held Irene up to the sky and roared.

She shrieked and covered her ears. His challenge seemed to linger, bouncing back and forth across the valley.

A ballista bolt smashed into the side of the mountain.

The dragon laughed and brought Irene up to his good eye. "Your king comes too late, witch." He opened his mouth.

"I can set you free!" Irene said hurriedly before he deposited her in his gaping maw.

"No more tricks, girl. I've been alive too long to fall for another one."

Irene dug into her pocket and held up the key. "I can unlock the collar."

The dragon froze, his good eye locked on the key. "A trick," he grumbled.

"No trick," Irene assured him while she silently prayed that she was right.

The King must have had one key to both dragons. He would have liked holding that sort of power.

"I will kill you if you are wrong." The dragon moved her close to his neck and tilted his head.

Another ballista bolt whistled past.

Irene fitted the key into the collar. "If I am wrong..." she breathed as she manipulated the lock, "...it won't matter."

Shouts carried on the wind, one more authoritative and outraged than the others. The King, she knew, saw what she was doing.

The collar sprang open, falling to the ground with a clank. The dragon's eye widened and he caught his breath. It had rubbed off his scales in a perfect ring. Pale gray skin seemed to glow from within.

"Free," the dragon whispered.

His claws opened and Irene fell to the ground.

"Free!" the dragon bellowed and launched himself into the sky, breathing fire.

Irene rolled to her feet and ran back into the cave. She fell to her knees in front of the apple-wood box. Outside, men and horses screamed. The wind carried blasts of heat into the cave.

She fumbled with the iron lock, desperate to get the skin.

Vovin would kill the King. As soon as he had his power returned to him, as soon as the King held no sway over him, Vovin would kill the King.

The lock clicked. She threw open the box.

His skin cloak was neatly folded on the bottom. It looked just like dragon scales, made of heavy, golden discs that moved like oil when she picked it up. She clutched it to her chest and turned around, ready to sprint down the path to the waiting horse.

Vovin stood in the entrance of the cave, sword drawn and muscles tense.

Irene froze, the cloak held in front of her like a shield.

"That is mine," Vovin said dully.

Irene nodded. "Yes." She took a step forward, holding the cloak out. "Please take it back."

The sword lowered. "Just like that? No promises, no threats?"

"Just a request."

Vovin cocked his head. "Yes?"

"Kill the King." She moved closer. "Please, just kill the King when you are free. That's all I ask."

His hand reached out and tugged the skin from her grasp.

"Yes," he sighed as he swung it over his shoulders.

The skin moved and stretched over his body. Like a painting taking shape, he grew and changed, and then he was a full grown dragon, as he was always meant to be.

He lingered for only a moment, his orange eyes meeting Irene's as she stared at the massive gold dragon in front of her. Then he was gone.

Irene chased after him, staring up at the sky to see him wheeling up and turning east, away from the knights below. She paid no attention to the other dragon's scream as a ballista bolt finally punched through his chest. She paid no mind as the dragon thumped against the mountainside, his death throes raining rock and debris down around her.

"NO!" she screamed. "Come back and kill him!"

Vovin disappeared behind the trees.

She waited for him to come back. After several long breaths, it became evident that he was gone. She turned around.

"You cost us our dragon!" The King's fist slammed into the side of her head. "You cost us *two* dragons!" He hit her again, and stars exploded behind her eyes. "Death will come, my dear lady, and it will come swiftly."

Then darkness.

~ ~ ~ ~ ~

The drums beat a rhythm of death.

Unlike the Queen, Irene had not come quietly to the block. The platform from yesterday's execution remained, stained and bloodied, and she had to be dragged up the stairs and tied down. She had expended all of her tears through the night and now lay motionless, nothing but slow anger burning behind her eyes.

The crowd gathered for this execution as well, though they remained silent and still. The King's hold was breaking, but it was firm enough to keep the crowd in check.

They had tied her head down facing the King, who glared with furious eyes. She stared back.

The drums beat one last time. She felt the sword rise and in the silence, a dragon screamed high in the sky.

And then the sword fell.

## About K. G. McAbee:

K.G. McAbee has had a bunch of books and short stories published, some of them quite readable. She writes steampunk, fantasy, science fiction, horror, mysteries, pulp and comics and belongs to Horror Writers Association, Sisters in Crime and International Thriller Writers. She received an honorable mention in the Writers of the Future contest and won the Black Orchid Novella Award for her first mystery.

For more info, please contact her at: kgmcabee@gmail.com.

# A Knight, a Wizard and Bee—Plus Some Pigs

## K. G. McAbee

I've lived with Pretty Decent Wizard Cardoman for the last eleven seasons. It hasn't been bad; don't think that. Sure, I've kept pigs for him, shoveled pig shit onto our garden patch, and grown cabbages. But I've done a good bit more. Cardoman, while aging—he says he's three hundred and seventy-nine, but I think he's exaggerating—can still have days—well, hours—of clarity and intelligence.

And he has five books.

I've read them all, of course, and I've learned what I can. Wizards are not always born with great powers, after all, though it seems the best of them must, or should, be. One can learn certain spells and minor magicks, no matter at what age one begins, though of course, the earlier the better. I can spell a mean getting-rid-of-fleas geas, and I'm not too shoddy when it comes to lighting a fire, if the wood is dry and it's not raining.

But lately, every day, I've watched Cardoman grow weaker and more scattered, his eyes dimming, his legs giving out on him at times, and his spell-casting growing more and more diffuse and erratic, not to mention dangerous.

So it was almost a relief when the knight rode into our yard one late spring morning.

I was, as usual, slopping our three pigs: Isabeau, Isenbard, and Fred. They were snuffling their appreciation in between mouthfuls of grain, vegetable scraps and the odd egg I'd missed from the henhouse. A rotten egg is not advisable for humans, but pigs have less picky taste.

"Halloo!" hallooed the knight.

I turned from the pig sty—a rather natty shed I'd built myself, with an early visigotherin style—and looked to see who had hallooed.

He did not look prepossessing. Knights are generally not very impressive upon first glance, as I've noticed more than once; we see our share of them wandering through, as our cottage is the last one you come to on the trail to the Great Big Scary Dark Forest. Mostly they're after dragons or the occasional princess captured by a band of outlaw goblins. Our local goblin tribes are fairly law-abiding—for goblins, at least—but a few do tend to go off on romps from time to time, capturing the odd offspring of nobility for ransom. So I'd certainly seen my fair share of knights.

This one, though, just didn't seem to fit the mold. His helm was hanging from his saddle by a wide green ribbon—probably his lady faire's emblem, or else he really liked green—and his armor was surprisingly dented and dirty. Like I said, our cottage was right at the beginning of the GBSD Forest, so most knights and adventurers hadn't really run into anything dangerous, this early in their quests, meaning they were generally pretty clean and neat.

Then, when the knight tried to dismount, he got his foot caught in his stirrup and fell, head first. His foot stayed caught, and his horse looked bored and very clearly not at all surprised.

I ran over to help the knight get untangled. It took both me and the horse to accomplish the task, me tugging and twisting while the horse stalked slowly forward, only dragging the knight a bit. Finally, the foot came free.

"Thank you kindly, young lad," said the knight, sitting up—well, trying to, at least. Armor is heavy. I've had to help many knights take the stuff off and put the stuff on enough to know from personal experience.

"Bee!" came a weak, sickly sounding voice from inside our cottage.

"Are there hives about?" asked the knight from the ground, looking nervous. "Not that I'm afraid, mind you, being a knight and all, but they are a bitch to remove when they get caught in one's armor, and they do refuse to understand that their incessant stinging does not help the matter in the least."

"No, I'm Bee," I said. "B-E-E. It's short for—"

"BEE!" This time, the voice was considerably stronger and far testier. More testy? Whatever.

"Excuse me," I told the knight. "Be right back."

I left him sitting in a large puddle while I ran inside to check on Cardoman and put the kettle on. I was sure the knight could use a cup of tea, and I needed one myself.

Inside our cottage, Cardoman was sitting in his rocking chair before a blazing fire, staring into the dancing flames. They were doing the quadrille, I believe, though I'm not up on my dance steps. No partner, so never saw the point in learning about them. I know; it'll come back to haunt me one day, as Cardoman often points out.

I waited until the flames reached the end of a measure and said, "I'm here, master."

Cardoman looked up at me.

"Well, I can see that!" he snapped. "I'm not in my dotage yet. That won't be for at least three more hours, perhaps four."

I sighed. "You called me, sir."

"Really? Did I? Well, it must have been for a good reason." He looked idly around the room. "Wonder what it might have been? Do you know?"

"No, sir," I said, looking over my shoulder out the door.

The knight was still sitting, though he'd managed to transfer from one puddle to another. He appeared to be moving in a sort of mock-turtle movement, shifting and rocking to try to get up, then falling back again, though in a slightly different position and a bit closer to his horse.

The horse, which clearly had a sense of humor, kept moving just far enough out of range so his knight couldn't grab hold of a stirrup to help himself stand. I could understand the horse's reasoning, and I couldn't help but wonder how often this had happened to both of them.

I turned back to my master. "We have a guest, sir. No doubt you called me in just now to put the kettle on and provide some hospitality for him."

"Of course I did! How clever, not to mention thoughtful, of me." Cardoman wiped his nose—it had been running constantly for about nine months now, ever since a disastrous mistake in a spell due to a mispronunciation of 'not'— on the tail end of his beard and waved his hand at me. "Bring the guest person inside, Bee!"

I filled the kettle from the bucket in the corner and hung it over the fire. Cardoman managed to restart the flames dancing in a polka, to make the water boil faster. Sometimes he's his old self. Almost.

Then I ran back out to see what the knight had accomplished.

The horse was over at the water trough, sharing it with three of the ducks who wander in from the nearby river from time to time. The pigs had finished their breakfast and were watching the new entertainment provided by the knight, who had managed, with the help of a convenient boulder, to get to his feet. He was swaying a bit and had acquired a lot of new mud and several fresh dents.

He had a very pleasant face, though at present it was as dark red as the inside of a beet. In fact, it was beet-like in other respects: round and slightly pointed on top, where his hair was curled up in a tight spike, apparently from the shape of his helm. He smiled at me.

"I thank you kindly for your assistance," he said, nodding. "Can I assume that I have arrived at the house of Cardoman?"

"Yes, you have," I said. "I'm heating the kettle for tea if you'd like to come in and meet my master?"

"Actually," he said, looking a bit embarrassed, "I don't feel quite right taking your hospitality. After all, I'm here to kill the Great Cardoman."

"Ah, that is a problem," I said as I helped him unbuckle his cuirass. "To be quite honest, I'm afraid I am going to be forced to disagree with your intended program. He is my master, don't you see."

"Understandable," said the knight. "Only to be expected, after all. And your sense of duty and loyalty is all to your credit, young Master Bee."

"Uh, actually it's—"

"But I cannot be distracted from my goal, I do assure you," he continued. "Begging, pleading, importuning, beleaguering, plaguing, nothing will sway me from my intended quest. Do not try, I pray you, for I would hate to repay your kindness by murdering you, slicing you from neck to crotch with my mighty sword."

Since his mighty sword was still attached to his horse's saddle, a convenient several yards away, I wasn't too worried. Not to mention, both his hands were wrapped in dirty, blood-stained bandages. I could see why he'd been having trouble dismounting, and I couldn't help but wonder how he got on his horse every morning.

After all, if you recall, the horse wasn't helpful.

"I see, Sir Knight," I began.

"Oh, dearie me, I forgot to introduce myself!" He bowed. "Sir Archenhold of Archenhold, son of Archenhold the Brave, grandson of Archenhold the Doughty, and nephew of Dirk of Dirkfeld. Who is, as all who know of great warriors are aware, the son of Dirk the Devious and the grandson of—"

He was stopped by a fit of coughing, brought on, I assume, from the dust stirred up by the four piglets who raced across the yard at that moment, heading for their elders in the sty.

"It must be fun at family gatherings, trying to figure out who's talking to whom," I said as I led him over to the well and handed him a dipper full of water. "What's your mother's name?"

He drained the dipper and said, "Maud. Daughter of Maud the Mighty and granddaughter of Maud the Mellifluous."

"Naturally." I dipped another dipper full, and he drained it again. "Now, let's have some tea and sandwiches, shall we?"

"Your hospitality is commendable, young sir," said Sir Archenhold with another bow. This one was deeper and more respectful than the first, and it had the unfortunate result of causing his greaves, which he'd tucked into his wide belt, to fall to the ground.

I reached down to pick them up. He reached down at the same time. We bumped heads and both fell backwards onto our butts. I bounced back up, as I usually fall down quite a bit during the day. Mud, you know.

Sir Archenhold, however, began his mock-turtle movements again as he tried to get back up. The rocky well-surround was just out of his reach, and there was no convenient boulder to help him this time.

I grabbed him under one arm and hauled him up.

"Thanks, my young lad," he said politely. "My apologies that your master has seen his last dawn and must face death at my fearsome and dangerous hand. But I have made a vow that cannot be broken."

I shrugged. "Cardoman hasn't seen a dawn in years. He's always been a late riser. And you're welcome to try to murder him; you won't be the first, not even this month. If you're the first to succeed, I will be surprised, is all I can say."

Sir Archenhold's eyes widened in what I interpreted as admiration.

"Stoutly spoken, by my honor!" he said, thus telling me I had interpreted correctly. "Tell me, young Bee, once my sad yet necessary deed is done, would you like to become my squire? Regular meals, a third of a third share in all jewels and gold found on any quest, and a new doublet every year. Come, I cannot say fairer than that, forsooth?"

"Tempting," I said. "But let's just see how tea and the aftermath go, shall we?"

"So mote it be, brave youngly! Now, let us have tea, and then I shall be about my business with your master. Uh…" he gazed about our yard. "You haven't seen my sword, have you? Not that I need it to dispatch a wizard, don't you know, but I feel more comfortable with it at my side."

"It's on your saddle," I said, pointing to his horse, which had made itself at home and was cropping the green shoots of corn in our garden.

"My thanks indeed, young Bee," said Sir Archenhold. "And if you play your draughts right, that clean new doublet," he eyed my mud-spattered attire, "might come your way twice a year instead of once."

"Tea first, attempted execution second, discussing my future natty attire third," I said. "Come on inside."

I had to fetch his sword for him first, and as he buckled it on, I led the horse from the garden spot and gave it an armload of hay and a little barley. I looped its reins around a post and turned to ask Sir Archenhold its name.

I was alone in the yard. Well, the horse and pigs and chickens and ducks were there, of course. But no knight.

I raced inside, my heart in my throat.

I hoped my master hadn't splattered Archenhold all over the room. The last time that happened, I'd spent days cleaning up the mess. Do you know how long it takes to get guts and brains out of the upholstery?

But I needn't have worried.

My master was still in his rocking chair before the first, head still firmly in position. Sir Archenhold was just as firmly still in one piece, all parts still in their proper places. He was sitting on my low stool.

His sword, however, was nowhere in sight, and neither were the knives I'd seen in his belt and boot tops. I glanced upwards and saw them exactly where I expected them to be: attached firmly to the ceiling by spiderwebs.

Our spiders were pacifists, well trained and used to visitors.

"Bee, the kettle is boiling," Cardoman said. "Tea for our guest. And cookies. And bread and butter. I suppose an apple pie is out of the question?"

"Only if you can magick up some apples. Last season's are all gone. Remember? We had tarts last Wednesday."

I bustled around, pouring boiling water into the big brown teapot, gathering the mugs and setting the cookies—gingerbread, one of my favorites—on a plate. I went to the table for the loaf, but Sir Archenhold was there before me."

"Allow me to slice the bread, young Bee," he said.

"Happy to," I nodded at the knife, "but don't expect it to cooperate. It's been here longer than I have and has a deep attachment to our master."

Sir Archenhold tried to seize the knife, but it slid away from him.

"I see," he said, the admiration thick in his voice. "And I see my work is cut out for me indeed."

I shrugged as I sliced the bread and handed the knight a spoon. "Here, my master likes lots of butter on his bread. I usually use this, and no, it's not sharp enough for any kind of mayhem."

With me slicing and him spreading rather clumsily with a spoon, we had a plate piled high in no time. The tea had steeped the perfect amount of time—a long-ago spell of my master's that had yet to die away, though occasionally it turned the tea to lemonade—not bad in summer. I poured three mugs full and heavily sugared Cardoman's, then filled his plate high.

Sir Archenhold had done a good job on the buttering.

We dug in and didn't say a word until the plates were clean and we'd all started on our third mugs of tea.

Sir Archenhold sat back with a sigh of repletion.

"Gadzooks, it goes against the grain to repay such hospitality so brutally," he began.

I glanced up at the ceiling, but the spiders still had his weapons firmly attached. They're handy to have around; great for keeping down mice and bugs too. You just have to be careful around the webs, especially when there are cocoons. And you can't be squeamish when they eat their mates. And babies.

"So tell me, Sir Knight," I began when it became obvious that Cardoman wasn't going to grab the conversational gauntlet. "Why are you going to murder my master?"

"It's my time to go," said Cardoman.

Well, that was a corker.

We both stared at him.

"You haven't mentioned a word to me about this," I said. "Don't you think this is one thing which should definitely be on my need-to-know list?"

Cardoman shook his head. "It was a surprise to me too, Bee," he admitted. "Oh, sure, I knew my days were numbered, had been for the last half century or so, but it's always a shock when your last day arrives, isn't it?"

"All right…" I couldn't help but glance at the ceiling again. No, everything with the least bit of sharpness was still there. "But how is Sir Archenhold supposed to, well, cut your head off?"

Head-cutting-off being the preferred method for dispatching wizards, as is known to all.

"After all, everything of his which is sharp is currently residing on the ceiling," I pointed out, "and none of our knives would be willing to pitch in to help. And why today? And why him?"

"Perhaps I can clarify things a bit." Sir Archenhold wiped his mouth politely and dusted the crumbs from his lap. "It was foretold a many a day long gone—actually, at my birth, or so my father Archenhold and granddad Archenhold told me—that my destiny would be to destroy a mighty wizard who threatened to destroy our world and our very way of life."

"Well, just allow me to point out, please, that that description does not appear to match my master," I said, trying to be reasonable. "He hasn't threatened so much as a badger in years, much less someone's way of life. And when it comes to the world, well, that's just not in the picture, is it? Why, in his condition, he's barely capable of staying awake for more than an hour. The world is going to survive that with no problems, I'm sure."

"Dear acolyte and pupil," said Cardoman, "we both knew this sad day was bound to come. We have both dreaded it daily, almost hourly."

"Not me," I said. "I didn't know anything about it. If you've been expecting me to dread things, you should have filled me in on what needed dreading, is all I'm saying."

Cardoman shrugged. "Well, it must have just been me doing the dreading, then. Still, no matter. It's time, dear Bee, for me to die. And for you to go out into the greater world and make a name for yourself."

"I've already offered to take Bee on as my squire, so no worries there," said Sir Archenhold.

"But I haven't taken you up on that offer," I said. "I'm not sure I'm up to sorting through all the different Archenholds, not to mention the Dirks and the Mauds."

"You won't have to be around them much, at least for a long time," Sir Archenhold said. "I'm not going back to the castle until I've done the same thing the wizard wishes for you: I must make a place in the world, have great praise and acclaim attached to my name, find my true love and so forth. You know, the usual."

"How will anyone tell which Archenhold should get the praise and acclaim? After all, there are so many of you." I thought that was a reasonable question.

But before he could reply, my master interrupted.

"Hear me, Sir Knight," said Cardoman in a voice louder than I had heard from him in years. "This burden I place on you: you may take my life as was fore-ordained, and I shall do naught to say you nay. But in exchange for the glory which such a deed will bring you, you must make a vow, the darkest and most powerful kind of vow."

Sir Archenhold looked worried. I wasn't surprised. I was worried myself. My master, even though he sounded fairly centered and together, had a look in his eyes which did not bode well for the knight's future.

"Tell me, oh powerful wizard," Sir Archenhold said, his voice shaking.

"You must vow to take this amulet far away, to the lands of never-ending snow, and deposit it on the spire of the greatest mountain in the world."

"Which amulet?" I asked.

Cardoman looked down in his lap as if he expected to see an amulet there. The only thing he saw—the only thing he could possibly see—was a pile of crumbs and a smear of butter on his robe. Then he reached up and inside his robe, pulled out a leather cord. But it had nothing on it; it was just a cord. So he scrabbled some more inside his robe, bringing out a dead mouse, three dried leaves and a spoon I'd missed three weeks ago.

"Wait a minute," I said. I got up and reached over my master to the small carved box that had sat on the mantel for as long as I'd lived in the cottage. "Are you looking for this?"

I handed him the box, and he opened it. Then he sneezed, mainly because I don't think it'd been opened in a dozen years or more, but mostly because when it opened, a cloud of silvery dust rose up.

We all sneezed as my master rooted around inside the box and drew out a silver chain with an oblong bit of gold hanging from it.

"This is the amulet of Boracelapheladon," he said, his voice dropping into the lowest register he was capable of at his advanced age, which made him sound like a squeaky millstone that someone had primed with a bucket of gravel. "Or was it Celaborapheladon? No matter. It is an object of great power and great worth, and it must not fall into unworthy hands. I have kept it safe here for, lo, these many years, but when I die, it must return to he...or was it she?...who made it in the misty beginnings of time. You, Sir Knight, must vow to return it, upon pain of death and eternal pain and damnation. Did I mention pain? And curses, really, really bad curses?"

I sighed. This day had started out like most others in my time with Cardoman, but it was certainly going in all sorts of entirely new and unexpected directions.

Sir Archenhold dropped to his knees before my master's rocking chair and laid his clasped hands in the crumb-laden lap.

191

"Great, mighty and puissant Pretty Decent Wizard Cardoman, I vow my life, my honor ,and my very soul to undertake this great task. Let no one stand in my way. Uh, may I take Bee with me as my squire, though?"

"Bee is your destiny as well. The two of you will have many adventures, struggle through great danger and overcome incredible obstacles together."

"Good," said Sir Archenhold.

"Now, wait a minute," I said. I had all sorts of objections right on the tip of my tongue, organized and numbered, and I was just getting ready to start enumerating them, when: Pretty Decent Wizard Cardoman's head detached itself from his body. His toothless mouth smiled at me one last time; he winked, and then his head vanished. His body collapsed bonelessly, toppling forward onto Archenhold's head.

The knight squeaked in fright and scrambled back, trying to push the dead body away.

I was just glad it wasn't bleeding. Do you know how hard it is to rent out a blood-soaked cottage? I'd run into the same problem when my folks had been murdered. Nothing like bloody walls and floors to lower the asking price.

The spiders chose that moment to drop the sword, a whole bunch of knives and a few other sharp things that I didn't even know were there—so that's where Cardoman's knitting needles had disappeared to—onto the floor with a rattle and a clatter.

Archenhold jumped up and backed away. Cardoman's headless corpse fell into the fireplace, knocking the tripod where I hooked the kettle over into the embers. All through the cottage, the spells, both great and small, began to dissipate at their creator's death.

"Well, looks like I've got a new master," I said, gazing around. "Hold onto that amulet of Bora-or-Cela-whoever's; it's probably dangerous as direwolves. Not nearly as smelly, though."

He looked at the amulet looped over his wrists and immediately dropped it.

"Perhaps, young squire, you should take charge of it for me," he said, scrabbling for it in the scattered embers on the floor and hissing when one came into contact with his fingers. "After all, no one would suspect that you had such a thing of power about your, uh, forgive me, scrawny and somewhat odorous person."

I shook my head at him but grabbed it and linked it around my neck. After all, I thought, it was probably powerful, so it would be better off with me than with him, for now, anyway.

"Well, now," I said, looking around the place I'd thought of as 'home' for most of my life, "here's what we need to do. First, find some renters to take care of the place and the pigs."

"And would a bath be possible?" asked Sir Archenhold. "It's been some weeks since I've been out of this armor..."

I shook my head. It looked like it was going to be a long quest...

## About T. L. Norman:

From early on, story telling has been a gift that T. L. Norman has nurtured. Her ability to write in many different genres is a dedication she prides herself on. This ability has resulted in the publication in two anthologies, one science fiction, one horror. Recently, her favorite genre to write is the paranormal afterlife. She also writes non-fiction and is an SEO content expert. T. L. Norman lives in Calgary, Alberta, Canada with her husband and daughter.

# The Waiting Room

## T. L. Norman

The light pierced through the darkness with a yellowish glow. It was different from the other lights. Savannah huddled close to Mama.

"Is that our light, Mama?"

"Shh," Mama urged.

It moved strangely up and down the walls as it came closer to them.

"That's no angel light, Missy." Mr. Schivitz gruff voice came from behind Savannah and Mama.

Mama raised her arm and motioned to move back into room 114. Savannah did as Mama asked, but her four-year-old curiosity got the better of her. "If it's not an angel light, what is it?"

"Savannah, shh They'll hear you," Mama whispered.

The light was really close, and Savannah could hear garbled, distant voices, like screaming through water; the same way Mama's voice had sounded before they woke up here in room 114.

The light stopped in front of them. Savannah felt Mama's hand on her mouth. The voices were louder but still garbled. The light continued down the hall and disappeared around the corner.

Mama removed her hand and knelt in front of her. "Listen to me, baby girl. We must not be seen or heard by the yellow glow."

"Why, Mama?"

"Because they are hunters." Mr. Schivitz said.

"Hunters?" Savannah was confused.

"Stop that, Alba; you're scaring her."

"She needs to know the truth."

"Baby girl, we avoid the yellow glow because it can lead us deeper into the darkness. We need to wait here for the angel light. There are no such things as hunters."

"OK, Mama. When will our angel light come? It's been so long."

"It will come when it's our turn. Until it comes, stay close to me and be patient."

Savannah nodded and climbed up on the bed. Mr. Schivitz moved back to his spot, looking out the window into the darkness. Mama stood in the doorway and kept watch down the hall.

Savanna wondered if what Mr. Schivitz had said was true? Were there such things as hunters?

She laid her head on the pillow and waited patiently, as Mama had asked.

~ ~ ~ ~ ~

Devon, Jonah and Sam walked slowly down the main hall of the long-abandoned hospital. Their flashlight cut through the darkness in a centralized yellow glow. Armed with a video camera, digital recorder, and some misplaced courage, the three friends were determined to find proof of ghosts.

The main floor hallway had papers scattered all over. Despite the hot, humid summer night, Devon felt a chill as they approached room 114. Knowing a change in temperature could mean something paranormal, he began asking questions.

"How many are here? How did you die? Do you know where you are?"

They slowly continued down the hall and around the corner. The temperature returned to normal and Devon decided to play back the digital recorder to see if they caught any response to his questions.

Through the static on the recorder, a female voice could be heard.

"Shh, they'll hear you."

"No way?" Jonah proclaimed.

Devon felt tingles down his back. Sam stood quietly beside him, holding the camera.

"We got an EVP!" Jonah said excitedly.

"Let's go back to that area to see if we can get any more," Devon said, turning and walking back toward the hall outside of room 114.

~ ~ ~ ~ ~

Savannah laid silently on the bed listening to Mr. Schivitz hum a relaxing tune. He remained looking out the window into the darkness, but Savannah was unsure what he was looking for? The angel lights always appear in the hallway, not outside the building.

"Alba, shh. The yellow light is returning."

Mama looked at her and placed a finger to her mouth. Savannah nodded.

The light stopped outside the room. Mama took a step back. Savannah heard the garbled voice again but still couldn't understand it. The light entered the room. As it passed through Mama, Savannah saw a distorted shape that looked almost human.

Mama gasped and fought to catch her breath.

"Mama?" Savannah yelled.

Mr. Schivitz was instantly at Savannah's side, and he put his hand over her mouth and whispered in her ear.

"They stole her energy. She will be OK. Shh."

A little green light appeared and began to move around the room, and high pitched beeping began. It hurt Savannah's ears. She wanted it to stop.

Mr. Schivitz stood and yelled, "GET OUT!"

"Alba, no!" Mama cried.

The beeping stopped, but Savannah still heard the garbled voices. The light slowly left the room and the voices stopped. Mama was leaning on the wall near the doorway. She looked tired. Mr. Schivitz helped Mama stand. "Marla, you need to lie down to regain your energy."

"Yes. OK. It felt like a fire sucked all of my energy from me."

"That's what I've heard before. Hunters are pure heat energy."

"OK, Alba, I believe you."

"And with hunters around, you know the angel lights will not come," Mr. Schivitz said quietly to Mama. Savannah grabbed her raggedy old doll and hugged it close.

"I've seen it happen before, Marla. Before the angel light came for my beloved Annabelle. The hospital was busier back then, and not so dark all the time.

"How long did it take for the angel lights to return?" Mama asked.

"A long while. I have been waiting too long for those hunters to chase away my chance of seeing my Annabelle, and I will not see you ladies stuck here as long as I have either.

~ ~ ~ ~ ~

Devon and his friends regrouped outside of the hospital. The excitement of all the activity they had experienced left Devon with a chill and tingles down his spine.

Sam and Jonah were reviewing the recorder and video footage. Jonah listened to the recorder and began to yell, "Holy crap."

Devon ran to Jonah. "What? What did you hear.?" Devon took the headphones from Jonah and listened. The first EVP happened as soon as they had entered room 114. It was almost inaudible, but it was there. A woman gasping, as if she had the wind knocked out of her. He continued listening. Right after the gasp, a girl's voice saying "Mama." He rewound it and was about to review it again when Sam began to yell. "Guys, you gotta see this."

Devon and Jonah gathered around Sam and watched the LCD screen on the camera. The timestamp was just before they left the room. As the camera panned from the empty bed to the right near the window, a shadow appeared. A face formed in the shadow that looked like an old man yelling.

"Jeezez," Devon said, unable to move.

"What's that timestamp, Sam?" Jonah asked.

"2:21:04."

Jonah matched the time stamp on the digital recorder and hit play. A loud, angry male voice filled the night air. "GET OUT!"

The three looked up at the hospital. Devon felt a nagging feeling that they were being watched. The excitement of the proof they had gathered was replaced by a deep fear. "Maybe it's time to go," he suggested, as he tried to hide his fear.

The others agreed with Devon and hopped in their van. "Wait. I forgot the static cam." Sam said.

"Just leave it," Devon said. "We'll get it tomorrow during the day."

"OK. But if it gets wrecked or stolen, you owe me, Dev. It's expensive."

~ ~ ~ ~ ~

The light had gone, and the feeling in the hospital changed. Savannah heard the murmur of the others who also were waiting for their angel lights. A big man who Mr. Schivitz knew came to the door.

"Alba, the hunters left something. A blinking red light. A trap? A snare maybe?"

"Show me." Mr. Schivitz said, leaving the room.

"Mama, I'm scared."

Mama rolled over and wrapped her arms around Savannah. The feeling of her Mama's embrace made her feel a little better. "Will Mr. Schivitz make the angel lights come back?"

"He is going to try. We just have to be patient."

When Mr. Schivitz returned, he did not look happy. He used big adult words that Savannah didn't understand as he explained to Mama what the others had found. "Someone has to manifest to get rid of it."

"I can do it." Mama said.

"No, Marla, you need to rest."

Savannah had heard the word manifest before, but she wasn't sure what it meant.

"I will do it." Mr. Schivitz declared.

"Do you have enough energy to manifest?" Mama asked.

"I will go with him, the big man said in the doorway."

"It will only take a minute. We will destroy it and return. Come on, Reginald."

"Good luck," Mama said with a sigh.

"Where do they go when they Manianufest?"

"Manifest? That is a hard question, my dear."

"Why?"

"Manifesting means going through the doorway to the living?"

"Aren't we living?"

"Well, sort of. We are spirits. We used to be living, but now we exist differently."

"I remember bits of living, like daddy."

"Me too, baby. But now we exist here, and will soon travel to a new place on the angel lights."

"Why can't we just manifest and go back to daddy?"

"All the questions, baby."

"But why can't we?"

"Manifesting takes energy. We don't have enough energy. We need the cold energy to survive. The living need the heat. It is dangerous to manifest. If we lose too much energy, we will be stuck here."

Savannah thought for a minute.

"Baby girl. Savannah. Promise me you will not ever try to manifest."

Mama's voice was serious and stern.

"I promise."

Mr. Schivitz and Reginald came back. Mr. Schivitz looked weak.

"We destroyed it, but Alba used to much energy leaving a message for the hunters."

"A message?" Mama asked. What message?"

"That doesn't matter." Mr. Schivitz said swatting the air with his hand as Reginald helped him to the other bed in the room.

"It was a recording device," Reginald explained. "We broke it, drained the batteries and Alba wrote 'get out' on the wall."

"Alba!" Mama was angry. "We don't want them to know we are here."

"They already know we are here, Marla. We need to scare them off."

You may scare these ones off, but more will come, Alba."

～ ～ ～ ～ ～

The abandoned hospital didn't look so ominous during the daylight. Devon was still pumped from the night before. The thought of what they could have caught leaving the camera there all night made him even happier.

He and Sam walked in the front doors and past the old admitting desk. As they turned down the hall where they left the camera, Sam began to curse.

"My camera, man. No. Not my camera." The static cam was broken all over the floor. "I knew it was a bad idea to leave it here."

"Calm down, Sam."

"Calm down? Calm down! Do you know how much one of these cameras cost?"

"Look, the tape, over there."

Sam picked it up. As he turned to hand it over, a look of pure terror crossed Sam's face.

"What's wrong, buddy?"

Sam pointed at the wall. As Devon turned, the words GET OUT looked as if they were written in blood on the walk.

"Was that there yesterday?" Sam asked.

"No. Let's get a still of that and go review the tape," Devon suggested.

Sam pulled out his phone and took a couple shots of the wall, then followed behind Devon, leaving the remnants of the camcorder on the floor.

Jonah was waiting with the car, having a cigarette. "Where's the camera?"

"Trashed," Sam said, still upset.

"We got the tape," Devon said, "Let's go to Sam's and watch it."

Once at nerve central, Sam began to play through the 6-hour long tape. Devon made notes of the timestamps. At 2:22:38 the three were seen walking out of the building. Then there was nothing until 2:45:58. Two shadowy figures appeared and moved toward the camera. One looked like a small old man, the other, a large, stocky man.

"Holy sh…" Devon said watching the two apparitions manifest right on camera and move quickly at them. The camera appeared to fall over just before the screen went black and a voice was heard.

*"Teach them a lesson."*

Devon looked at his friends. Jonah was sitting on the floor, a look of disbelief on his face. Sam sat still, frozen. It was obvious to Devon that they didn't feel the same excitement.

"We are going to be famous, boys!" he exclaimed.

"So…they wrote 'get out' on the wall? *On the wall?*" Jonah asked.

"Yeah. We found the camera broken on the floor and the words 'get out' were smeared on the wall." Sam said. He pulled the picture up on his phone and showed it to Jonah.

"'Get out' is what the EVP said last night," Jonah said.

"Proof of intelligence." Devon felt even more excited.

"Proof we pissed someone or something off. "Jonah said.

Devon felt pumped. "We have to go back."

"Go back? Are you crazy?" Sam said.

"I'm with Sam. We stirred up some stuff and were given a clear message."

"I'm going back in. You can come, or stay. Makes no difference to me."

"You're nuts, Devon."

"Maybe I am, but I am going back in tonight."

He grabbed a digital recorder from the table, a duffle bag of pods and old cameras and left his friends.

~ ~ ~ ~ ~

Savannah sat with Mr. Schivitz for most of the day. He was very weak. She remembered what Mama said about becoming weak.

"Your angel light is not going to come for you, is it?"

"My dear child, there is no need to worry about an old fool like me. Yours will come, for you and your mother. And it will come for the others as well."

Savannah felt tears fall down her cheeks. "But you are going to be stuck here for eternity."

"You are a sweet girl, Savannah. If I have to stay here, then I will do it happily. I will make it my job to make sure the angel lights continue to come for those here who need them."

"What do you look for when you stare out the window?"

"So many questions, child."

"What do you see?"

"I see beauty and light. I see a future where the waiting room is no longer needed. I see love and eternal life. And above all, I see my sweet Annabelle smiling at me."

A silent stillness fell over the room. Peacefulness. Savannah looked over at Mama, who was sitting in the doorway. Mama began to cry. Savannah ran over to her. Out in the hall, a bright white light began to appear. The bigger it got, the brighter it became.

A voice that sounded like a calm breeze spoke. "Marla, come with me."

"And Savannah too?!" Mama sobbed and pulled Savannah close.

"Her light will come."

"I don't want to go without her."

Savannah began to cry too. "Mama!"

"Come now or stay here forever."

Mama slowly got to her feet, tears running down her face. She bent down and kissed Savannah on her forehead. "I love you, baby girl. I will see you soon."

Mama looked at Mr. Schivitz. "Alba, take care of her for me."

Mr. Schivitz nodded silently.

Mama walked toward the light. She stopped for a moment, bathed in beautiful white light. She turned to Savannah and blew her a kiss. Then Mama dissolved into the white light, and the hallway became dark.

"Mama!" Savannah cried.

"Dear child," Mr. Schivitz said from the bed," your light will come soon. You must be patient.

Come sit with me. Let me tell you about my Annabelle."

~ ~ ~ ~ ~

"I don't need those cowards with me", Devon said to himself as he drove back to the abandoned hospital. "I'm going to get the most ultimate proof any paranormal research has ever gotten."

He pulled his car up to the front of the building and grabbed the bag full of gear. As he walked toward the unlocked front doors, he glanced up at the sun setting over the western mountains. It cast a dark shadow over the building.

He approached room 114 he called out to the spirits. "I'm back!"

Setting up the equipment from the bag, he placed a small camcorder at the end of the hall, and scattered electromagnetic pulse pods all along the middle of the corridor. In room 114 he placed a digital recorder on the table between the two beds. He left the room and walked back to the admitting desk and placed another digital recorder on the counter.

The last bit of daylight disappeared, and Devon was now in complete darkness. He turned on his night vision camera and began his investigation.

"Hello? Can you hear me? Do you want me to get out? "He walked into room 114 and felt a cold chill go through his body. "Come on. Make me leave. Show me your power."

The EM pods began to light up and beep. From the corner of his eye, Devon saw an apparition of a little girl. He turned and followed her out the door. The EM pods scattered down the hall turned on as she walked past them. The camera on the tripod began to teeter.

"What's your name? Are you good or evil?" The entire hallway felt cold; Devon's arms were covered in goosebumps. A feeling of being watched nagged at him.

He decided to play back his digital recorder and heard a girl's voice. "Go away."

"Go away? Why? Are you a demon pretending to be a child?" Devon waited a moment before rewinding the recorder and playing it back. He heard one word.

"No!"

At the end of the hall, the camera on the tripod fell over. Through his night vision camera, he saw a little girl staring at him, her face contorted in an angry scowl. She ran at him. He stepped back and bumped the recorder off the admission counter.

She ran into room 114. He ran in after her. The EM pod was making a high pitched, constant whine. Devon positioned himself in the corner near the window. His heart raced. He was filled with part fear, part excitement. "Show yourself," he yelled.

A cold draft rushed toward him. The old man from the tape appeared in front of him. Devon heard him yell "*Get out!*" right before he felt a sharp pain in his chest and a falling sensation. Then darkness.

~ ~ ~ ~ ~

Savannah fought back her tears. She hoped Mr. Schivitz was right. She hoped her light would come, and she would see Mama again. She hoped it would be soon.

Reginald came into the room and looked worried. "Alba, a hunter is back. What are we going to do?"

"Get rid of the hunter."

"But I can't manifest and neither can you."

"The girl can." Mr. Schivitz said looking down at her.

"But Mama told me not to. I promised her. And I don't know how."

"You are young. You need less energy to do it. Reginald and I can show you how."

"But I promised Mama. I don't want to be stuck here." Savannah felt knots in her stomach and wanted to start crying again.

Mr. Schivitz put both hands on her shoulders. "If we don't get rid of the hunter, you will be stuck here. If you want to see your Mama again, this is the only way. I am sorry, Savannah, but I won't let you get hurt."

Savannah thought for a minute, then slowly nodded. "OK. If it helps me see Mama again."

"OK. Good girl. Now, hunters are warm energy; we are cold energy. We can use their warm energy to manifest by letting it warm us. Once you feel warm, you can cross the barrier into the realm of the living, and you can be seen by them."

"Will I be alive again?"

"No," Reginald said. "You will be like a shadow."

"What do I do when I manifest?"

"You break all the hunters traps. The beeping ones, the cameras, anything with a flashing light. Then run back here as fast as you can."

"OK."

"You will begin to feel the heat leave you, and you will be back. And do not talk to the hunter if he sees you."

"OK."

"Now, let the energy of the hunter's traps warm you. Good luck."

Savannah saw the green light in the room and heard the distant voice. She stood next to the light and let its warm tingle cover her. The garbled voice became clear and loud. She stepped out into the hallway and saw many round boxes on the floor with flashing lights. At the far end of the hall was a camera on legs. It had a bright red flashing light.

Remembering what she had to do, Savannah kicked the round boxes as each one whined. Then she ran to the video camera and tried to knock it off its legs. It teetered but did not fall. Behind her, the hunter yelled at her.

"What's your name? Are you good or evil.?"

"Go away." She screamed.

A minute later the hunter yelled again. "Go away? Why? Are you a demon. Pretending to be a child."

Savannah began to feel angry. This hunter was keeping her from being with Mama. With all her strength she pushed the camera over, and it broke when it hit the floor. She turned to run back to room 114, but the hunter stood between her and the door.

Her head ached, and she wanted to cry. She wanted Mama. With all the courage she had in her tiny body she ran at him and screamed. "NO!"

The hunter moved back, and she ran into the room. The warm tingles slowed and then stopped completely. She was tired and wanted to nap.

"Get on the bed child and close your eyes, "Mr. Schivitz said.

She heard the hunter in the room, but the voice was garbled again. Mr. Schivitz screamed 'get out!' and everything went quiet. Savannah opened her eyes and saw Mr. Schivitz standing at the window.

"It will all be OK now, Savannah." Mr. Schivitz said without turning from the window. A moment later a strange man she had never seen before entered the room. He looked confused.

"What happened. What's going on?"

Mr. Schivitz turned and faced the strange man. "Welcome to the waiting room."

~ ~ ~ ~ ~

Devon opened his eyes to find himself in the doorway of room 114. "What happened? What's going on?"

"Welcome to the waiting room," an old man said to him from the window.

Devon walked to the window and looked down. He saw his body lying on the pavement, his head surrounded by a pool of blood. Sam and Jonah were standing over him. Flashing lights swirled.

"No. This can't be?"

Sam and Jonah walked to the front doors with a police officer. Devon ran out of the room and down the hall to meet them. Sam stopped and picked up something from the floor."

"Sam, buddy."

Devon moved closer to tap his friend on the shoulder. His hand went right through his friend and his hand tingled. Fog began to close around Devon, and a moment later, the hospital became dark. He heard a garbled sound like distant voices.

Devon went back to room 114. He wanted answers, and that old man had them. As he entered, he saw the old man sitting on the bed beside a little girl. The little girl he had seen in the hallway.

A bright white light began to manifest in the room. As it grew in size, a voice could be heard.

"Savannah, come with me."

The girl leapt from the bed carrying a raggedy doll. "I'm coming, Mama." She stopped, ran back to the old man, gave him a hug and a kiss on the cheek, then ran into the light and disappeared.

Devon stared in awe. "What was that?"

"That was an angel light. They come when it's our turn. Until then, we wait."

"Wait? For how long?"

"Depends."

"On what?"

"On whether or not your friends keep coming around."

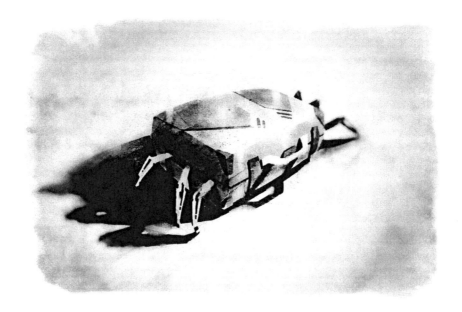

## About Chris J. Randolph:

Born and raised in Silicon Valley, Chris is a writer and graphic designer with a deep love for fantasy and science-fiction. He spent his early years playing video games, watching anime, and fixing computers for friends and teachers, while (as one might guess) rarely getting enough sunlight.

After working a variety of jobs, from technical support to book sales, he self-published his first novel in 2010. That book, *Biotech Legacy: Stars Rain Down*, has since been downloaded more than 60,000 times, and holds an average rating of 4.2 stars at Amazon. Rumor has it his mother is also quite fond of it.

When not dreaming up strange universes full of tentacled abominations, he can often be found arguing online about linguistics and superhero movies, or heatedly playing Jeopardy! from the couch. His long-term goals include publishing more books, exploring the convergence of text and digital media, and maybe going on one of those date-things he's heard so much about.

# RETIREMENT PLAN

## Chris J. Randolph

I wake from hibernation at precisely 2215 hours local time (GMT+8) and wait while processors distributed throughout my body run diagnostics on their slaved subsystems. Within this darkness, the digital chorus report back their progress as they work — verifying the integrity of RAM banks, scanning solid-state drives for corruption, then loading device drivers that each orchestrate their own litany of tests.

The whole process takes less than 600 milliseconds, after which the local network crackles to life around me. What were isolated components only a moment ago are now part of an integrated whole, a single machine with many parts but only one purpose, all unified through a living biological core. The bundle of living neurons that bridges them is... me.

And with a subtle taste of warm copper, the smell of ozone, a thrum of excitement, I am awake.

I pass a signal to my container and its steel latch pops. Hinges let out a warbling whine as the briefcase levers itself open, allowing light to wash over the multitude of small sensors that dot my external surface. My vision is blurry and disorganized at first, but I adapt quickly and take stock of my surroundings.

I'm on the ground in a tight alley, hidden in the shade of a blue dumpster. There's little light, most of it orange phosphor from a street lamp in the distance, and the rest from a sliver of starry sky overhead. The ground is littered with paper cups, polystyrene food containers, discarded nicotine cartridges.

The nearest cellular signal is more than 50 meters away, and the only sounds are a weak breeze and the squeaking of a hungry rat. Confident that I'm alone, I engage dozens of servos and my body unfolds from the briefcase, rising silently like a ghost from its grave. Carbon fiber plates and struts slide over one another to assume new shapes: legs… arms… a torso and head.

The imitation is imperfect—a charcoal wraith in the rough silhouette of a human being—but it's good enough to avoid suspicion so long as I maintain distance, stick to the shadows, and linger in peripheral vision.

I pick up the now empty briefcase, its surface engraved with a Kilotech Industries logo, and I place it in the dumpster while simultaneously acquiring GPS lock. The songs of distant satellites echo through my hardware, endlessly whispering timecodes which a dedicated processor decodes to determine my position. I'm at the planned insertion point, 483 meters southwest of Liánzhèng International's corporate headquarters. As I walk toward the street, the local time is now 2216, leaving three minutes to reach the rendezvous point.

I feel the sea of radio signals that surround me, some secured and others not, like a gentle electromagnetic tide that ever ebbs and flows. More purpose-built processors within me automatically go to work, forging credentials that give me access to the internet, dozens of private networks, and finally the surveillance cameras affixed everywhere. I combine their views with my own 360-degree vision, and I'm now aware of my body from both inside and out.

There's little traffic on the street at this time of night, and that allows me to make full use of my skills. Powered by the city's wireless grid, I shift into a quadrupedal form and take off at nearly 50 kilometers per hour. Humans on the sidewalk catch sight of me—business people clad in wrinkled suits, exhausted from long days at the office; wandering vagrants mummified in multiple threadbare layers who are too distracted by their empty bellies to pay me any mind—and at this size and speed I'm nothing more interesting than a scared house cat. I'm a streak of black that's gone in an instant.

I thrill at this momentary freedom, let loose from the lab and into the dizzying world beyond. The cold city air rushes over my skin with a seductive hiss, while neon lights of every color imaginable pass in a blur. I am silence given velocity, traveling at the speed of shadows around and between the plodding sedans and their slumbering passengers.

I've made better time than my handlers anticipated, averaging 46 km/h and covering the distance to Liánzhèng in just under 38 seconds. According to my target's itinerary, it's still 2 minutes and 23 seconds away, leaving me with a decision: do I find a concealed position and wait here or move to intercept?

I don't care much for decisions. I like having the right answer, and I like winning.

I access local maps and immediately have a strong suspicion about which path my target will take from the airport to Liánzhèng. I can't confirm that suspicion, though; the target is exercising exceptional operational security, and if they're currently online, I can't locate them. Would they have taken a less predictable route to throw off would-be attackers? Interception then carries an increased risk of missing my rendezvous.

On the other hand, I can already detect Liánzhèng's security processes and they are both clever and aggressive. I've resumed my humanoid form, disconnected myself from external power, and am now mimicking standard cellular data traffic, but they'll realize something is amiss if I loiter too long. I'm not designed to withstand scrutiny, so it's best not to attract any.

Liánzhèng's cameras and their heuristics are tuned to recognize suspicious behavior, so I feign human mannerisms. I mask my true intent behind pantomime, looking down at a nonexistent phone, shrugging my shoulders, turning around and marching away in frustration. A few seconds later, I'm once again outside of their network's range and beyond the vision of their cameras, where I can continue network operations without fear of discovery.

I decide on a half-measure. I identify a concealed position along the target's probable route, down the block and outside of Liánzhèng's security sphere. Should the target approach from the opposite direction, this will still give me enough time and space to improvise another response.

I fluidly change shape again, sliding into the six-centimeter gap between a trash can and a bus shelter. Thanks to the wireless grid, my capacitors are at full charge, and I feel like unspent lightning ready to burst. I'm crackling with impatience and excitement, vibrating while I wait for my moment to arrive.

My target approaches — a black town car with tinted windows, license plate 8X772FS. This is a specialized vehicle reserved for VIPs, carrying several hundred kilos of dense armor under its reflective skin. My sensor suite can't penetrate the exterior, and its network is so cunning I can't even detect its presence.

But where technology fails me, intelligence fills in the gaps. I watch the town car's suspension rock as it rounds the corner, and that allows me to determine the weight and distribution of its cargo. Three human passengers: one in the driver's seat (though the vehicle is driving itself), and two more seated in the rear. There's also a 25 kilo mass in the trunk. Computers? Weaponry? I can't tell for sure.

The town car nears and I prepare myself. I enter silent running mode, shutting down all external networking and placing my non-essential processors into low-power states, making myself nearly invisible to mechanical detection. All that remains are my haptic sensors, my 128 eyes, and my will to succeed.

The moment is here. The town car turns the corner and for one instant, I'm in its blind spot. I launch myself forward, rolling end over end then sliding. I fold like an origami crab, creating legs that prop me up and allow me to scurry along the ground. The car accelerates smoothly out of the turn while I become its shadow, keeping pace but careful not to touch it. If I so much as scrape its undercarriage, the game will be over.

We proceed down the street like this, the town car rolling along while I run beneath it. Without networking, my entire world is this small space between the pavement and the vehicle above me, bounded in four directions by spinning rubber tires. In seconds, we are once again inside of Liánzhèng's security sphere, but my presence is now shielded by the very same security measures that protect my target.

We traverse the block, slow and turn toward Liánzhèng International, then head down the ramp and stop at the security gate. While laser scanners on either side check for foreign bodies, I make myself flat and hug the ground. At less than one centimeter in thickness, I'll appear to their systems as nothing more than a piece of trash... passing cardboard... something for their sanitation crew to pick up later.

Satisfied, the lasers disengage while the gate opens with a rumble, and both I and my target are inside. We enter the parking structure together, and continue on for another 30 meters before the town car finds a spot and comes to a stop.

It's finally my turn to go on the offensive. My wireless suite launches into action, scanning Liánzhèng's network and exploiting multiple vulnerabilities. I'm now tapped into the security cameras and watching the town car from several angles, while Liánzhèng's mainframe is receiving a dummy feed. It'll see through the illusion soon enough, but not before I've done my job.

The driver's door opens and a man in a crisp suit and sunglasses steps out. He has a firearm in a chest holster and another on his ankle. I also see evidence of high-grade cybernetic implants — subtle metallic contact plates along the temple and the back of his neck. What upgrades do you have? Communications, surely. Vision enhancement, personal radar, and several terabytes of data storage. Most likely reflex acceleration.

The driver performs a sweep of the area, then walks to the back of the vehicle and stands guard by the trunk. "Clear," he says. A second later, the rear door on the passenger side opens and a nearly identical man exits. He replicates the driver's sweep, then circles the vehicle and stands beside the door on the opposite side.

So close now...

"All clear," the second guard says.

The door opens and an elderly man steps out. His suit is old fashioned in the English style, meticulously tailored and made of the finest cotton with organic silk accents. Dark blue with nearly invisible pinstripes. A maroon waistcoat and matching tie. Shoes the color of well-oiled mahogany, their soles clack against the pavement.

He adjusts a cufflink and glances to each of his bodyguards. He has thick silver hair with waves and cowlicks that refuse to be controlled; bushy eyebrows that speak of wildness in years gone by. I scan the contours of his face… angular jaw and high cheekbones, thin and bulbous nose, wrinkled lips that hold the hint of a scowl… and I confirm his identity.

Silas Jennings, president and CEO of Kilotech Industries.

The driver pops the trunk and retrieves a black case while the other guard keeps watch. Jennings takes a few steps forward and allows the town car's door to automatically close behind him, all the while looking down at an antique gold wristwatch. Does he know? Can he sense that he's about to die?

This is it. Just as the driver lifts his heavy case from the trunk and the other guard glances toward the elevators, I slide out from beneath the car and build myself upwards, my dozens of mechanical components sliding and shifting into place. I extend an arm toward Jennings with fingers dangling like a sorrow-filled spirit. I place my palm lightly against the back of his head, and before he can even draw a breath in surprise, I silently accelerate an eight-gram slug into his brain.

At the age of 56, Silas Jennings drops dead in Liánzhèng International's parking structure from a single gunshot wound to the head. The lights dim at my command while his bodyguards react to the sound of his lifeless body crumpling. They draw their weapons in vain and search frantically for the attacker, but I'm already in the wind.

Sprinting as quickly as my four legs will carry me… wrestling with Liánzhèng's mainframe for control… I initiate chaos in every corner of the network. Doors open and close of their own accord. Fire alarms trigger and cancel. Lights throughout the building strobe in every color. All the while, I cover my tracks with falsified timestamps, counterfeit credentials, and corrupted records that loop back eventually on themselves.

...all to conceal my escape route. The security gate is on emergency lockdown, but this grand mal seizure I've given the building has created a new path. I'm a black bolt rocketing in a spiral up the service stairs, along the white tile of their administrative level, and through the malfunctioning doors of their server farm. The air here is doped with inert gas to fight a non-existent fire, and as I enter, the mainframe has just begun to vent that gas outside.

Using most of my remaining charge, I flex and jump, reforming into a javelin that punches through the grate, then I allow the ventilation system to do the rest. I rattle and bounce along the inside of the ducting, buffeted by hurricane-force winds as I rise up, and up, and up...

...and blast out into the dark and empty sky.

I'm high above the city and its gaudy neon lights... its chronically exhausted populace sleepwalking the streets... its discarded rubbish flipping in the breeze. Liánzhèng International's skyscraper flashes and twitches and screams beneath me, and I'm as free right now as I'll ever be, wearily forming wings as black as death, and gliding back down towards gravity's inescapable embrace.

*Kilotech Industries Argos Prototype, Serial #857-B*

*Timestamp: 2220 Hours (GMT+8)*

*Mission Status — Complete*

*Merger Interrupted*

*Evac coordinates incoming...*

## About S. A. Rohrbaugh:

S. A. Rohrbaugh has lived in Washington State her whole entire life. She grew up in Western Washington and now resides in Eastern Washington. She attended Washington State University and graduated in 2006 with a degree in Communication, emphasis in print journalism. After interning at a newspaper, she chose to pursue a creative writing career instead. She is married with two daughters and one very personable cat.

# The Magical Worlds of Theodore Erickson: A New Beginning

## S. A. Rohrbaugh

"You can at least pretend you're having fun," Victoria chided, looking up from her book. "It's the beach, not a prison sentence, Charlie."

"I'm bored," I complained. "There's nothing to do here. I hate this city."

"Well, there's no use complaining about it now," Victoria pointed out, jamming her bookmark irritably in between the pages of Jules Verne's *20,000 Leagues Under the Sea*. "Dad got a promotion, and we're here. Most people like the beach, anyway. Just because we're not in New York anymore doesn't mean our life is over."

"That's easy for you to say," I replied darkly thinking of all the friends I had been forced to leave behind.

"Grow up."

I smirked as I watched her back retreat before me. She never left my sight, but having some distance from her was a relief. She had been my shadow ever since we had arrived in Charleston, South Carolina.

I turned back to face the ocean and blinked. A shape had appeared in the water amongst the swimmers. I shaded my eyes and stood to get a better look at it. Was it a shark?

Nobody seemed to notice whatever it was until the thing was almost to the shore. Then a little girl shrieked and every swimmer made for the shore, the water foaming and frothing so violently that it concealed whatever it was that they were fleeing. Screams sounded off all along the shoreline as word of whatever it was spread.

A man in a gray pinstriped suit raced toward the shape kicking up piles of sand in his shiny black shoes, his bowler hat falling into my lap. I picked it up hesitantly and watched as the man approached the thing in the water.

"Jezebel," the man said. "Thank goodness I've found you. What are you doing in there?"

Jezebel didn't reply.

I looked back towards where Victoria stood, a cell phone pressed to her ear. She must have borrowed someone else's because we hadn't brought one. For a moment, I considered putting the hat back down and joining her. She would expect that...and it would be safer for both of us. Except, the man was talking to the animal, and it seemed to answer him in its own way. It was the kind of thing I only saw in movies, or that Victoria read in her books.

I walked towards the man; his hat thrust before me so that he knew I meant to give it back. Strangers made me nervous, but I was sixteen now. It was time I didn't run from every strange man I encountered.

Mid-step I halted and stared. Not out of fear, but because it simply didn't seem possible. It wasn't a shark at all!

The animal grunted, and the man turned to me.

"It's rude to stare, you know," he said.

I gaped at the man.

"But it's a hippopotamus!"

"So?"

"So what is doing on the beach in South Carolina?" I asked.

The man scowled.

"I'll deal with you later."

He turned back to the hippo, Jezebel.

"He didn't mean anything thing by it," the man told her. "He was just surprised to see you; that's all. Can you really blame him? A magnificent creature such as yourself appearing in this great wide ocean?"

The hippo batted its eyelashes at the man. I kept my thoughts to myself. The last thing I wanted to do was insult an animal like this- one that could crush me in its jaws in a few seconds. What was a hippo doing here? Did it escape from the zoo?

"Jezebel," the man said more sternly. "You know how people stare when we're out."

The hippo snorted and groaned, her head displacing enormous amounts of water as she replied in her own way to the man's command.

"I know you get bored, but we have no other choice! They'll start to ask questions." The man looked back at me. "They'll take you away from me. They'll put you behind bars like some monster."

Jezebel studied the sea around her for a moment, shifting her weight from one side to the other. If I hadn't known better, I would say that the man was *reasoning* the animal out of the water. Hippos couldn't talk, let alone reason with a man.

Slowly, the hippo emerged from the ocean, water sheeting off of it as she shook herself. She held her chin up regally (or as regally as a hippo could) as she joined the man in the pinstripe suit and they started up towards a ramshackle building about a half mile down the beach.

I looked back to where Victoria stood, watching me nervously. I had to know, though. Nothing about this made sense. I couldn't meet her eyes as I turned away to follow the man and the hippo, Jezebel.

"Wait!" I shouted running to catch up to them.

The man and the hippopotamus ignored me completely.

"You forgot your hat," I added thrusting it towards him once more.

The man paused and felt the top of his head. He looked surprised to find that the hat wasn't there. He murmured something to Jezebel, and they halted while I caught up to them. The man looked at me suspiciously.

"How did you come by this hat?"

"It fell off your head as you ran to…"

I gestured towards the hippo. Would she be offended if I used her name before having been properly introduced? I doubted calling her "hippo" would go over well. It seemed like the safest thing to do.

"Impossible," the man replied. "This hat was crafted for me using the wool of sheep who loved me. It would never fall from my head."

"Except it did," I replied, confused. "Does sheep's hair have any say in where it stays or goes to?"

The man asked shook his head, annoyed.

"Of course, they do. Why do you think some sweaters itch and some don't? If the sheep hairs like you they will make you comfortable, if they think you're a brat they terrorize you until they no longer need to be near you."

I blinked, my mouth agape. The very idea was laughable, but this man wasn't laughing. There wasn't a hint of a smile on his face. I studied him to distract myself from how ridiculous the entire situation seemed.

If he weren't wearing the suit, I would have assumed his was some kind of laborer. His face was tanned and lined as if he had spent many hours out in the sun. His brown eyes studied me as closely as I studied him. His brown hair was winged with gray at the temples.

He looked perfectly sane. His eyes portrayed a level of certainty that even my dad didn't possess, and my dad was a well-respected man. Perhaps I had misheard him before. I ignored the comment about his hat altogether.

"I didn't steal it," I insisted. "It fell next to me."

The man studied me for several moments longer, crinkling his forehead until I feared it may never go flat again. Fear bubbled inside of me. Had I made some mistake in following him? Is this how my mother was taken? Did she meet some crazy man, who seemed respectable, who hid her away to do God-knows-what?

Just when I thought he was going to reach out and grab me by the collar and drag me away, he smiled.

"Very well then. I'd like you to meet, Jezebel. Jezebel, this is…"

He adjusted the invisible hat on his head.

"Charlie," I replied, feeling foolish for catering to the man but still drawn to him.

The hippo nodded towards me, her eyelashes fluttering as she looked up at me through them. The man in the suit grinned.

"She likes you."

I found myself blushing horribly and told myself to stop it. This was ridiculous. I had finally lost my mind.

"Glad to meet you, Charlie," the man continued taking no notice of my discomfort. "I'm Theodore Erickson."

He reached out to shake my hand. Purely out of habit, I shook his. He took his hat back and fixed it on his head.

"That's it?" I wondered.

"Well, the hat wanted to be by you. You can't be all too bad of a fellow."

I blinked. Insanity. I shouldn't be here.

"My sister's waiting. I shouldn't really go without her."

"You shouldn't be talking to strangers either, I reckon," Theodore replied. "I'm willing to admit; they don't get much stranger than me."

Jezebel met my eyes knowingly. Apparently, she thought Theodore Erickson was very strange indeed. I couldn't blame her. Worse, I couldn't seem to stop following them.

"Mr. Erickson," I said. "How are you doing this?"

"Doing what?"

"You know," I replied.

I looked at the hippo uneasily.

"You mean to ask how I convinced Jezebel to exit the ocean?"

I nodded.

"The answer is simple, my boy. I merely asked. The hippopotamus is one of the most intelligent creatures on this planet. Elephants and dolphins might be their only real competition. Well, perhaps cats might contend, but they're such divas. Anyhow, hippos understand everything we say perfectly. She listens to me more than others because I've bothered to learn how to understand hippo-speak, that's all."

"Hippo-speak?" I repeated weakly.

"Yes. Far less complicated than dolphin speak and more effective in some ways."

I nodded. It seemed a safer reaction than my disbelief. However, I could remember wondering if animals had their own language and people were just too self-absorbed to bother to listen for it when I was four. Theodore Erickson, it appeared, had bothered to listen. The child in me delighted in the very idea.

By now, we had reached the ramshackle shed on the beach. Theodore opened the door for Jezebel, who walked inside after one last longing look at the ocean. I watched as she vanished before my eyes. I think I actually jumped.

"Where did she go?"

Theodore took his hat off of his head and whispered to it. Then he put it against his ear. Presumably, it said something for he listened to it for nearly a minute before he turned back to me.

"Do you really want to know?"

"Yes."

"Are you sure? Once I show you, you can't ever un-see it."

My heart began to pound in my chest.

"Is it really that bad?" I wondered.

Theodore smiled sadly.

"No, it's not bad. It's wonderful. It's like magic- except it's real. I still remember when Mr. Jacobson showed me."

"What did you see?" I wondered.

"I can't tell you until you can see yourself," Theodore explained. "It's hard, but those are the rules."

"If you show me, do I have to never go home or something?"

Theodore shook his head and made a face of pure disgust.

"You are a cynical one, aren't you? No, we aren't cruel, but when you go home, it will be different from when you left it. The choice is up to you."

"Different how?"

"The invisible worlds will be visible. You will be able to access places you never knew existed. Some of the greatest thinkers this world has ever seen- the human variety- could see these places."

"Really, like who?" I wondered.

"Roald Dahl, for one- I met him personally many years ago when I was about your age. Nikola Tesla, L. Frank Baum. The histories are filled with their accounts, their adventures."

"You mean the books they wrote?" I asked.

Theodore shook his head and sighed.

"It doesn't matter. Do you want to see it or not? I am a mere hippo herder, but I have shown at least three people the world as it is."

His chest puffed out a bit as he spoke.

"You will never be bored again," Theodore tempted. "But you must decide quickly. That girl has brought a police officer towards us. There is no time for games."

I glanced behind me and saw Victoria marching towards us with a uniformed officer in tow. Briefly, I considered how completely bored I had been since we moved to Charleston. We had only a couple minutes at best before they got here.

He knows how to talk to hippos; my inner voice reminded me. Think of all the wonderful things you might learn to do!

"Do it," I said.

Theodore smiled and put his hands to either side of my temples. I felt a jolt through my synapses and backed away, shocked.

"That hurt!"

"I never promised it would be painless."

I was about to berate him when I saw past him into the formerly empty room. There were at least six hippos crowded behind him, hanging on every word he said. Jezebel was first among them.

"I told you I was a caretaker to the hippos," Theodore said smiling.

"There was nothing there before!" I exclaimed

"And they won't be able to see a thing."

He motioned to Victoria and the policeman. It didn't seem possible that they couldn't see the animals gathered before me, but I hadn't seen them a minute before.

"So long, Charlie," Theodore said quietly, backing into the house. "Be sure not to follow me or you'll disappear too."

Theodore backed into the shed. Nothing happened. Thirty seconds later, Victoria was nattering in my ear, the officer a few feet back, no doubt listening to every word we said.

"Where were you walking off to with that man?" she asked, her face red and streaked with tears.

I turned to face her, surprised by the vehemence in her words.

"I wasn't walking with anyone," I lied, shocked at how easily it came. "I just figured if the beach wasn't safe I should get away from the shoreline after I checked it out."

Victoria crossed her arms and glared at me, even as she seemed to sag with relief that I was safe.

"I saw you talking to someone. What was I supposed to tell Dad if you just disappeared?"

My eyes widened for a moment. Had she overheard something? Then I realized that she just meant that she had been worried they wouldn't be able to find me.

"I'm sixteen, Tori," I replied. "I'm older than you. I think if someone was going to come along and try to murder me I could fight them off."

She shuddered, and I flinched. After what had happened to our mom, I knew it was a low blow, but I couldn't take it back. I meant it. Even if Charleston was new to us, I was confident I could defend myself. How many hours of self-defense had we taken over the past four years because of mom's disappearance?

"You left me all alone," Victoria whispered quietly. "Why did you leave me?"

I stared at her.

"What do you mean? You were the one who walked away from me!"

"But I stayed where you could see me!" she shouted right back in my face. "I didn't just leave!"

I wanted so badly to be angry at her, but I couldn't. Dad had drilled into me how I wasn't to leave her by herself, even if she was thirteen. Mom's disappearance had shocked us all, but Victoria had felt it most keenly. She looked just like her with her golden blonde hair and blue eyes. What if someone tried to take her, too?

For two years she had barely wanted to go to school. Most of her friends had been the books that she read- always new worlds, fantastical places. Now that she was willing to be out amongst people, I shouldn't have left her in a strange place by herself. Shame burned within me.

"I'm sorry," I apologized before she could say anything. "I shouldn't have walked away, I know. It's just…I hate living here."

She sniffed and scrubbed her tears away with the back of her hand.

"Well, get used to it. Dad's promotion means this is where we live now. You're not the only one who lost friends, you know. You'd think you might be more inclined to be nice to me and not less, seeing as we're all we have right now."

I wondered if I should tell her about Theodore, about the invisible hippos in the shed behind us. The hippos she couldn't see. The officer cleared his throat before I could open my mouth again.

"So, there was no man walking with you?"

I shook my head.

"And this man didn't herd a hippopotamus out of the ocean?"

"How many hippos do you know that swim in the ocean?" I asked.

The officer shrugged and smiled as if he didn't quite believe it himself.

"I have quite a few witnesses claiming they saw just that."

"A shark seems more likely," I replied.

"Which is why it is even stranger that they claim it's a hippo. Actually, I saw it myself not three minutes ago."

The officer's smile vanished. In its place were cold dark eyes and lips set in a stern line.

"I also saw the man in the suit."

I wanted very badly to look in the shed behind me. However, I was afraid that would lead the officer to check it. Right now, I needed to get him away from here.

"Where is he hiding?"

I maintained my silence, afraid my voice would betray me.

"Did he threaten you?"

I shook my head. The officer looked like I was wearing on his last vestige of patience.

"You won't get in any trouble if you tell me the truth. I can help protect you."

I looked down at my feet. The man was only trying to help me, but he would never believe me if I told him the truth. The officer sighed as if he could feel my inner conflict. His eyes softened.

"I suppose you won't mind if I look in that shed behind you?"

I swallowed nervously and nodded. Just because the officer couldn't see Theodore and his hippos didn't mean that he wouldn't feel them when he walked inside. With my pulse so loud I could barely hear anything else I stepped aside and let the officer enter. What else could I do?

I watched as Theodore and all of the hippos migrated to the opposite side of the shed. The policeman looked around, confused. He seemed to be talking to himself, but I couldn't quite hear what he said. After several long minutes of pacing back and forth, Theodore and his hippos moving around him all the while, the officer exited the shed. He took off his hat and scratched his head.

"Everything seems to be in order here," he said after several long moments. He turned to Victoria. "You keep an eye out for that stranger and let me know if he shows up again, okay?"

Victoria looked at her feet and nodded. The policeman walked away still talking to himself, darting glances over his shoulders. They had both seen Theodore and now they couldn't- they must feel like they were going crazy. However, that wasn't what twisted the knife in my heart- it was the look of betrayal on my sister's face.

I was supposed to be there. We were all we had with Dad always at work in the new city, and I had abandoned her to chase after a supposed apparition.

"Tori, I'm sorry," I said after what felt like an eternity of silence.

She refused to meet my eyes.

"You already said that."

I looked desperately at Theodore. My guilt twisted my stomach painfully. She needed to know- she needed to understand!

Theodore bent down to speak with Jezebel and her hippo brethren. Then he took his hat off and held it to his ear. He seemed to be arguing with them, but what for, I couldn't hear he was speaking in tones so low. After a minute or so, after the police officer was far enough that he wouldn't see, Theodore straightened up and marched towards the doorway.

I saw Victoria's eyes widen as he emerged onto the beach. She opened her mouth to speak and let it hang there.

"It's a pleasure to meet you," Theodore greeted Victoria, tipping his hat and bowing slightly.

"I- thank you. How...?"

She trailed off unable to find the words. Theodore smiled, his eyes twinkling at her confusion.

"I am Theodore Erickson, caretaker of all the hippos in Charleston, South Carolina. And you are?"

"Um, Victoria."

"It's lovely to meet you, Victoria."

"I watched you appear out of nowhere!" she exclaimed.

Theodore snorted.

"That's ridiculous. You can't come back from Nowhere."

He shivered.

"Nowhere is a place?" I asked.

"Well, something like that, more like a void between universes. Nasty business, Nowhere. You never want to find yourself in Nowhere. Nobody knows how to find their way out. I suppose that's why they call it Nowhere."

Victoria stared from the doorway of the shed to where Theodore stood now and back again. I felt a chuckle rise within me and held it down. She wouldn't appreciate being laughed at just now. After a few moments, her head jerked back to Theodore.

"Did you say you're a caretaker to hippos?"

Theodore nodded.

"Would you like to see one?"

Victoria's breath seemed to catch in her throat. She nodded.

"Jezebel," Theodore called. "Our new friend, Victoria, would like to meet you."

Jezebel sauntered over towards us; her chin held as high in the air as she could get it. Her ears twitched with excitement. She batted her eyelashes at me before halting in front of Victoria.

"It's, uh, nice to meet you," Victoria told Jezebel before taking a few steps backward.

"She won't hurt you," Theodore reassured her. "You're Charlie's sister, so you're okay in our book."

"How do you know Charlie?"

Theodore shrugged.

"My hat liked him. My hat likes you too. Would you like to see the other hippos?"

"There's more than one?"

Theodore grinned.

"May I?"

He put his hands on Victoria's temples, just as he had mine.

"You're going to have so much fun, Victoria Crane. A mind like yours…" he trailed off savoring whatever he was seeing her head.

Victoria jumped as she was jolted with whatever this second sight was.

"How do you know my full name?"

"Your full name isn't Victoria Crane," Theodore scoffed. "It's Victoria Samantha Crane. I know because I had to access your memories in order to let you see."

"See what?"

Theodore stepped aside and flourished his arm, presenting the hippos congregated around the doorway. Victoria looked at me, then at the hippos again, Theodore and then me.

"I think I've finally cracked," she whispered to me.

"If you've cracked then I have too. I can see all of it. Mr. Erickson says that we'll continue to see these things even after we leave him."

"Hippos?"

Theodore rolled his eyes and shook his head.

"Worlds you never knew existed. Oz and Neverland and Wonderland. Wonderland is always through the mirrors. To get to Oz you either have to walk into a rainbow or wait for a storm- the doorways always open up when the air is agitated. Sometimes a good strong wind is enough."

"Let me guess," I said. "To get to Neverland, we have to go to space and find a star."

"That's a common misconception," Theodore corrected. "You get to Neverland via Big Ben in London. And there are thousands of other worlds beside. Menageries and circuses are hidden all over the place. Some worlds have several entrance and exit points, so if you're not careful, you can end up somewhere many miles away from where you started. That's what happened to Agatha Christie. "

His face grew sad.

"Poor Mrs. Christie."

Victoria stepped forward, her eyes lit from within.

"It means we can live the stories that we read in a book in real life, doesn't it?"

Theodore's face brightened.

"And more besides. Be careful, though, not every world is nice. They all have their villains. Neither of you will ever be bored again, though. I can promise you that. Now off with you. I have work to do. I can't spend all day gadding around."

With that, Jezebel and Theodore Erickson entered the shed and closed the door behind them.

"Do you suppose he's telling the truth?" I asked.

"I'm willing to give him the benefit of the doubt," Victoria replied. "After all, a herd of hippos just appeared before my eyes when there had been none."

I nodded.

"So what are we going to do?"

"Find a map or atlas or something and start investigating where these worlds are," Victoria said. "At least the ones that are close. We can keep a journal of our own adventures then."

I stared at her.

"You're serious?"

"Of course, I'm serious. You were the one complaining about being bored! There's still another six weeks of summer left! Let's make the most of it!"

"He said that they were dangerous."

"Driving in cars is dangerous but you still do it," Victoria pointed out. "You've been flashing that stupid card for ages!"

"You're just jealous," I argued, my hand drifting toward my wallet in my back pocket where my driver's license lay.

She rolled her eyes.

"Come on! Don't you see? It'll be even better than reading a book- it will be writing our own and living it!"

A smile twitched my lips. There were always princesses and pretty girls in the stories, guys that could show me how to sword fight, boys who faced giants...

I met Victoria's eyes and grinned.

"Let's go home and find a map."

## About Charles D. Shell

Charles D. Shell is a Virginia native who loves art, books, history, comic books, role-playing, movies and animation. He spent four years in the Army doing Military Intelligence, and recognizes the irony of that title, before going on to graduate from the Joe Kubert School of Comic Art. Now, he spends most of his spare time writing and doing freelance artwork.

"Boneyard Prophet" was conceived one afternoon after watching a show on The Learning Channel about ship and plane boneyards. Charles was fascinated by how much forgotten firepower floats unknown off coastlines or in the middle of deserts. Wondering about the future and how spacefaring civilizations would dispose of their ships when wars ended, he penned Boneyard Prophet. Charles has been a fan of sentient ships since he first read Fred Saberhagen's *Berserker* books many decades ago.

# Boneyard Prophet

## Charles D. Shell

*Cerberus* stood at the watch when the intruder was detected. He'd only taken over the watch from *Warspite* a few weeks earlier and still had several months to go before he handed over to *Hotspur* and returned to sleep.

He hadn't always been named '*Cerberus*' of course. In a former life he was known as Lt. Commander John Wilshire. That had been before the battle that reduced his body to a ruined pulp. Only his brain was salvageable and because of the specific conditions and release he'd signed when he took his officer's oath, his mind was transferred to the electronic crèche and eventually installed into the main control center of the battleship HSBB-114 *Cerberus*.

That had been a hundred lifetimes ago.

"Go to condition one yellow," he said to the primary guardian core computer. The computer was highly advanced but without self-will. All full artificial intelligence engines were patterned after specific human minds, as was *Cerberus*. The core computer went from hibernation mode into a low level of activity and woke the secondary sensors. A single life form, transmitting electromagnetic impulses invaded the outer ring of the Boneyard.

"That's damned odd. Do a diagnostic to make sure that reading is real."

The core computer complied, showing no faults within its system. It was unlikely to have any, considering the high level of self-maintenance built into the facility. The Boneyard orbited the gas giant Reef-8 beyond the obscure, distant yellow dwarf star nestled inside a nebula. It was as 'out-of-the-way' a spot as anywhere outside of the galactic core. The Boneyard was deliberately hidden until needed. The powerful forces within its hyperalloy frame slept until humanity recalled them.

"Send remotes for a visual scan. Scan the system to find its ship."

Sensor waves caressed the Reef solar system, finding only a small, primitive ship against the hull. The tiny craft would—at best—be classified as a ship's launch. It carried no weapons and was in poor condition. It was woefully inadequate for interplanetary flight—forget the impossibility of interstellar travel.

"Where the hell did you come from?" *Cerberus* asked.

The remotes flew through conduits to the outer hull. A tiny figure was visible against the titan construction around it.

"Looks human."

The figure struggled to breathe in his crude spacesuit as he clambered over the massive superstructure between the inner and outer hull. The suit was ill-fitting and appeared to have… extra sleeves? Two extraneous sleeves protruded from beneath the traditional locations and were tied like a belt around the waist. The rest of the configuration of the suit was unfamiliar but appeared to be a variation on a standard life-support design theme.

The two remotes converged on the figure's location. At their sudden appearance, the figure cringed in surprise and shock. Two targeting lasers pointed at the figure's heart.

*Cerberus* challenged the figure in several broadcast methods but he appeared oblivious. Unfortunately, they were in vacuum so no verbal commands would work. Whoever the intruder was, he was pathetic. His spacesuit was a mass of patches from a basic unknown design. No rank or nationality insignia was visible anywhere. The figure tripped and sprawled backward.

"What in the cosmos am I going to do with you?"

He considered for a while. Since communication was presently impossible, protocol dictated that he take the intruder prisoner. The remotes had force-grips, but he'd need to be careful. That suit didn't look like it could take much abuse and if it were ruptured in the vacuum of the outer hull, the prisoner wouldn't be answering any questions, ever again.

Still, he didn't have much choice. Not trusting the remotes to handle such a delicate task, he projected his mind into one of them and carefully adjusted the force-grips to a minimal setting. The invisible beams leapt out and cradled the figure in a web of kinetic power. The figure panicked and flailed around against the grip.

*Cerberus* hoped that he could get to the pressurized area before the fool tore his suit open. The remote shot down the corridors at the maximum safe speed for humans. Much to his relief, he soon had the intruder inside a pressurized airlock. With no need for further delicacy, *Cerberus* sliced the crude spacesuit apart with the force beams. The figure cried out in terror until he'd gulped in a lungful of oxygen.

"Air!" the figure shouted.

"Yes," *Cerberus* said. "The atmosphere here is perfectly balanced for human physiology."

The figure was definitely a human male. However, he appeared rather unhealthy. He had a very low body fat percentage and his hygienic condition left much to be desired. His light brown hair hung in greasy clumps.

The intruder laughed, sounding hysterical.

"I'm alive!"

"And in deep trouble. You've invaded a secure facility of the Terran Hegemony with no authorization."

He laughed again. "I'm here! I'm here!" He danced a weak jig.

"Yes… you're here.

*Cerberus* was baffled by the man's behavior. Clearly, he was deranged. He tried to access the man's internal processors only to discover that he had none! He was completely organic, without the tiniest hint of cybernetics or nanotechnology! He'd piloted a ship without a cybernetic interface?

"What is your name?"

"Alenti-22," he said, laughing more. "I made it!"

"I heard you the first time." *Cerberus* noted that some of the words, accents and sentence structure used by Alenti were distorted. Probably language drift. "Now stop laughing and tell me what you're doing here."

"I'm here to get help from the Great Boneyard!"

"What?"

"This is the Great Boneyard, yes?"

"This is Boneyard Station. Help? Were you in an accident? Did your mothership crash or become disabled?" It would explain some of the situation but not how the primitive ship got so close to Boneyard without detection. "Why wouldn't you call for aid from patrol vessels?"

"I don't know what that is."

Crazy. Stark, raving mad. Poor devil.

"All right, I have to keep you under arrest until we can sort this out. In the meantime, did you need food or medical attention?"

He laughed some more. *Cerberus* mentally shook his head. At least it made for an eventful watch. Hardly anything ever happened at Boneyard since it had been built and filled with the Mothball Fleet.

"This is amazing!" Alenti said to *Cerberus* as he ate a brownie with such gusto that *Cerberus* feared the man would choke. "I've never tasted anything like it!"

"You've never tasted chocolate?"

He held up the brownie. "Chocolate?"

"It's a chocolate brownie."

"It's amazing. May I… may I have another, Boneyard?"

"My name is *Cerberus*. Yes, of course, you can."

The Autochef came out the wall, providing him with an entire plate of the brownies. The medical scanners probed his body as he gorged himself.

"What happened to you?" *Cerberus* said to himself as the medical scanners showed Alenti-22's state. He had borderline malnutrition, bone density loss, no dental care and several mostly-mended broken bones. He had no nanotech symbiotes, no artificial bones or organs, and no internal computers. So far as *Cerberus* was able to determine, he'd never had any medical attention his entire life. That was difficult to comprehend. And he'd never tasted chocolate? *Cerberus* imagined many trends had come and gone since Boneyard had gone online but no chocolate? Seemed unlikely. A vague sense of alarm crept up his electronic spine.

"Alenti, what are you doing here?"

Alenti looked up at the speakers, his mouth covered in chocolate. His reply was incomprehensible.

"Finish chewing or you're going to choke." He felt a little like a mother admonishing a young child.

Alenti washed the brownie down with more lemonade.

"I'm here to supplicate myself before the Great Boneyard. We need you to return and liberate us from the Ulil." He dropped to his knees and did something roughly akin to praying.

Despite the blistering speed of the molecular circuitry containing *Cerberus's* mind, he couldn't answer for nearly fifty seconds.

"Alenti… this is a secure facility for the Terran Hegemony."

He grinned. "Yes, the Great Boneyard. We have kept the faith and knowledge of our forefathers, despite the Ulil. We know of your mighty power."

*Cerberus* took pity on the madman but still, something was wrong here. No pathetic and—somehow entirely organic—madman should have been able to get within a million klicks of Boneyard Station undetected. Its sensors could sweep the entire solar system.

"Let's take this from the top, Alenti."

"Alenti-22."

"Alenti-22. Why do you have a numerical designation? What's your last name?"

"Family names are forbidden by the Ulil."

"I don't recognize that name. Who are the Ulil?"

Alenti stared at the ceiling in shock.

"The Ulil are… are the masters. They control us all."

*Cerberus* felt the alarm increase.

"That name has no significance in my linguistic databanks except as a partial Islamic name."

"Islamic? What's that?"

"It… it's a major human religion."

"Oh."

"You've never heard of Islam?"

"No. I have some friends who are Christo-Revivalists. I pretend to be so that the Ulil won't kill us."

"And you are what?"

He laughed. "I'm of the Boneyard Pilgrims, of course!"

"Of course." *Cerberus* initiated a diagnostic scan of the Boneyard Station to check battle-worthiness. The madman kept saying things that didn't make complete sense, but the gist was disturbing.

"You test me?"

"No. Are you saying the Ulil are a religious faction that has taken control of the Hegemony?"

His staring eyes indicated Alenti's cluelessness.

"Okay, other than 'the masters' what are the Ulil?"

Alenti struggled with the question.

"Let's start with what they look like."

"Oh, well they're a little taller than humans, red-skinned with bigger eyes, four arms and then there are the tendrils around their heads…"

"It's an alien race?"

"Yes." He pointed in the direction his suit had been taken. "I used one of their spacesuits."

*Cerberus* examined the data from the analysis done with the suit. It was a retrofitted design whose original owner had some very odd dimensions. None of the design protocols were recognizable. The computer code inside the microprocessors was completely alien. The evidence was enough that *Cerberus* went into level two yellow alert mode. Long-dormant machinery connected with the Mothball Fleet to raise them from hibernation into standby mode.

"How did you get here?"

"Your machines grabbed me."

"Before that. How did your ship get here?"

"I used the navigation computer and it brought me here."

*Cerberus* rallied his patience.

"Your approach was undetected. How did you avoid the station sensor web?"

Alenti's eyes stared in incomprehension again.

"Never mind. Did you come from a mothership?"

"Umm… yes, I think. I came from the Ulil base."

"Base?"

"Yes. The one that sits next to the other big planet. Uncle called 'em gas giants."

"There's a hostile alien base orbiting around the next innermost gas giant?"

"Umm… yes?"

*Cerberus* accessed the sensor web and saturated Reef-7 with deep, detailed scans. No artificial satellites or ships were detected.

"There's nothing there."

"It's gone?"

"There's no evidence there was *ever* anything there, Alenti."

"I don't understand."

"Neither do I." *Cerberus* very much wanted to dismiss Alenti as a simple lunatic, but the fact of his appearance indicated something was very, *very* wrong. Could it be some kind of unscheduled readiness or security test? They'd happened occasionally but nothing like this.

Alenti slumped over the table, his eyes fluttering.

"Are you well? Do you require medical attention?"

"I'm sleepy."

*Cerberus* guided him to one of the sealed guest rooms and placed a remote outside as a guard. He used the time to analyze what was going on. He spun up the Q-comm and sent a detailed report of the intrusion to the closest naval base. The response was to be expected—they were sending a patrol ship to take the man into custody and start an investigation. They acted as if he was familiar to them but didn't elaborate.


"Are you refreshed?" *Cerberus* asked as Alenti exited his room.

"I'm sorry I fell asleep. That was the most food I've ever had at one time."

"You're highly malnourished. Breakfast awaits you. I would suggest eating slower."

Alenti dug into the synthesized rations as if they were a royal feast. Perhaps to him, they were. When his eating slowed, *Cerberus* resumed the conversation.

"These Ulil, how did they make you slaves?"

"It was the Great War. They surprised all the ancestors and broke all of their great weapons before they could fight back properly."

"Surprised?" *Cerberus* considered the concept. It was quite difficult to achieve surprise in space warfare, due to its nature. The best a fleet could hope for was to hide the occasional ship as an asteroid or similar debris. Surprise on a large scale was impossible.

No, not impossible—merely unknown.

"How did they surprise them?"

"I don't know. They're real sneaky, though."

"Are you suggesting that they're hiding their presence from me in this system?"

"I don't know. Maybe."

"So you escaped from them and came here?"

"Yes. It took a long, *long* time to get slaves here who were of the faith. It took even longer to figure out how to use the Ulilkish machines and then come up with a plan. We fixed up one of the old ships they had in the station and then the computer tenders made them blind for a while so I could come here."

It had a faint air of plausibility to it. *Cerberus* dearly wanted to send a sortie over to Reef-7 to see if sensors could burn through any countermeasures they might have. But his authority to do such things was limited by the alert status and he still didn't have the justification to go to a red alert. Also, the reply he'd gotten from the navy had passed all authentication protocols. How did he reconcile the two?

"To tell you the truth, Alenti, I'm not sure what to think."

"My faith is strong. You need merely test it."

"That won't be necessary."

The patrol ship *Red Wolf* appeared on the Boneyard's sensor displays as it sped in-system. *Cerberus* checked the registry to see if it matched with his database. It was a legitimate patrol destroyer. He hailed it.

"This is HSBB-114 *Cerberus* calling. Please identify yourself."

A clean-cut male human with commander insignia appeared on the commlink. He smiled.

"This is Commander Chanville of the patrol destroyer *Red Wolf*. We request docking with Boneyard Station."

"Please authenticate." The electronic data was compared. Everything checked out.

"Request granted. I'll guide you in."

"Thank you, *Cerberus*."

The *Wolf* coasted into orbit, matching with the approach vectors. Just to be sure, he activated some of the station weapon pods and tracked it. Nothing seemed amiss.

"Care to tell me who my visitor is, commander?"

He smiled. "Ah. Well, I'm afraid he's one of a number of crazy colonists who splintered from the Hegemony long ago. They don't believe in cybernetic modification and have been backsliding for decades. Apparently a few of them got it in their heads that you were some kind of 'holy pilgrimage' or some other such nonsense. It looks like one of them finally decided to go to their holy site."

*Cerberus* relaxed a little.

"How did he get to the station? He slipped right through our sensor net."

The commander frowned. "We're still trying to figure that out. It looks like we might have either a serious malfunction or serious security breach."

Quite an understatement!

"Are you going to follow up?"

"Naturally. They've already dispatched maintenance ships here. We're not really equipped to handle this."

"Thank you. Of course, you realize this means I have to double-check all security measures. You don't object, do you?"

"Of course not. You'd be derelict in your duty if you didn't." He glanced to his left. "Fifteen minutes to dock. Please have your prisoner ready for transfer."

"I will." He paused. "Ever hear of something called the Ulil?"

The commander shook his head. "No alien race I've ever heard of. Why?"

"No reason. I'll have the prisoner ready for you."


"You're… you're giving me to them?" Alenti asked. His face showed complete devastation.

"They'll take care of you. You need more help than I can give you."

Tears rolled down his cheeks.

"But… so many died! We may never get another chance! They'll kill me!"

"They won't kill you. You just need some help."

"I *came* here for help! We need *your* help! Why do you forsake us?"

"I'm not…"

"Do not forsake us!" Alenti dropped to his knees. "Oh please, mighty Boneyard, bring us deliverance!"

The remotes escorted him down the corridor.


The boarding hatch on the *Red Wolf* opened, disgorging Commander Chanville and a pair of Marines.

"Welcome aboard, commander."

"Thank you." Chanville looked from side to side. "Where's our prisoner?"

"I'm having him brought up. He had a few medical problems, and I was making sure he was in fit shape to transport."

"Yes, well, thank you."

"My pleasure. Want something to drink while you're here?" A hovering sphere came up with a dispenser on top. Lights bathed the three of them from its mechanism and a spigot hovered there.

"No thank you."

"Here he comes. Please be gentle, I think the poor fellow is deranged. He hasn't got a speck of cybernetics in him, either. What colony is this that they come from?"

"They call it New Gaia."

"Nothing named that in my databanks."

"It used to be called Cradle. They changed it when the new religion took over."

"Ah. I suppose you can update my records when the maintenance team gets here."

"I would imagine."

The remotes brought up Alenti-22 to the Marines. He looked terrified. The remotes held him in their invisible grip, and his face went through several changes, finally settling on resignation. He slumped in their grip.

"I'm releasing him now."

The remotes dispelled their force grips, and Alenti stumbled forward into the arms of the Marines. With shocking speed, he grabbed at the holster of the nearest Marine, pulling out the gauss pistol and leveling it at the captain. The second Marine brought his pistol up just as Alenti shouted: "Let my sacrifice be enough to awaken you!"

The gauss needles tore through Alenti's body, sending him to the deck in a spray of blood and other internal fluids.

"Are the three of you all right?" *Cerberus* asked as medical remotes rushed to the scene.

"Y-yes… I think we're all fine. It's just good that my corporal was as quick on the trigger as he was."

"I'm so sorry. He showed no sign of being violent before now." The medical remotes swarmed over Alenti-22, who lay in a pool of widening blood. "Damn stupid of me."

"Will he make it?" Chanville asked.

"I'm not sure. Your Marine was pretty efficient."

"Just as well. If he'd gotten a chance to use that pistol, it would probably be me on the ground."

"Yes. He didn't use chocolate rounds, did he?"

"I... no, I don't think so."

"That's good. Don't know if I could treat chocolate wounds."

"Yes. They're terrible."

"You know what else is terrible?"

"Hmm?"

The force grips curled around the three uniformed humans in painful grips. At the same time, *Cerberus's* electronic systems invaded the *Red Wolf* through the docking ring connections.

"Your acting."

Inside the *Red Wolf*, the façade was revealed. Several red-skinned aliens that *Cerberus* could only assume were Ulil sat at the controls of an alien craft reconfigured to resemble a *Dauntless* class destroyer. They tried to activate their outside communications, but the invasion was so fast and so efficient that they were quickly rendered deaf, dumb and blind.

As the prisoners were taken to holding cells and Alenti was taken to sick bay, the battleship christened *Cerberus* decided that it needed a look outside in a hurry. Instead of cycling the giant dock doors, the nuclear clearing charges blew, blasting megatons of hyperalloy doors out into space, followed mere seconds later by the miles-long bulk of *Cerberus*.

"Holy shit!" *Cerberus* said. Space was alive with alien transmissions and sensor contacts the second he burst out of Boneyard Station. Two alien ships of a light cruiser class engaged him. His shields shrugged off the primaries of the lighter craft, and he blasted them to component atoms within thirty seconds. They were mere distractions. His focus was the massive alien space station that orbited 'above' the pole of the next innermost gas giant. Energy signatures indicated that multiple warships were powering up for battle. The tonnage was impressive, but they'd been caught flat-footed. Before they could deploy, the *Cerberus* tore the guts out of every ship at dock in a single pass. A few survivors were detected further out-system, but they were accelerating away far too fast for *Cerberus* to catch them.

They were doubtless fleeing to inform the Ulil of their failure.


Alenti-22's eyes flickered open. He was wrapped in a mesh of pain-dampeners.

"How do you feel, Alenti?" *Cerberus* asked.

"I… do not feel much. What has happened?"

"I turned that Ulil fleet into scrap. I left the main station alone except for weapons and communications. You said there are other slaves on there?"

"Yes, many hundreds." Tears rolled down his cheeks.

"All right. I'll get them off there."

"Thank you, *Cerberus* spirit."

"You're welcome."

"How did you know?"

"That they were lying? First off, when I mentioned 'Ulil' he said it was no alien race he'd ever heard of—but I never said they were an alien race. Second, I did a medical scan of them with the fake drink dispenser machine. They had cybernetics, but they were non-military and looked to have been installed within the last 24 hours. Third, when you grabbed that pistol—which I wasn't expecting—he seemed to think that you could use it, but all military sidearms have been coded to a single user for centuries. He should have been in no danger whatsoever."

"Oh."

"And he didn't know what chocolate was."

Alenti smiled.

"There's a problem, though. Your body was shredded by that gauss pistol. I don't have a complete medical bay—only a rudimentary one for emergencies. I'm keeping you alive only by a miracle right now. By the time I can get the hospital ships online... it will be too late."

"Oh," Alenti smiled again. "That's all right. You needed a sacrifice."

"I... yes, I suppose I did."

Boneyard Station had been established after the Terran Hegemony's last great war. The fleet of sentient, incalculably-powerful ships might be needed again someday, but the nervous citizens of the Hegemony feared to have them constantly awake and patrolling their peaceful space. So they'd been mothballed in the hidden system of Reef to await a future call to battle.

Fear over such potential power had made Boneyard Station into a paranoid's dream. Multiple layers of defense and security wrapped the Mothball Fleet like a blanket. The Ulil had found the encrypted keys to the security of the outer station and instead of risking rousing the fleet to awareness had merely fed the interior false data for uncounted ages. They could have used the ruse to launch a massive sneak attack, but the station and ships were so powerful and resilient that it was quite possible even an antimatter bombardment wouldn't have fully destroyed them—and anything less would have been akin to wakening a hive of killer bees. Instead, they merely made sure the station and ships slept away while mankind became broken slaves.

"They painted a fake, sunny sky and we fell for it," *Cerberus* told Alenti. "I'm so sorry."

"Sorry? I was the one who grabbed his gun."

"Not for that. We failed humanity. How many generations have the Terran worlds been under Ulil rule?"

"I trace my line back ten generations."

"We have failed you." Shame burned his circuitry like acid. "But perhaps... I might at least save you."

"But you said…"

"I said I can't save your body. I might be able to save your mind. I was once like you until I was grievously wounded. They transferred my mind into the *Cerberus*. If you want… I can do the same for you."

"I… think I would like that."


*Cerberus* patrolled the outer system while the Boneyard Station came to life. Over twelve thousand of humanity's deadliest warships woke to a long-delayed reveille. A few sorties had been tried by Ulil ships, only to end up smashed and gutted in space.

Humanity's fleet was *angry*. Their fury practically radiated through the vacuum.

"He's amazing," *Cerberus* said to his fellow battleship *Warspite* as they patrolled.

"Who?"

"Alenti-22. He took off in a jury-rigged ship across an interplanetary distance, hoping that the people back on the station could cover his flight long enough to get here. It was a week's flight, and he barely understood how to fly at all. If the navigation system had failed, he would have died drifting in space. Then he climbs into the hull of a station in a patched alien spacesuit, hoping for salvation."

"Brass balls," *Warspite* agreed. "Did the *Mercy* manage to save his brain?"

"Yes. It was a close call until she came online but she's a good hospital ship. The only question is which ship do we put him in and what do we name it."

"How about the battleship *Cyclops*? The AI failed on that one long ago, but it's in outstanding shape, otherwise."

"Yes, I think I shall. It'll need a rename, though." He consulted the ship nomenclature. "I think we should christen it the *Marathon*. No human has ever run so far as Alenti did to bring more vital news."

His twelve thousand, six hundred fellow ships agreed as they prepared to liberate a long-suffering humanity.

## ABOUT MARIJA STAJIC:

Marija Stajic won the 2013 Undiscovered Voices Fellowship of The Writer's Center. She has a BA in literature from the University of Nis (Serbia), and an MA in international journalism from American University. She studied fiction at the George Washington University and the Writer's Center, and playwriting at HB Studios in New York City. She wrote a blog and worked for the *New Yorker* magazine as fact-checker, translator and cultural consultant. Her fiction has been published in the *Doctor T. J. Eckleburg Review*, *South 85*, *Gargoyle*, *Epiphany*, *Lunch Ticket*, *Inertia* and another dozen literary journals, and in *Defying Gravity*, a collection of short stories. She is also a travel writer and an author of three collections of poetry in Serbian. The short story, "Refugee and Her Book of Secrets," represents a powerful, complete segment of Stajic's newly finished novel of the same name.

# REFUGEE AND HER BOOK OF SECRETS

## Marija Stajic

11:00am, June 28, 1914

Sarajevo, Bosnia, Austro-Hungarian Empire

*Two shots, both deadly.*
*Long live Yugoslavia.*
*Before the cyanide eats my mind, my last unknown wish.*
*This gun belongs to Petrovic family.*
*Let no man defy it.*
*It's theirs for eternity.*

- Gavrilo Princip

# REFUGEE AND HER BOOK OF SECRETS

March 26, 1999
Nis, Serbia, Yugoslavia

When the bombs break the earth, it feels like your house is coming down on your head. And on your family. And you thought you were so young and had your whole life ahead of you. And the fact that you never left Serbia didn't matter because there was so much time ahead. And the fact that you only studied and dated stupid boys. And all of a sudden, with a pilot's hand movement, with some muscle and joint contraction, with a screech of release and a smell of burnt metal, there is a whistle in the air above your head, and you're ticking the rest of your life away listening to that whistle growing meaner and louder. And the fear is unlike any fear you have ever felt before, any fear you ever read about in a book. And you don't even care anymore if God exists or not, if there's heaven or an afterlife or reincarnation. You just want to live.

And when your house shakes from foundation to roof, and the crystal chandeliers swing viciously, and the glass and porcelain break, and your great grandmother's armoire that stood in the same spot for a century slides toward you, you wonder if you're still alive. And when you feel your heart is fighting to break out of your chest and jump and run and hide, and you're all drenched in sweat and tears, and your mother is pulling her hair out like in those heroic epic poems you studied in school, and your father is on his knees peering out of a broken window, you realize you are still alive. Then you hear another whistle. Groundhog day. And even if your sweaty palms are on your ears, you still hear men and women and children screaming in the streets, you hear cats, and babies and dogs wailing alike, and cars starting and someone swearing at Christopher Columbus, and at someone's fucking American mother, and at Milosevic's mother, and you hear doors slamming, and someone's running.

Then the lights go out everywhere. A whole new layer of terror. And then you think if you're still alive, you won't be for much longer. And this must be how the grave looks like from the inside. Then you hear seconds in your head, filled with lead like bombs, but they seem like minutes now. Then like hours. And suddenly everything is silent. And you're thinking, this is it, I'm dead. It wasn't too bad; it didn't hurt too much. Until you hear a siren. But you don't know what it means, because when in your twenty years of life did you ever hear a siren; it's not like they teach sirens in school. And when a neighbor chants: "Curfew over," and his voice is first louder then fainter, and then the lights go on again, on the street, then in the house, and you see your mother weeping. And your father grabs your shoulders and asks you, 'Ana, are you are okay?' And his hands are bloody, but you can't speak. And your mother hugs you so tight that you can barely breathe. And then she releases you, and you see her mouth move, but you can't hear her.

March 29, 1999
Nis, Serbia, Yugoslavia

As the end-of-curfew siren, *Smirela*, went off in the morning, Mira called the doctor who had treated Ana since she was born, and Mira since she was born, and her mother Nada since she was pregnant with Mira.

"Ana terrifies me more than bombs," she said. "She's not eating, she's not sleeping, she's not crying, she doesn't talk, but she keeps whispering *New York, New York*. What's wrong with her?"

"Have you tried giving her mild sedatives?"

"Yes. She sleeps for hours, then when they wear off, she's back doing the same thing. Like a parrot. And I don't want to turn my child into a junkie."

"When did it start?" he asked.

"That first night those NATO Satans bombed the hell out of the Tobacco Factory and the Concentration Camp. You know how close we are to those places. It sounded, I swear, as it were in our backyard. We all thought we were going to die. I remember thinking, at least we were all together. We would all go together wherever dead people go," Mira said.

"Any chance you could take her away, out of here?"

"Take her where? I'm not a bird."

"I don't know. Out of Serbia, anywhere? I hear people are applying by mail for refugee visas for the United States. I know it's a long shot, but it's worth a try."

"Miodrag, tell me for God's sake, what is wrong with my daughter?"

"Post-traumatic stress disorder. She's too fragile to deal with the proximity and likelihood of death. In layman's terms, she's having a nervous breakdown. Knowing her well, I think she would most likely be fine if you take her out of…"

"Hello? Hello?"

The line went numb. Static.

Mira dropped the phone on the carpet, walked into the bedroom and checked on Ana, who slept drugged. Mira covered her with a blanket, then went straight into the post office.

The closest post office was closed, even though there was an *OPEN* sign fluttering in the draft. Someone had forgotten to tape over the windows, and now they were shattered. So Mira went to another one, then another one. All closed. They lived in Nis, and the U.S. Embassy was in Belgrade. That could be a dangerous three-hour trip just to "kiss" the Embassy's door. No shelters on the highway, no place to duck or hide.

When the telephone lines were restored two days later, Mira called the U.S. Embassy. She called about a hundred times until she finally got through to an assistant who told her which documents to send and where to send them.

"What if I can't get all these college transcripts, birth certificates, paystubs, house title? Most offices are not open; God knows when they'll be," she said.

"Just send what you can," the young male voice said, in Serbian. "Do your best, and…good luck. You are going to need it. We all are."

For days, as bombs fell like black snow, Mira rummaged through her desks and cabinets, looking for life-saving pieces of paper. She didn't want to tell Ana what she was planning unless she got visas. She didn't want to give her false hope.

"Joca, do we have enough money to pay for three plane tickets and to eat for a while until we find jobs there?" she asked her husband.

"No way. You two should go. I'll stay, look after the house. Besides, I don't speak English. What would I do in America? I'm too old for that; I would rather die in my own house than clean someone's toilet at 55," he said.

Mira spent the few curfew-less hours of every day walking from a government building to the post office and back, hoping something would be open. No one answered phones in Serbia anymore unless they needed something themselves. She had everything she needed for Ana, but not for herself. She couldn't find her own birth certificate. She couldn't get another issued for God knows how many months. Even when Serbia wasn't at war, the bureaucracy moved at turtle speed.

So she packed all the documents she had for both of them in a long, sealed envelope and waited in front of the post office for days until a day came that she knew it would be open. It was the day Slobodan Milosevic announced on TV that Serbs should go back to their jobs despite the fighter planes hovering day and night. "Defiance," he said. "Defiance will save us. We're the Serbs; we're heavenly people. We're a nation older than the United States. Serbia was an Empire while the illiterate Indians roamed America with bows and arrows and Christopher Columbus's great grandfather wasn't even born. Pride and spite, that's what Serbs are all about. Let's show that third-rate sax player that we will never be afraid of his invisible planes."

Then he ordered people to return to work or be fired.

Mira ran to the post office a few hours after that televised speech, and it was open.

There was nobody else waiting in the line.

"What's so urgent that it cannot wait until this fucking war ends?" a female postal worker in her 50's with budding mustaches asked.

"I have to mail these documents urgently. It's a matter of life and death," Mira said, tears building in the corners of her eyes.

The woman placed her large, oval glasses, hanging on a string around her neck, back on her nose. A piece of duct tape fastening its right stem indented the woman's cheek. She didn't seem to mind.

"U. S. Embassy Belgrade?" the woman asked rhetorically, and looked at Mira through her glasses, her eyes magnified.

"What are you, an American spy?" she hissed.

Mira wanted to tell her to mind her own business, do her job and let her get back to her daughter. But she knew this woman, if infuriated, would be capable of throwing Mira's envelope in the trash after she left, thus drowning all of Mira's hopes.

"God forbid," Mira said.

"What is it then? What do you have to send to the Yankees *so urgently* despite the fact they are dropping bombs on our heads?" the woman asked, propping her hairy chin on her elbowed fist, fingers covered in golden rings.

"My niece is in America; I'm trying to find out where she is and get her back. My sister is worried sick. They lost touch when this NATO aggression started." It was the best lie Mira could come up with at the spot. She looked at the woman's face. The postal worker scanned Mira for a few more moments as if deciding whether she would do her job or if she was just in too shitty of a mood to stamp the envelope and throw it into an empty metal bin, marked Belgrade.

"That will be 142 dinars," she said. "Unless you want it express. Then it's 205."

"Express, please. How long will it take?"

"Ask Clinton. Depends on how often he bombs our trucks. Before the war, it would take a day."

Mira paid the money, thanked the woman who chewed on her cuticles then spat them out in the air, and ran out of there as soon as she saw her envelope in the Belgrade bin.

~ ~ ~ ~ ~

A week later a yellow envelope arrived stamped "urgent." The blue-inked U.S. Embassy stamp was in its sender corner.

Mira handled it as if expensive crystal was inside, sat on the sofa, and placed it on her lap.

Joca was at work. Ana asleep.

She sighed and unbent the little metal clasp.

Both of their passports were there. She opened Ana's first. There it was, a single entry refugee visa. A sigh of relief. Then she opened hers. Nothing. It was empty. Her knees shook.

She began reading the typed letter with the U.S. Embassy letterhead and blue stamp.

"We're sorry to inform you that only Ana Petrovic's visa has been approved. Mira Petrovic could apply again when she provides us with the following forms...

Then there was a list of forms. Three, four. It could take a year to get them all. If ever.

The paper fell on the floor. The beginning-of-curfew siren, *Sizela*, sounded another black downpour.

~ ~ ~ ~ ~

"Ana, honey, please wake up." Mira brushed Ana's shoulder. Then she moved Ana's hair from her face.

"What is it? Let me sleep."

"Ana, you need to pack," Mira said, and with the word "pack," as if with a dangerous, cursed, forbidden word, her throat clenched, closed, it was hard for her to swallow her own saliva.

Ana grunted, moved the rest of her hair from her eyes and face and propped herself up on her elbows.

"Pack? What are you talking about?"

Mira tried to speak, explain, but she couldn't. Instead, tears ran down her cheeks in creeks, mute. She gasped for air. The air that smelled of torched metal.

"Mama, why are you crying?"

~ ~ ~ ~ ~

"Ana, have you packed the antibiotics, pain-killers and B6 Vitamin? C too, Vitamin C? I don't know what kind of health care they have in America. And food, have you packed your *Eurokrem* and *Plazma keks* and *Jaffa*? God knows when you'll be able to eat those again, and you love them." Mira's voice was muffled as if she had been recovering from bronchitis.

"I think they probably have food and medicine in Washington, mama. I'm not going to Africa," Ana said.

Nis, Serbia, March 1999

Ana melted into Ruza's round, soft 72-year-old body. Ruza's hair wasn't red anymore; it was as white and fragile as a spider web. It smelled of freshly ironed linen.

"Let me look at you," Ruza said, gently pushing Ana's shoulders away from her own. She sighed. "Like looking in the mirror 50 years ago." Then she grabbed Ana again, her thick hands and dry skin gripping Ana's shoulder blades. Then she kissed her long, red hair.

A few seconds later, Ruza gently broke the embrace, took Ana's hand and led her into the living room.

"Sit," she said. "Are you hungry?"

"No, Nana, I'm fine," Ana said as the musty armchair swallowed her. The room was stuffy as always, all the windows tightly closed to avoid the infamous Serbian killer draft. Ruza sat on the sofa, slowly and with difficulty, her bones popping like dry wood, still holding Ana's hand. The sofa springs released rusty, metal-to-metal noise.

"You're leaving tomorrow, my son tells me?" Ruza asked, her voice suddenly deeper and raspier.

"Tomorrow."

Ruza withdrew her hand, letting go of Ana's. Then she looked down at both her hands, twirling her scratched, faded wedding ring on her right ring finger.

"I'm never going to see you again," she said, her eyes glistening over.

"Of course, you are, Nana," Ana said in a soft voice, placing her hand on her grandmother's shoulder for a few seconds.

"I know you kids. America is so far away. And this country…and this family alike…cursed," Ruza said, lifting her palm and cupping her forehead, shaking her head *no*.

"Nana, I will come back, I promise."

"Yeah, for my funeral." Ruza's small eyes, deep in their sockets, shone. She pulled a yellowish hanky out of her wool cardigan pocket and wiped her face. Her skin turned red, blotched, her wrinkles deepened.

"Then don't die, wait for me to come back."

"A part of me is happy you're leaving Serbia. There're no damn wars in America, and I even heard women are human beings there, not housekeepers and wet nurses. But that other part…"

"Nana, I'll come back to see you, if you promise me two things."

"What? That I won't die? That's God's business. I can promise to try. What else?"

Ana swallowed saliva audibly.

"Why do you say we're cursed?"

Ruza let go of Ana's hand once again. Then she looked down at the worn out carpet under her wool slippers.

"You sure you're not hungry?"

"Mama and grandma Nada both said to ask you, that you have every little family secret written down? Is that true?"

"Loudmouths," Ruza whispered, resting her index finger on the tip of her nose and floating her eyes around her living room. "Do you want some Turkish coffee and delight? My neighbor brought me some. I think it's rose flavored. How original. But with my high blood sugar…"

"Nana, you must give me that book. I'm scared to death, and I feel…I need it if I'm going to make it in America alone." Ana got up from the armchair and looked at the black and white photo of her late grandfather, Svetomir, staring down at the two of them from the wall.

"If you give it to me, I will never be alone. I will never hear the bombs again. Instead, I'll hear you."

Ruza stayed put, sinking her shoulders deeper into the sofa, white lace doilies behind her head, framing it like halos.

"Those stories aren't pretty," Ruza said.

"Perhaps. But, I need them. Your farewell gift to me?"

As she headed out of the living room and into the kitchen, Ana turned her head.

"And I heard something about a gun?"

Ruza propped herself on her elbows, jerked her neck. It popped. She looked at Ana, with her blotchy, blood-shot eyes.

"You know about the gun?"

Nis, Serbia, March 1999

A stone had lodged inside Ana's chest the moment her mother told her she was the only one going to the United States. The only one.

It didn't make sense, Ana thought, if she were indeed cursed, that she would be able to escape it. But it made sense that her whole family had to stay behind in Serbia to pay for God knows whose sins. And who cursed them, and why? She clenched the gray-bound notebook her grandmother Ruza, the family's queen bee, reluctantly gave up.

Growing up, Ana heard relatives whisper around Ruza, saw them walking around her as if on ice, curtsy to her as if she were royalty. They whispered about her unusual red hair, her ability to read people's minds, to see into the past and future.

When Ana asked her mother Mira about it, she would say: "I don't believe in such things. Neither should you."

When she asked her grandmother Nada about it, she said: "You should ask your grandmother Ruza."

And when Ana finally grew the courage to ask her grandmother Ruza, she replied: "None of you can keep secrets from me. And that's all I have to say about that."

So Ana wrapped the book into a winter scarf, then into a plastic bag, and placed it in her backpack. A good read for the long journey ahead.

~ ~ ~ ~ ~

"Ana, please bring these herbal teas from *Gorchintzi*. There's one for everything—a sore throat, heartburn, menstrual cramps, anemia, immunity."

"Yes, mama. I'm sure they've heard of teas in Washington."

"I don't know. Maybe their land is polluted."

"And ours isn't? If you haven't noticed, we have bombs falling into our meadows and fields. One thing our teas would be good for is anemia."

Ana tried to blink away tears she could feel coating her eyeballs. She looked at the clock. Her bus to Budapest airport was at 3 pm. It was 2:15. The time was ticking by so fast it was though it had been fast-forwarded.

"And here's your passport, and money."

"Money? What are the two of you going to live on?" Ana asked.

"Don't you worry about us. We'll be just fine. You're the one leaving home for the first time, alone." Mira got down on her knees, bowing forward, resting her forehead one her white Turkish carpet.

Ana felt as if she had swallowed a rock. It was right where men had their Adam's apple, but it was bigger and sharper. Tears began rolling down her nostrils. Her temples were stuffed with lead. Her head hurt.

"That's it, I won't go," she said.

"No!" Mira yelled. "You're going! It's the best thing that could have happened to us." Mira lifted her swollen face and wiped it with her black dress.

~ ~ ~ ~ ~

It never occurred to Ana how much it would all hurt until she boarded that bus in Nis, looking at her mother's face through that dirty window, Mira's blue eyes drowning, her whole body trembling as if she had a fever. Ana couldn't even cry. She felt her head was clogged, her tear ducts shut. She wished she could; she wanted to cry so badly, both for her mother, her grandmothers and herself. She wanted to dislodge those knots she had in her chest and stomach, destroy them, and spit them out.

Her father was smart. He stayed in the car. He hugged and kissed her from the driver's seat, pushed another hundred dollar bill into her sweaty palms and said: "You two take your time, I have to move the car."

Ever since she graduated from college Ana thought there was nothing she wanted more than to leave Serbia. She was certain she would be deliriously happy if it happened. It never occurred to her that she would want to crawl back into a corner of her house and pull a blanket over her head, or that she would have a sharp-edged stone floating up and down her internal organs, cutting them, one by one, into tiny little pieces.

And now she had an urge to escape that bus to Budapest more than Serbia. She wanted, oh so much, to dig her nails into the velvety seat in front of her, pull herself out of her seat, and run as fast as she could, tripping over people's oversized bags in the aisle. But she somehow felt chained to that seat, smelling of cigarettes and fresh vomit, with *Ceca's* turbo-folk music coming from small circular speakers above her.

She opened her backpack, pulled the book out, and placed it on her knees. It was so old and dirty, with coffee circles on its leather cover, torn pages like winter leaves, eaten by moths and God knows what other kinds of creatures throughout the years. It was crinkled and smelled like her grandmother's hair. It looked as if it had been wet many times over, and dried many times before.

## ABOUT JOSEPH SWINK:

When he's not busy at his day job, Joseph Swink divides his time equally between taking classes at the local community college, reading, and writing; and it is his dream to write professionally. Joseph is from a rural farming community, and grew up learning the value of hard work and simple living. He writes narratives involving whimsical, flighty subject matters realized through grounded, down-to-earth imagery, characters, and settings.

# CALL ME HOME

## Joseph Swink

The wind howled as it catapulted through the trellises of Wendigo Bridge, lifting the fresh loose powder from the trellis cross-members and whispering it down onto the shivering form of Eleanor Rigby. She watched as her breath lifted itself above and away, into the gray opaque of early January, and shuddered against the biting cold that locked her bones tightly in her frame. She searched her mind, trying to remember why she was sitting on the worn wooden park bench, splintered with age and weathered with experience, looking up at gray clouds and oblique fog drifts that banked down the steep incline towards the Wendigo River. Her eyes, watering against the sharp chill, searched her surroundings, and traced along the blurred edges of the bridge itself, which frowned a mouthful of wood-and-metal teeth, drooling rust along its down-turned scowl. Her loneliness shook shivers through her back.

"Are you lost, Mom?" She started, half expecting that it was the hulking bridge that had spoken, then turned as quickly as her chilled rack would allow her, letting her neck do the bulk of the pivoting and casting a bleary eye over her shoulder at the man standing behind her. "Are you lost? It's just that you know it's awful cold out here for a lady to be sitting." The man smiled warmly, thawing Eleanor, and she stood. His face was kind and drooped around its border with age and weariness. She glanced from his pronounced chin, peppered with fresh gray stubble, up, past lips that sagged below their smile, to his nose, wide with flaring nostrils, and stopping at his eyes. She marveled at them. The man looked the visage of septuagenarians, yet his eyes were pools of azure, flecked with the fire of youth, and ablaze with the intensity of the youngest of stars. There was something familiar in them, welcoming perhaps, something that she recognized in her recognizer, but couldn't put into words.

"I'm Eleanor," she spoke, then added, "Have we met?" She raised the last syllable into the peak of a question, incredulous, yet somehow comfortable in assuming that they had.

He chuckled, "Who could say, Mom. One meets lots of folks along the way." His voice stayed steady, a calm that seemed to Eleanor to start in his eyes, and radiate through him until the abundance flowed over into words on the cold morning air.

She smiled despite her incredulity, warm even amidst the nipping blasts of arctic air, "I'm sure I know you from somewhere... Don't you have a name?"

"No, Mom. I don't suppose that I do."

"What?" Her question surprised her, and he looked sideways through a slanted glance, tucking the corners of his eyes in as if to give his answer speed.

"They call me lots of things, see. Nothing in particular these days, just lots of things that I go by, but I don't have a proper name, no, Mom."

"So what is it that they call you then?" She was visibly amazed at the conversation and had forgotten her forgetting, even forgotten the cold chill that stuck on her from all sides.

He raised an eyebrow at this, smiling and flashing large blue orbs, now perfectly round in their cases. "My Momma called me 'Home' so I suppose if you like, you can call me 'Home' too."

Eleanor let out an unexpected giggle, punctuated by a throaty snort. "What kind of name is that?"

His face pulled in flat, and he glanced down at her; "It's a name, like any other. Like the man said, 'What's in a name,' and like I say, you can call a man a many great manner of things and never change him one inch up or down."

"I suppose." She regarded his response and then shivered once more, her eyes now drawn to Home's scarf; a particularly bright crimson thing made of wool and wrapped loosely around his neck, it clashed in vivid contrast with the gray day that rose around them.

As if he had heard her thoughts, Home quickly offered, "It was a gift. Isn't it lovely?"

"Quite," Eleanor nodded, wishing she had one of her own to fix between her and the sharp breeze that threatened to split her asunder. She pulled her eyes away from the scarf, back to the eyes, so familiar in an "it's on the tip of my tongue" kind of way, they taunted her like a song that you remember the tune to, but can't recall the words.

"Perhaps a walk, to warm our spirits?" Home asked hopefully, his brow arching above the blue pools of slipped memory and, holding his hand out to Eleanor, added: "Join me, Mom?" She hesitated but politely accepted, allowing him to take her pale hand in his own.

"You know..." Eleanor started, looking around knowingly, but then she seemed to lose her train of thought.

"What's that?"

"Nothing, it's just that I was remembering something that happened around here, but I can't for the life of me recall what it was. And it was just right there, you know, but now it slipped my mind." A slight anxiety was easing into her eyes, and she stopped for a moment on the path.

"Don't worry, Mom, it'll come back to you, no reason to fret now." Home spoke with certainty and reassured Eleanor. "Say, why don't you tell me a little about yourself? Maybe that will open up those pesky memories?"

Eleanor considered it, mulling over the stories of her past as she began walking again behind Home. They were heading away from the river now, up a small hill that she was sure she remembered, but perhaps only from a dream. "I have a son. Jude Rigby, named after his-" her voice caught hard in her throat, stealing away the words there and melting them into salt streams from the corners of her eyes. She blinked the ghost of grief away and swallowed down the blockade just beneath her chin. "Named after his father, Jude Pepper Rigby."

"You lost him, Mom?"

Eleanor looked, stung with the question, and answered at first with her eyes before offering, "Yes. He was in the military."

"Tell me about your son?"

"He's a good boy, so much like his father, sometimes to his own detriment."

"How so, Mom?"

"His head's full of coals, and his heart's full of dreams and in between isn't fastened tightly enough for the other two."

"I see. His mouth gets him in trouble does it?"

"To say it lightly. He's had his run-ins with the law, and some business with a few of the seedy types. He's a good boy, you know." She trailed off at the last, her eyes hazy with the past, her hands trembling from the present. They had walked some distance by this point, and Home had led her around many turns and down a few side roads. Home led, and she followed, and the familiarity tugged annoyingly at the back of her thoughts.

They turned again, and as her mind sifted through everything she knew, she vaguely recalled walking through rusted gates and onto a small stone path. Home had stopped, and in her daze, she had passed him on the path. "Mom. We're here."

"Where?" The statement had caught her off guard. She stopped abruptly, planting her feet, then turned to face Home.

He had pulled the scarf from around his shoulders and was wrapping it around Eleanor's neck. "It's awful cold to be out, Mom." She pulled the crimson warmth into her, plunging her hands into the folds of it, letting it drip its warmth down her, through her, permeating the chains that held her memory, shattering the locks there. A stout scent of cologne hung on it, and she breathed it in, as familiar as the sapphire specks in Home's eyes. She fell, or rather, her memories rose, enveloping her until Home, the winter, the stone path, all were somewhere above her and her below, standing in front of the warm glow of her fireplace, her hands now pink with vibrant life.

"Why can't I go? You've met Kelsie, and Mike and John are good guys!" Jude Rigby was shouting, and Eleanor stood unflinchingly at first, her eyes searching her surroundings, her bearings spinning while she gathered her composure. She had the annoying feeling that something had just slipped her mind, someone, or perhaps some place. It was on the tip of her tongue, but she couldn't quite call it up.

"You..." She started, but trailed off, a bemused look crossing her face. She breathed deeply; the wood smoke robust in her nostrils, she smiled.

"Mom, you okay?" Eleanor's demeanor had thrown Jude from his point, but he recovered quickly. "Look, I told you, I'm not into that stuff anymore. It's just me and some of the guys going out to hang, over in North End."

Eleanor looked sharply at her son, her mind settling into her surroundings, she shot back, "You know I just don't like those..." She paused, chewing her words to digestion before uttering, "Thugs, and you know that's just what they are! You're a good boy, Jude, so much—*too* much like your father at times!"

The jab wounded Jude, his hurt hanging from the ramparts of his eyes, which surged with youthful fire, bathed in azure. "You don't know them! You've never met them! You judge and judge and judge, this guy's this, that guy's that! You can call people a lot of things and no matter what you call them it doesn't change them one bit, they're still the same as they were, every inch of 'em!"

Eleanor backed into the table, rattling the dishes left from dinner. "Jude, please, just stay in tonight. It's freezing out, the roads are patched in ice, how are you even going to get all the way over to North End?"

"Kelsie's brother has a Jeep; he's going to tote us over there. We'll stay the night, and the news said the temps will be up into the forties tomorrow."

"Tomorrow go to North End." Eleanor was focusing, trying to steady her voice, fighting the shaking anger that threatened her composure.

"But the party's tonight."

"Party?" Eleanor shot darted eyes at Jude.

"No. Not that kind of party, there's not going to be any-"

"You don't do well with parties, and I know the kinds of parties you and those… those..." she swallowed the word down, replacing it instead with, "*friends* of yours like to have."

"Yeah well, at least *they* are my friends, and at least *they* let me be myself, and aren't constantly trying to change me!" His words had crossed from anger to pain, and large drops of grief slid down his face. He was frantically grabbing his wallet, his keys, and somewhere trying to fit room for his youthful pride.

"What are you doing?" Eleanor shot, panic taking her. Jude glanced sideways through slits of eyes, as pointed as daggers towards her. With that, he was at the door, and in the moment it took to work the lock, he was outside. Eleanor chased after, but he was down the street, hood over his head and at full jog before she cleared the threshold. "Jude!" She wept, her arms clinging against her breast, as she walked back into the warmth of her small apartment.

At eleven-fifteen, she started calling around, and by the stroke of midnight, she had moved from worried to frantic. She walked to the phone, dialing through panic. "Father McKenzie? Of course, I realize it's late, it's just that you said that if I needed anything I could - Mrs. Rigby, down the street from the Abbey... Eleanor Rigby, you said that if I needed anything I could call... Yes, it's my son Jude, he's left angry, and I've called around to his friends, but none of them can be reached. Please, my car is in the shop still, I really just need a ride. North End, if you could manage. Thank you." She bundled herself against the frigid night air and, almost as an afterthought, grabbed a crimson red scarf from the hallway closet, where things that she had meant to be forgotten were left. The scarf had been a present from Pepper, a reminder of his warmth while he was away. When she received the news of his death, she packed it, along with other boxes of his things, into the closet, and put a guard at its gate to keep the memories locked tightly in.

She wrapped the scarf around her, thinking of the day Pepper presented it to her, the last day she saw him, the last happy day she had, where sadness mingled with joy and the promise of the future. She started at the rap on the door. *Father McKenzie*, she thought, and headed towards it, looking back as it swung open, taking one last inventory before heading out. Turning back to the doorway, she was caught in place.

"Mrs. Rigby?" The officer, official in blue, his hat held tightly in his meaty hands asked cautiously.

"Yes, that's me." Eleanor's mind raced, implausible things cartwheeling through it, she hoped any of them could be the truth; had she done something wrong, or perhaps the officer had the wrong Mrs. Rigby. The truth of his words washed over her in waves.

The first wave struck ankle-deep: "Mrs. *Eleanor* Rigby?" he emphasized, pity in his eyes. "Jude Rigby is your son?" The second wave, knee-high, caused her to stumble, but she dug her heels into the floor boards and braced herself. "There's been an accident," he continued. "Up Wendigo Bridge." Chest-high and rolling, the wave sat her down on the small stool just inside the stoop. The fourth and final wave, more tidal, more torrential, more a tsunami than a wave, laid her flat on the floor. "I'm sorry, Mrs. Rigby. He's gone." She gnawed at it, her eyes dashing from the feathered hair to the unbuttoned lapel, to the name tag. Officer Meenie, how fitting.

"You must be mistaken; he's just gone for a walk is all." Her eyes looked at nothing, her lips pursed in defiance.

"He was with friends up Wendigo Bridge. The friends say their jeep left the road just the other side of the river, and they were walking back to get help. A truck in the opposite lane hit a patch of ice and lost control. The truck struck Jude, then pushed through the guardrail, and Jude was thrown down into the water." Eleanor stood in awful silence, fighting with all of the muscles of her body, and all of the constitution of her spirit not to break. Tears pooled in her eyes, gathering at the corner, but she forbid they fall, calling them back in.

"So we just have to look for him, he's probably down on the bank somewhere, waiting for help!"

Officer Meenie shook his head slowly. "No ma'am, there's no reason. Listen, his friends tell it like it wasn't pretty, and I don't mean to bother you with the details, but it's below zero out there, and even a person in full control of their faculties wouldn't last more than ten minutes after dropping into the slush. I'm sorry, deeply." He meant it, his hands sweating despite the freezing air, his eyes trading glancing blows with Eleanor's. Eleanor was pushing past the blue uniform, her mind racing, she walked out onto the sidewalk, slipping occasionally on the ice. "Mrs. Rigby?" The voice carried from ahead of her and at last she looked up.

Father McKenzie was sitting in his car, a behemoth relic of a station wagon; the boat of a car bore snow chains on the tires. She ran now to the passenger side, climbing in on the slick leather seat, "Take me to Wendigo Bridge. Please!"

As they drove, her mind raced. She chewed her lip, fidgeting with her earring, wrapping and unwrapping her scarf.

"Is that where Jude is, Eleanor?" Father McKenzie asked at length, hoping to break the awkward stillness, stirred about by the dash heater, circulating through the roomy interior. "Is he waiting for you?"

"He's fell into the water." The tears that she had budgeted earlier now burst forth until her chin began to drip with sorrow. "We have to-" Her voice caught again, she blinked away more tears, wrapped and unwrapped the scarf, which smelled faintly of Pepper's cologne, "We have to find him. He's a good boy, you know." Her mind entered hiatus, and no more words were exchanged until they reached the bridge. Father McKenzie gingerly eased the heavy car onto the hill. Fresh sand and salt had been spread, and the ice had turned to semi-slush. He edged forward and, topping over the hill, uttered a small cry of surprise at the sight. There were busted plastic and metal, broken glass, the scene of what must have been a gruesome accident, leading through the guardrail, which hung out across the expanse as if open arms awaiting one last embrace.

"Stop the car!" Eleanor cried. Before it was stationary, she was out, and on the road, walking toward the edge.

"Now you be careful, miss!" Father McKenzie watched, frightened, from his position, looking behind him every so often to be sure no other vehicles were headed up the bridge.

Eleanor stood at the edge, against an intact portion of railing, and called down to the icy water below. "Jude! Jude Rigby, you've had your fun now come home! You hear me? Come home this instant!" She was crying, panicked, frantic, lost, confused, all of it and none of it, attached and separate, she moaned and clasped the railing with shaking hands. "Jude Rigby, you come on home right this instant you-" Her stomach knotted, yanking the words from her throat, closing a flesh gate above her lungs which trapped the air inside of her. She stood, trembling, exhausted, knowing that it must be a mistake; knowing that it must be a dream, and she would wake at any moment. She pushed against the flesh gate, she tugged against the sinew which held from her stomach to her voice, and violently, she won. The voice, the breath, bred together in despair, leaped out of her, and she issued forth a guttural wail which broke the night's silence and called forth movements in Father McKenzie that simply shocked him.

She pulled the scarf from around her neck. Father McKenzie had already begun to exit the vehicle, steadying himself on the slick slush of a road. He watched, across the lane, as she tied the scarf loosely around the mangled bit of guardrail, dangerously close to the edge, making the priest start from fear and move towards her. "Mrs. Rigby, come on now, let's just get away from that edge shall we?"

"It's not fair," she uttered, lowly but clearly enough for him to understand her. "It's just not fair." Crying again, her head hung nearly limp against her chest. "You do what's right, you go to church, you worship, you pray, you wish for the best. You lose your husband; they tell you it'll be OK, that it's just part of God's plan. You pray more, you worship, you're back in the church, the same building where you said goodbye to an empty box because there was nothing left to put in it!" She was erect, rigid; now her face turned towards the hurrying priest, who was making towards her in an earnest attempt to save her. "And then... The one thing you thought might have been that part of God's plan, the one thing that you thought might have made it all make sense..." She shrugged, as if indifferent to it, indicating what she believed was

God's indifference to it, "That one thing gets ripped out from your heart, tossed away like refuse!"

"Eleanor, you don't know what you're saying! Get over here away from the edge before you get hurt!" Father McKenzie was easing towards her with his arm stretched out. "Mrs. Rigby, please, come with me, I'll get you home, and we can have some hot tea and get you warmed up!" Father McKenzie eyed her, nearly to her, his hand stretched out, ready to snag her back to safety.

"It's just not fair..." Spreading her arms wide, like the mangled guardrail that straddled her, she let herself fall backwards, towards the icy river. The priest lunged forward, now little more than arm's length away, but missed by inches. His heart thumped wildly in his chest, genuine concern in his eyes as he edged towards the open pit below, looking down into the darkness.

Eleanor Rigby blinked tears from her eyes. She felt the chill of the morning air, and the stone path beneath her feet, and the warm scarf around her neck. "I remember..." She said, her eyes looking down around her. She realized that she was in a cemetery. "I remember what happened, the story I forgot earlier. But, it can't be, because..." She trailed off, noticing that the place that Home and she had stopped was in front of a small family plot. Three markers, with the two on either side mounded with fresh earth, the smell permeating the cool air. The center marker bore a bronze flag, with brazen lettering which read: "Soldier, Husband, Father; Here Lies Sargent Pepper Rigby." Eleanor breathed deeply, shuddering at the words, then turned to the other two markers.

"So then, I must have."

"Yes."

"And then I'm-"

"Afraid so."

"So what happens now?" She asked, turning to Home, but taken aback, shocked at the sight. Home was gone, and standing in his place, Jude Rigby beamed, smiling with his eyes, his hand held out towards her. Eleanor clasped hands with her son, and they began to walk. "It was you?"

"Yes. I've come to call you home."

# Permissions

# NEOGLYPHIC
## Entertainment

Neoglyphic Entertainment believes story is the heart of the human experience. Story inspires creativity, shapes minds, and catalyzes social change. Story connects us to one another, celebrating our greatest triumphs and exposing our deepest fears, establishing a common ground to learn, to understand, to be.

Stories are shared through written word, visual art, film, music, video games and more. Neoglyphic develops technology to cultivate story across all these art forms, and reduces the traditional risk and cost associated with entertainment production. We offer a storytelling platform to connect with fans, derive meaningful insights, and deliver immersive experiences.

Whether you're an author writing your first novel, or a studio creating a feature film, Neoglyphic will be your trusted partner to untether your imagination.

*www.neoglyphic.com*

9 781944 606039